The Paternoster Ruby

Her face went suddenly white. The hand holding the card dropped to her lap. She sat bolt upright, and directed at me a look of surprised bewilderment.

We both started and looked at the front door.

"Listen!" Miss Cooper whispered.

Light, stealthy footsteps sounded upon the porch. Next instant the knob was being slowly turned by a cautious hand.

We sat rigid and breathless, with our eyes glued to the slowly revolving door-knob. At last a faint click announced that the latch was released. The door opened a few inches, to reveal the slender figure of Alexander Burke.

Manifestly he was ignorant of our presence. Neither I nor Miss Cooper stirred, and Burke was for the time blinded by having come so abruptly from the snow glare into the comparative dimness of the hall.

I regretted that we were not in position to follow his movements unobserved, for of course he must be attracted to us the instant that either of us stirred. I was exceedingly curious to learn what had brought him back to his employer's house.

And now he did a singular thing. His hand was still on the knob, and only his head and the upper part of his body projected through the doorway. His attitude was that of a strained listener; and had I not been there to testify to the contrary, one might have sworn that he received a warning not to enter. The silence, however, remained absolutely unbroken.

All at once a shudder convulsed his frame. He slowly withdrew his head, as if fearful of disturbing the house's lifeless occupant. Next he deliberately closed the door without entering at all.

Miss Cooper turned to me in blank amazement, and for a moment I confess that I was nonplussed myself by such singular conduct.

The Paternoster Ruby

By Charles Edmonds Walk

Originally published in 1910

The Paternoster Ruby

© 2010 Resurrected Press

Published by Intrepid Ink, LLC

Intrepid Ink, LLC provides full publishing services to authors of fiction and non-fiction books, eBooks and websites. From editing to formatting, to publishing, to marketing, Intrepid Ink gets your creative works into the hands of the people who want to read them.
Find out more at www.IntrepidInk.com.

ISBN 10: 0-9843857-5-4
ISBN 13: 978-0-9843857-5-1

Printed in the United States of America

FOREWORD

In 1892, the time that the events in Paternoster Ruby take place, Chicago was already well on its way to becoming the "City of Broad Shoulders." It had become, as it is today, a transportation hub through which much of the grain and livestock of the upper Midwest and the plains of Canada passed on the way to market. Fortunes were made and lost speculating in wheat and hogs. With ready access to both the railroads and shipping on the Great Lakes, Chicago was also becoming a center of manufacturing and mercantilism. The two financiers depicted in the novel had numerous real life counterparts.

After the great fire of 1871 the city had been rebuilt in a completely modern mode. Chicago was the birthplace of the skyscraper. By 1892 Frank Lloyd Wright and his contemporaries were already starting to develop the "Prairie School" style which was to become America's first indigenous architectural style. The elevated trains provided rapid transportation for the common man. In 1893 the city would hold the World's Columbian Exhibition which would be one of the most influential world's fairs in history.

Chicago was becoming a cosmopolitan city with a diverse population. The original settlers had been joined by waves of immigrants, first by Germans and Irish, then Poles, Italians. It was also gaining a reputation for a brand of local politics that it maintains till today.

It is worth remembering that while the story is set in 1892 it was in fact published in 1910. The treatment of the female characters has a more modern feel to it that reflects the sensibilities of the early twentieth century rather than the latter part of the nineteenth. In particular, Miss Genevieve Cooper, proves to be a modern, independent woman.

This then is the background against which the novel is set. Read it and enjoy.

About the Author

Charles Edmonds Walk was born in Indiana in 1875. In addition to *The Paternoster Ruby*, he wrote a number of other books, *The Silver Blade* (1908), *The Yellow Circle* (1909), *The Time Lock* (1912), *The Crimson Cross* (1913) with Millard Lynch, and *The Green Seal* (1914). He also wrote a number of stories published in Blue Book and other magazines. His date of death is unknown.

Greg Fowlkes
Editor-In-Chief
Resurrected Press

Table of Contents

1
The Sheridan Park Mystery

With a screaming of brakes, the elevated train on which I happened to be jerked to a stop, and passengers intending to disembark were catapulted toward the doorways – a convenience supplied gratis by all elevated roads, which, I have observed, is generally overlooked by their patrons. I crammed the morning paper into my overcoat pocket, fell in with the outrushing current of humanity, and was straightway swept upon the platform, pinched through the revolving gates, and hustled down the covered iron stairway to the street. Here the current broke up and diffused, like the current of a river where it empties into the sea.

This was the first wave of the daily townward tide – clerks, shop-girls, and stenographers, for the most part intent upon bread and butter *in futuro*. The jostling and crowding was like an old story to me; I went through the ordeal each morning with an indifference and abstraction born of long custom.

The time of the year was January, the year itself 1892. A clear, cold air with just enough frost in it to stir sluggish blood, induced one to walk briskly. It was still too early in the day for the usual down-town crowd, and I proceeded as fast as I wanted to, allowing my thoughts to dwell undisturbed on the big news topic of the day, which I had just been reading. And so I did, as I strode along, with the concern of one whose interest is remote, yet in a way affected.

So the great wheat corner was broken at last! The coterie of operators headed by Alfred Fluette had discovered to their dismay that the shorts were anything but "short," for all day yesterday the precious grain had been pouring into the market in a golden flood. Grain-laden vessels were speeding from Argentine, where no wheat was supposed to be; trains were hurrying in from the far Northwest; and even the millers of the land had awakened to the fact that there was more profit in emptying their bins and selling for a dollar and sixty cents a bushel the wheat that had cost them seventy-six cents, than there was in grinding it into flour.

It was another pirate of the pit who had brought disaster to the bulls – no other than that old fox, Felix Page, himself a manipulator of successful big deals, and feared perhaps more than any other figure on the Board of Trade.

But his spectacular smashing of the memorable corner has passed into history. While Fluette's brokers were buying and sending the price soaring – skyrocketing is more descriptive, though – Felix Page was selling in quantities that bewildered and, since it was Page, alarmed the bulls. Insurance on the lakes had ceased with the advent of winter; the granaries of the world were supposed to be scraped clean; so it seemed that he must be rushing headlong to certain destruction. Still, seeing that it was Felix Page who was doing most of the selling, Fluette's crowd was nervous.

And the sequel, in all conscience, warranted their anxiety. For more than a week Felix Page's iron-prowed ships had been crushing and smashing their way through the ice, opening a way for other ships; yesterday they had steamed into port with their precious cargoes, demoralizing the bull clique with a deluge of golden grain.

Page settled; he had sold five million bushels, and he delivered the goods. This was the opening fissure. Fluette was soon overwhelmed, and today he and his crowd would be holding a melancholy wake over the corpse.

This, however, is not a story of stupendous battles in the arena of Commerce. I have merely gone behind my proper starting-point by a matter of ten minutes or so – no more – to lay before you one of those inexplicable coincidences which, when they are flung at us, shake us from our self-possession. The stage was already set for me; serenely unsuspecting, I was headed straight toward it.

Police headquarters was my destination, and I had no sooner stepped across the threshold than I was told that the Captain was wanting to see me at once. So I went direct to his private office, where he was deep in conference with a party of four men, who, in spite of a general air of gloom which seemed to envelop them, looked like a quartet of prosperous brokers. It occurred to me that they might have been struck by the stick of the spent rocket.

As the Captain abruptly broke off an earnest speech to wheel his chair round and address me, the four men stared at me with a curious, unwavering interest.

Fancy how I was staggered by the first words. My chief thrust a card in my direction, on which was pencilled a street number.

"Go to this address at once, Swift," said he. "It looks like murder – old Page."

"Page!" I almost shouted. "You can't mean Felix Page!"

"What's the matter with you? Know anything about it?"

My stupefaction was pronounced enough to excite his wonder. I assure you, we are not often astonished at the Central Office.

I caught my breath and shook my head. Of course, I knew nothing about it. But it was something besides the amazing, unexpected intelligence of Felix Page's death that struck me right between the eyes. With the mention of his name, my mind cut one of those unaccountable capers which everybody has at some time in his life experienced.

The names of Felix Page and Alfred Fluette had been before me in one way or another for days; I had followed the remarkable wheat deal with about the same degree of interest that animated everybody else who was not immediately concerned; but not until this moment had it impressed me that I knew something respecting Page which had not appeared in the papers in connection with the corner. What was it?

But I could not remember. This was the scurvy trick my mind was playing. I stood there staring at the others, and they sat staring at me. A question was halted provokingly upon the very tip of my tongue, which, despite a most earnest whipping of memory, remained obstinately elusive.

Felix Page! What particular, unusual circumstance was associated in my mind with that name? Why should it come to flout me at this juncture without revealing itself?

My ineffectual effort to remember was cut short by my chief. He scowled, manifestly in perplexity at the way the news had affected me.

"These gentlemen," he said, with a gesture indicating the funereal quartet, "were more or less associated with Mr. Page; he don't seem to have had any close friends; but they can tell me nothing. Whatever line you pick up, you must find the end of it at the scene of the crime – the house. The address is on that card.

"Here's all I know about it: It must have happened sometime during the night; the report came in from Sheridan Park station about daylight. Three men from there, Patrolmen Callahan and O'Brien and a plain-clothes man named Stodger, are at the house holding two suspects until somebody shows up from the Central Office. Stodger's in a stew; can't seem to make head nor tail of what's happened.

"You hurry, Swift," he curtly concluded; "this is too important a matter to waste time over."

So it was. I saluted and hastily left him.

My brain was still in a whirl; my musings and the blunt, surprising announcement had come too close together for me to regard the supposed crime with unshaken equanimity. Then, too, I was still vainly striving to drag from memory's hiding-place the tantalizing circumstance which I somehow felt was pregnant with possibilities in the light of the financier's death. What on earth was it? I thought of everything else I had ever heard or read about the man.

But I was young – not only in the service, but in years as well – and this was one of my first hard rubs with that heartless old pedagogue, Experience.

Felix Page had enjoyed – I use the word advisedly – a widespread reputation for eccentricity. The word, I held a secret conviction, was merely a polite euphemism to cover his unscrupulous nature. Many acts of his were condoned, or even laughed at, which would have been nothing short of outrageous if performed by another. He had been widely exploited as a "character"; in reality he had been a merciless old skinflint, with a supreme disregard for the rights or pleasures of others.

Still, it is not to be denied that his eccentricity did reveal itself in certain ways. After business hours he retired to a forlorn old mansion, where he lived alone, without kindred (if he had any) or servants, save for an ancient dame who came of mornings to prepare his breakfasts, and to discharge, under his nagging supervision, the few domestic duties necessary to meet his requirements.

Something like a half-hour after leaving the Central Office, I arrived at the Page place. Stodger, a short, fat, good-natured chap, was awaiting my arrival – evidently with some impatience, for he was stamping to and fro before the gate for warmth. As soon as he learned my business he conducted me up to the house.

On the way he gave me a hasty account of the crime, concerning which he frankly and whimsically confessed to be very much at sea.

A description of the house and grounds is in order. The location was all that could be desired, and would have been an ideal place of residence if rehabilitated from its sorry condition of neglect. The house faced the north end of Sheridan Park, a glimpse of whose lagoons could be caught here and there among the leafless trees. It sat well back from the wide boulevard, and, surrounded as it was by fine old elms and beeches and maples, it reminded me of some antiquated English country home, such as I have seen in pictures.

There were any number of chimney clusters; but the general air of the place was extremely cold and forbidding. Notwithstanding it was mid-winter and that an inch or more of snow lay on the ground, there was not a wisp of smoke above any of the chimneys to indicate the welcome presence of a fire below.

A high iron fence extending along the front of the property was divided by a carriage entrance and a smaller gate for pedestrians. The former, barring the way to a weed- and grass-grown drive, was hermetically sealed by rust; while the other was just as permanently fixed open by the accumulation of earth and gravel about its lower part. Two parallel rows of ragged, untrimmed privet designated the tortuous way of the drive to the unused *porte-cochere*.

"Nasty case," Stodger was imparting, in queer staccato sentences. "Shouldn't have much difficulty, though; responsibility lies between two men. Here all last night. Nobody else. Callahan and O'Brien holdin' 'em. One's Page's private secretary; fellow named Burke – Alexander Stilwell Burke. Peach of a monicker, ain't it? Has all three sections on his cards.

"The other's a young lawyer chap; calls himself Royal Maillot. I can't pry out of either of 'em what *he* was doing here."

"And nobody else, you say?" I asked when he paused.

"Nope – so *they* say. Either one of 'em might have done it. They're down on each other for something; glare at each other like – like – you know – cat and dog."

"Go on."

"Well, this fellow Burke – Alexander Stilwell – he comes to our shack some time after two this A. M. Told the desk-sergeant old Page'd been croaked; wouldn't say anything more. Dippy? Say! Acted like somebody'd slipped him a round o' knockout-drops. Sure thing, he did. Wouldn't budge till old Grimes sent me back with him. I'm only a license inspector, too. This is what I – h'm-m – I butted into. Dev'lish cold, ain't it?"

He had opened the front door and ushered me into a deep, wide hall. A broad stairway, with carved oak balusters, rose on one side to a landing which formed a sort of balcony over the rear end of the hall, and thence continued up to the second story.

With his concluding words, Stodger pointed up to the landing, through whose balusters I could see a hand and a part of a motionless human form stretched out at full length upon the floor.

"Felix Page – b'r-r – dead as a door-nail," Stodger now added. "Slugged over the head with a heavy iron candlestick; find it lying there by him. Think of all that wheat – and them ships crunching through the ice. Say, it's pretty tough, ain't it? He was – but would you rather make an examination first? Or shall I go on?"

I smiled at the man's air of vast importance, which discriminated not at all between grave matters and light. With his queer "hum's" and "haw's," his funny little exclamatory noises and quick, jerky manner of speech, he reminded me of a jolly diminutive priest who had just dined well. Never was mortal freer of affectation. And his cheerfulness? It was as expansive and as volatile as ether. His buoyancy was a perpetual, never-failing tonic for doubt and discouragement, and I have yet to witness him confronted with a situation that could in the least dash his spirits.

He awaited my reply to his question with an air which suggested that nothing less important than the well-being of his very existence was at stake.

"Tell me what you have learned," returned I. Things usually acquire a more comprehensible aspect when you have a few facts by which to measure and weigh them, and I wanted to hear Stodger's story.

"Yip!" he cried cheerily. "Might as well sit here as anywhere else; nobody to disturb us."

Weighted as he was with surplus flesh, his agility was amazing. He wheeled round and plumped down on an oak bench, not unlike a church pew, which stood against the panelled stairway beyond the newel. As I followed I drew my overcoat closer about me, for the hall was cold and dismal.

"This fellow Burke – Alexander Stilwell; queer chap. Close-mouthed? Say!" – he squared around and tapped my chest with an impressive forefinger – "a clam's real noisy compared with him. Fact. Watched me steady all the time I – you know – looked at the body."

Stodger stopped abruptly, with the manner of one to whom has occurred a sudden brilliant idea. He thumped one fat knee with a pudgy hand, and whispered with suppressed eagerness:

"By jinks, Swift! I have it! I'll get Burke – Alexander Stilwell. Let him talk – in there" – with a violent gesture toward the opposite side of the hall – "library. What say? There's a – you know – alcove – curtains. I'll hide behind 'em and listen; if he don't tell the story just like he did to me, why, we'll call the turn on him. See?"

For various reasons I thought the idea not a bad one, and said so. Stodger was off up the stairs like a shot. He went nimbly round the prostrate figure on the landing without so much as a look toward it, and disappeared.

He and another man appeared, after a while, at the back of the hall, having evidently availed themselves of a rear stairway.

I surveyed the private secretary with much interest, and must even now confess, after no inconsiderable study of the human face, that I have never since beheld one that was so utterly baffling.

He was a slender man of medium height, and of an age that might have been anything between twenty and fifty; his eyes, hair, brows, and lashes were all of a uniform shade of pale yellow – excepting that the eyes had a greenish tint – while his face and thin, nervous hands wore a dead, unwholesome pallor.

The effect was extraordinary. The ageless face looked as if it did not know how to conform to or mirror any inward emotion; and furthermore, one was never precisely positive whether or not the pale eyes were following one, for they somehow, in their uncertain fixedness, suggested the idea that they were windows behind which the real eyes were incessantly vigilant. So it was when Stodger introduced him; I could not tell whether he was watching me or my colleague – or, in truth, whether he was watching either of us.

"Mr. Burke, Mr. Swift," said Stodger, with a grand air – "Mr. Alexander Stilwell Burke." Then, in a hoarse aside to me:

"Little matter I want to look after; just 'tend to it while you two are talking."

2
THE PRIVATE SECRETARY

Stodger at once left us together, having, I surmised, his own method of getting into the curtained alcove of which he had spoken. In order that he should have ample time to reach it, I held Burke with a question or two in the hall.

"Mr. Burke," said I, "who besides yourself and Mr. Page was in the house last night?"

He replied promptly, but with a deliberate precision, as if he were making a weighty confidential communication, and wanted to be exceedingly careful to convey an exact interpretation of his thoughts.

I might now add that this cautious, reflective manner characterized all his speech, and in time it grew extremely aggravating.

"A young man named Maillot," he said; "Royal Maillot."

"And who is this Royal Maillot?" I next asked.

Was Burke returning my intent look? Or did he have an eye for some fancied movement behind him, or off there toward the closed library door? For the life of me, I could not have told with assurance.

"I can't tell you much from my own knowledge," he presently returned; and now I was pretty positive that he was meeting my regard. "Mr. Maillot is still here, however; he can speak for himself."

"I know that" – curtly; "but I prefer to be informed beforehand – even if it's only by hearsay. Who is Mr. Maillot?"

Again the furtive, wandering look behind the blank of the clean-shaven, ageless features.

"I've gathered the idea that he's a young lawyer, and that some business affair brought him here to confer with Mr. Page.   He arrived only last night.   The whole circumstance was very unusual."

"What do you mean by that?"

Some moments elapsed before he replied.   "Why," presently, "Mr. Page was not in the habit of seeing people here, or – as far as that's concerned – of considering any business matters whatever after he returned home in the evening; this was his invariable rule, excepting – " He paused.

"Excepting what?" I urged.

"Well, occasionally – very rarely – he would have me here. Last night was one of those occasions; he expected to be absent from the city, and there were special instructions that he wanted to give me, concerning certain matters that had to be looked after to-day.

"But, without an exception that I can recall, everybody else who had any business with him was required to go to the Drovers' National, or to his office in the same building.

"Even *our* relations – our acquaintance – practically ended with each day's business, not to be renewed until the next day; and I suppose I approach nearer than any of his other employees to being what you might call a confidential clerk, or secretary."

I rose briskly to my feet.

"Let's go some place where it's more comfortable," suggested I, throwing open the library door; "in here will do."

He entered unhesitatingly, for it is an easy matter to influence people to your will in such trifling maneuvers; and as I followed, I glanced about the spacious apartment.

Its walls were wainscoted with oak, save for a narrow painted frieze, and while very few books were in evidence, the place would have been cheerful enough had there been a fire in the wide, handsome brick fireplace, or had there existed any indication at all that the room was ever used by human beings. Before the cold and empty hearth stood a table, where, very likely, Mr. Page had been in the habit of working on those rare occasions of which his secretary had spoken. On the right of this table was the curtained alcove.

Now Burke's conduct during the next second or so was destined, later on, to give me an idea concerning that gentleman, which indirectly aided me in clearing up a puzzling feature of the case. It was this.

As I indicated the chair where I wanted him to sit – one near enough to the alcove for Stodger not only to hear what Burke might say, but also to have the additional advantage of watching him without much likelihood of being observed in turn – I could have sworn that Burke hesitated and bent a doubtful, inquiring look toward the alcove; yet I am not positive that he ceased for a moment his blank, unblinking scrutiny of me. At any rate, he was no sooner seated than he bounded up again.

"We can have a little more light here," said he, starting toward the alcove, behind whose curtains Stodger was at that moment, I daresay, hastily planning a means of precipitate retreat. I was already seated myself, and I stayed his progress only in the nick of time.

"Burke!" I called sharply.

He wheeled about, a trifle disconcerted, I imagined.

"Please sit down," I went on authoritatively. "You are not precisely at liberty to go just where you please; for the present I'm responsible for your movements."

He shrugged his shoulders and returned to his chair, remarking in an unemotional way: "I forgot that I was under arrest."

I didn't trouble to define his position. At best it was at that instant an anomalous one; so far as I knew there were no grounds upon which to hold him at all; and while I would have hesitated to say that he was actually in custody, at the same time it is also true that I would not have permitted him to walk out of the house and away, had he desired to do so.

"Now, Mr. Burke," I went on, "tell me just what you know about this matter. Don't slur details; take your time."

"I know very little, Mr. Swift."

"Let's have it, nevertheless."

"About one o'clock last night I had just completed sorting some papers in my room. They had been in a file-case so long that they were very dusty; so when I was through I went to the bath-room – one door from mine – to wash my hands, and while I was so engaged I was startled by a crash, as of someone falling heavily outside.

"I picked up my candle, and looked into the hall. At first I saw nothing, and everything was perfectly quiet; but in a moment I noticed that an *etagere*, which had always stood at the head of the stairs, was tipped forward against the banisters, and at the same time I heard Mr. Maillot moving about in his room. I was much perplexed to account for such a disturbance at that hour of the night, and for a time I stood motionless, waiting to see what would occur next. I admit that I was even somewhat frightened; but as nothing else happened, I crossed over to Mr. Maillot's door – directly opposite my own – and rapped.

"He threw it open at once. He was holding a hand to his right eye, and glared at me with the uncovered eye. He evidently had slipped hastily into his clothes; his candle was lighted, and I noticed that his hands and face were wet, as if he too had been washing."

"It strikes me that there was an unusual amount of hand-washing," I here observed, "considering the hour of night. Had the household retired?"

"Why – yes, sir – we were supposed to have done so. But Mr. Maillot at once explained why his hands were wet. As he threw open the door, which he did in an angry manner, he asked me what the devil was the matter. I replied that I didn't know. He then stated that he thought the roof had caved in; that the tumult had awakened him, and that in springing out of bed he had nearly knocked an eye out by colliding with some piece of furniture. The pain was for a moment so intense, he said, that he had forgotten all about the noise; so he had lighted a candle and bathed the injured eye. It was already beginning to swell and show signs of discoloration. On my remarking that it was strange the noise hadn't roused Mr. Page, Mr. Maillot at once seized his candle and preceded me into the hall. He was the first to find Mr. Page's body.

"So far as we could determine, he was quite dead. Mr. Maillot at once warned me not to molest anything – he's a lawyer, I believe – and we agreed that I should notify the police while he remained to guard the house."

Such was Burke's story of the midnight tragedy. Further questioning elicited the assertion that he was utterly unable to account for Maillot's presence in the house; that he had never seen him before, and that he was sure the young man's call had been unexpected by Mr. Page, as the latter had, the last thing the previous evening at his office, instructed Burke to procure a number of specified papers from the file-case, and bring them to the house after supper.

Burke believed it to have been his employer's intention to go through these documents with him, for the purpose of selecting certain ones which had to do with a contemplated business trip to Duluth; but Maillot had arrived about seven o'clock, and he and Mr. Page had at once repaired to the library, where they remained until after eleven o'clock.

Burke had busied himself with other matters until convinced that, as his employer had doubtless given over the Duluth journey, his services would not be required; whereupon he had retired to his own room.

Such minor details were added: the only servant was a woman who came to the house of mornings, and departed before the master went down-town; there was no telephone in the house; and the millionaire's "eccentricities" included, among other things, a preference for candles over any other means of artificial illumination, and a strong disinclination to consume any more fuel than was absolutely necessary.

Learning that the woman servant was at that very moment in the house, I speedily saw to it that a rousing fire was kindled upon every hearth and in every stove; nor were they allowed to die out, as long as I remained beneath the roof. Felix Page would have no further use for his coal and kindling.

When Burke returned from discharging this errand, I continued my questioning.

"So it had been Mr. Page's intention to go to Duluth last night, eh? What for?"

"I don't know. About vessels or his wheat shipments, I suppose; something too important to entrust to the mail or telegraph."

"Did the coming of Mr. Maillot upset his plans?" "I can't imagine what else caused him to change his mind at the last minute; the journey must have been unusually important to take him away from the city at this time."

Then Maillot's mission could not have been without exceptional weight, I reflected. And unless I was much mistaken, the deferred journey had seriously disarranged some material plan for Mr. Burke. I had nothing more to say, however, for the present.

I sent Burke back to the custody of Callahan and O'Brien, to await the completion of my investigation; for, until I became reasonably sure that I held in my hand all the available facts, it would be rank carelessness on my part to send the whilom secretary about his business.

I would have been hard put to it to interpret the impression which Alexander Burke had made upon my mind, if Stodger had demanded my opinion at that moment. As his round, cherubic face emerged between the curtains, I turned to him with considerable curiosity.

"Told it word for word as he did to me," was my companion's comment. "Couldn't have told it better if it had been a piece learnt by heart."

"Oh, he couldn't, eh?" observed I, thoughtfully, leading the way to the landing.

But I could not permit myself to theorize at this stage – an indulgence which, when premature, inevitably colors one's opinions, and prejudices all attempts at clear, logical reasoning.

3
SOME DISCOVERIES

But I was not yet permitted to begin my examination of the body and its immediate surroundings. I had no sooner arrived at the landing than I heard a man's voice, somewhere above in the second story, speaking with a note of determination that demanded some sort of recognition from the person addressed. The clear, ringing, resolute tone made me involuntarily pause and listen.

"Where's your headquarters man?" the voice was irately demanding. "I want to see him, d' ye hear? You blithering idiot, I'm going down those stairs; if you want to rough it, just try to stop me."

Another voice was raised in expostulation. Stodger, at my elbow, suddenly chuckled.

"That's him!" he whispered, with an unaccountable excitement. "That's Maillot!"

"He must be a tartar," I observed.

At that instant a stalwart young man, very angry and with one discolored eye that lent him an uncommonly truculent appearance, looked down on us from the upper hall; then he deliberately ignored the arguing policeman, strode to the head of the stairs and descended to the landing.

"It's all right, Callahan," said Stodger to the discomfited blue-coat.

The young man halted before us. "Ass!" he growled, staring hard at me.

Stodger made the epithet exclusively mine with a bow and a broad grin.

Instantly the young fellow flushed and stammered an apology.

"I didn't mean either of you chaps," he explained, in embarrassment.

"It's that chuckle-headed hod-carrier in a blue uniform. If he gives me any more of his cheek, I'll take his club from him and hand him a wallop over the head with it – dashed if I don't."

He looked eminently capable of doing it, too. He paused, his look resting upon me with an interrogation.

"Are you in authority here?" he bluntly demanded.

"I suppose so. Are you Mr. Maillot?"

"I am. And I'd like to know how much longer I'll have to stay in this beastly cold-storage warehouse. I'm plenty tired of it right now, if you want to know."

I smiled at the resolute young fellow; there was something decidedly likable in his frank and handsome countenance, and his blunt, intense manner.

"It all depends, Mr. Maillot. You and Mr. Burke are the only ones who can help me to some sort of solution of this crime – if crime it is; I take it for granted that you are willing to do what you can."

He favored me with another stare, then stood thoughtfully pulling at his lips and gazing at the body.

"Poor chap!" he muttered at length, in a hushed voice. "A ghastly way to die; I'd give a lot to know how it happened." Then he looked brightly at me, and asked with an almost boyish impulsiveness:

"Are you a detective – like Stodger here?"

"I'm a detective," I told him; "though I don't know how closely I resemble Stodger." A sound came from that worthy that made me think he was strangling. "Swift is my name."

Maillot suddenly thrust out his right hand.

"Glad to know you, Swift," he said heartily. "You look like a sensible chap. I'm willing to do all I can to help you – of course I am. It won't be much, I'm afraid. But if any thick-headed cop says I can't do this or can't do that, there's going to be trouble. They can't bluff me, and I know they haven't any right to dictate what I shall do."

All of which was quite true. Maillot glanced at the body again, and lowered his voice.

"Say," he said, "can't we go to a more appropriate place to talk matters over?"

"Yes – the library," suggested I.

He drew back, and his face darkened.

"Library!" he echoed.

"There's a fire there now," I informed him, wondering at his quick-changing moods. Next instant he was talking again, eagerly.

"But – look here, Swift – you haven't examined the body yet, have you? I'm curious to see whether you discover anything. Queer old chap he was; I don't think anybody ever understood him." He broke off and eyed Stodger severely.

"What the deuce are you laughing at, Stodger?" he demanded.

Stodger laid a hand upon his arm, and asked with husky eagerness:

"On the level, Maillot – between us, you know – just what did you say last night when somebody pulled the shade down over that lamp of yours?"

"You go to thunder," Maillot retorted, turning his back upon him.

"Pshaw! I'll bet it was hotter than that," said Stodger, in a disappointed tone.

Now, then, here were the parts of the puzzle I had to piece together in order to gain some conception of the manner in which Felix Page met his death.

The still form lay, as I have already stated, on the landing which extended across the rear of the hall like a balcony. The stairs continued thence up to the second story, but in a direction exactly the reverse of the first flight and on the opposite side of the hall therefrom.

Standing midway upon this landing, I had a view not only of the entire spacious hall, but could also see the top of the *etagere* tipped forward at the head of the stairs. It had evidently been a receptacle for old magazines and newspapers, all of which, that had not been checked by the balusters, now lay in a confused heap upon the floor just as they slid from the shelves.

Even across the distance which then separated me from this article of furniture – twelve feet, I should say – I could see that the top was coated with dust, save for two spots where the rich red lustre of the polished mahogany shone conspicuously: one about five inches in diameter and forming a perfect octagon, the other much smaller, and ragged in outline.

Here at my feet was the explanation. The base of the iron candlestick accounted for the octagonal design; while the fragments of a shallow, saucer-like sea-shell, which had been utilized as a match holder, accounted for the smaller spot. These two articles manifestly had reposed upon top of the *etagere*. The matches, to the number of half a dozen or so, were strewn upon the stairs and landing.

I picked up the candlestick from where it lay upon the landing, and examined it with much interest. It was a solid affair of ornamental iron, about fifteen inches high, and weighed some six or eight pounds – clearly a nasty weapon if wielded by a strong arm.

The bit of candle which it had contained lay nearby, one end flattened out from having been crushed under somebody's foot. At the time of his tragic death Mr. Page was in his sixty-first year, but a large and very vigorous man. He had been garbed in his street clothes (save for a frayed and faded purple smoking-jacket), thus contradicting Burke's belief that the household had retired. On the right temple the mark clearly showed where the candlestick's base had crushed the skull beneath. Death certainly had been instantaneous.

While I held the candlestick in my band, Maillot suddenly exclaimed: "By George, Swift! the old gentleman's death may have been owing to accident, after all!"

I looked keenly at him.

"Suppose he was here on the landing," the young fellow went on enthusiastically; "suppose somebody knocked that book-case affair suddenly forward – might've stumbled against it in the dark, you know – why, that heavy candlestick would have put a quietus on any man, falling on his head that way."

But I could not encourage this idea.

"I thought of that as soon as I saw the overturned whatnot," said I; "but several circumstances disprove it.

"In the first place, if the candlestick slid off the top, the dust would show it. Now the shell did slide, for you can plainly see where it scraped the dust in doing so.

"Again, considering your supposition, the candle-stick would have struck about half-way up the flight; if Mr. Page had been at that point on the stairs – in the line of its fall – his head would have been too high to have encountered it. And then, Maillot, look here." I pointed to the object of interest itself.

"If you were carrying it while the candle was lighted," I said, "your thumb would be uppermost, and your little finger nearest the base – wouldn't they?"

"Naturally."

"Very well. Suppose, now, I reverse my grasp – my thumb toward the base, the little finger toward the top – I now have it in a pretty effective position for use as a bludgeon, eh?"

He was following me intently, and now nodded his head in token of comprehension.

"Look at those drippings," I went on; "the hand that last grasped the candlestick did not try to avoid them, although they were yet soft and warm from the flame. It doesn't require a trained eye to determine that the *thumb* was nearest the base."

"I declare!" he wonderingly interrupted. "Blest if you're not right, Swift. The candle was burning when somebody grabbed it up for use as a club. Whoever it was he caught hold of it with a pretty firm grip."

"An additional argument," I added, "that it was put to some violent use. It isn't necessary to hold it anything near so tight merely to carry it.

"However," I pursued, "the circumstance is in a way unfortunate. While I can gather the idea that the hand wasn't inured to hard labor, and that it was a rather long and slender one, it closed so powerfully upon the drippings that the pattern of little lines – the vermiculations which differentiate one man's hand from everybody else's – is merely a blur. As a wax impression of the murderer's hand it is not a success."

My audience seemed to be immensely interested.

But I was not yet through with the wax impression.

"One peculiarity is suggested, though: this is unmistakably the impress of a right hand, and the owner of the hand wore a broad ring on the second finger – an unusual place for a man to sport that sort of jewelry."

The third finger of Maillot's *left* hand was adorned with a modest signet ring, while the private secretary's abnormally long, bloodless digits bore no sign that they had ever been encircled by any ring at all.

The situation was serious enough, however; the imprint which I assumed to have been made by a ring was so blurred as to leave wide latitude for error respecting any deduction that I might make from it.

I gravely regarded young Maillot, and tried to picture him to myself in the role of a murderer, but was obliged to own that such a thing was exceedingly difficult to do. Still, all things are possible; and the next few minutes had to determine whether I should take him or Burke into custody – maybe both – or permit them to go about their business.

"Mr. Maillot," I said by and by, "I'll tell you frankly: this business looks pretty bad for you and Burke – unless between you you can help me to place it in an entirely different light."

He paled, but met my level look steadily enough.

As I have already said, he was a good-looking chap, dark of hair, his eyes gray, and he possessed an honest, open countenance that stood a whole lot in his favor. He was tall, with a well-knit, athletic figure that made me fancy he had been an heroic member of his university football team.

But I have known just such men – steady, upright and governed by high standards of conduct – to become in the twinkling of an eye red-handed assassins.

Your man of lofty ideas and honor, in truth, is the more deeply sensible of injury and sometimes the easiest incensed. He is the more keenly hurt when his most sacred feelings are suddenly outraged. Finish off his equipment with a hot, passionate temper, and his resentment is likely to strike as blindly and as effectively as a bolt from a surcharged thunder-cloud. It is the motive that either palliates or makes the crime. A moment's previous reflection often stays the hand from a deed which a lifetime of after regret can not recall.

I could associate these possibilities with Maillot, and yet extend to him my sympathy; for controlling impulses are infinitely various and sometimes not to be held to account.

And so, too, could I have done with Burke, if he had betrayed one trait of a nature to inspire sympathy or engage my goodwill. Still, I meant not to be in the least influenced by my own feelings in the matter, nor do I now believe that I was; I determined to be as just and impartial as possible. Bear in mind that, as yet, I had been given no hint of possible motive.

After a bit Maillot said very soberly: "The possibility of such a thing never for instant occurred to me; but – Swift – I suppose must meet it somehow."

"You're beginning excellently," I returned sincerely. "That's the way to look at a thing of this kind. If you'll not forget that I'm inclined to be kindly disposed toward you, why, I dare say we can, between us, clear up whatever mystery there is in one-two-three order.

"For example, why you came here last night – your business with Mr. Page – when you tell me that perhaps – "

I stopped. Maillot's face had suddenly become a mirror of consternation.

"Good God, Swift!" he gasped, recoiling, "I – I can't do that!"

I promptly grew grave. And then, from the head of the stairs, came the slow, colorless voice of Alexander Burke.

"How about the Paternoster ruby, Mr. Maillot?" inquired he. Maillot's hands closed spasmodically; his teeth clicked together; and he slewed round like a released spring.

Next instant, had it not been for the intervening stairs and Stodger's and my quick interposition of our bodies between the two men, matters certainly would have gone hard with the private secretary. Maillot's temper was like gunpowder; the quiet question seemed to sting him to an unreasonable fury.

"You – you spy! You dirty sneak!" he snarled viciously.

4
THE RUBY

Unless I wanted affairs to get away from me entirely, it was high time to assume complete control of them, and immediately to abandon all temporizing measures.

I turned Maillot about without ceremony.

"Go with this man to the library, Stodger," I peremptorily directed. "Burke, you come with me."

In the next ten seconds I had the big library table between the two, Burke impassive, while Maillot glared at him savagely. I wanted to give them time to cool – Maillot, at any rate; so I took advantage of the opportunity to scribble a note to the Captain, hinting at the complications promised by Felix Page's death, and requesting that I be permitted to retain Stodger as an assistant – for I liked the stout, cheerful man who was willing and quick to act upon no more than a hint, and at the same time not disposed to interfere at all with my own modes of procedure. This message I gave to him, requesting that he entrust it to either Callahan or O'Brien for delivery. "Tell 'em to clear out," I added; "I have no use for them here."

Then I thrust my hands into my coat pockets, and fell to pacing the floor while I reflected. That is to say, I reflected after I had secured a good, firm grasp upon the thoughts which scurried helter-skelter, like a flushed covey of quail, through my brain.

The Paternoster ruby!

Here was the very thing I had tried so futilely to recall when the Captain first mentioned Felix Page's death! Like a flash, the phrase had opened up to me an illimitable vista of possibilities. I went over in mind all that I had ever heard of this famous gem, and wondered –

indeed, to tell only the bare truth – I thrilled with the very idea: could it have had any part or place in the financier's death?

The Paternoster ruby!

Those three words were an illumination; memory was flooded; and I glowed with a satisfaction that, in accordance with my custom in such matters, I had collected and preserved every available scrap of information which had in any way to do with this same Paternoster ruby. And right here some of that data must be presented.

First of all, this magnificent gem's known history hinted at no religious association whatever, as its name might seem to imply. In more than one journal I have seen it seriously affirmed that at one time it was a property of that celebrated pope, Alexander VI, Rodrigo Borgia, father of Caesar and Lucrezia – thus investing it with an antiquity and romance which the facts did not warrant.

But, after all, am I not premature in making this last assertion? Perhaps it will appear before we are through.

The gem first became known to the world and acquired its name through one Luca Paternostro, an Italian dealer in precious stones having his place of business in London, who claimed to have purchased it in the rough from some adventurer whose name is unknown to history. This occurred in the early '80's.

Subsequently it was carefully cut in Amsterdam, a paste replica made for purposes of display in the course of trade, and then added to Paternostro's stock – perhaps not because he expected to dispose of it to the first chance customer, but rather by reason of the prestige which the ownership of so superb a jewel would give him; it was an excellent advertisement.

On the fourth night after he received the cut ruby from the Dutch lapidaries, Paternostro was murdered and the gem stolen from his apartments in Hatton Gardens.

Of course, a stone so celebrated was easy to identify; not alone by means of the paste replica and an accurate preserved description, but its extraordinary and distinguishing features – to say nothing of its value – were not likely to be forgotten by experts who had seen and handled it.

And so, when it appeared in Paris a few months later, Paternostro's heirs and successors in the gem-importing business were promptly on hand to claim their property; an enterprise in which they succeeded after the determination of some legal complications; and the Paternostros started with the ruby on the return to London.

Incidentally, the assassin and thief – an Oriental of undetermined nationality – was also apprehended and, the red-tape of extradition having been gravely untangled, conveyed to England and duly hanged.

Ill-luck, however, followed the ruby. On the boat over from Calais to Dover a confidential employee of the gem merchants, who had accompanied them to Paris, was lost overboard while the vessel was entering the home port. Although this man was known to be an expert swimmer – notwithstanding the attempts at rescue, the proximity of land and the numerous craft of all sorts in the vicinity – a strange fatality seems to have carried him straight to the bottom. After the man vanished beneath the waves, no sign of him was seen again.

In the following year no less than four attempts were made to steal the stone from the Paternostros; but as they had learned caution from their unfortunate predecessor's death – to the extent, at least, of keeping such treasure in bank – these attempts were abortive.

Later several tentative overtures on the part of one of Europe's richest monarchs toward the purchase of the Paternoster ruby came to naught; the price set upon it by the Paternostros was prohibitive; and gradually it came to be forgotten by the public, until the year '84, when interest concerning it was again revived, this time to fever heat.

And now we have Alfred Fluette and Felix Page arrayed against each other once more. Everybody, of course, still remembers the sudden rivalry between these two American citizens, which sprang up in June of that year, for the gem's possession. The complexity of causes which simultaneously inspired them with an inordinate desire for the Paternoster ruby – a desire which seemingly could be appeased only by possession, regardless of cost – was much of a mystery, and afforded the energetic correspondents a fruitful text for many a day. Both, as is well known, had unlimited means with which to indulge their sudden whim; where kings and princes resigned themselves to the melancholy fact that the gem was not for them, these two men battled for it with an unlicensed tendering of fortunes that amazed the world; and one may easily imagine the sleepless anxiety of the Paternostros, as first one and then the other of the millionaires ran up his bid with true American prodigality.

Only – and this the mystifying feature of the episode – Felix Page could never honestly be accused of prodigality in any circumstances. He secured the ruby – at a fabulous price; but in the operation he made at least one bitter, implacable enemy. Alfred Fluette returned to the United States, smarting with the stings of defeat, and pledged to a commercial warfare on the successful millionaire speculator. It waged merrily thenceforward.

Why did Felix Page want the Paternoster ruby? It was impossible even to surmise a tenable theory. His parsimony was notorious; he was a bachelor without known kith or kin, and had never before been known to evince the slightest interest in precious stones.

On the other hand, Mr. Fluette was not only a collector of gems, but his collection was and still is one of the most famous in the world. Perhaps Page was willing to sacrifice a fortune merely to thwart a rival's ambition;

perhaps he was only satisfying some old grudge about which the world knew nothing – it was all speculation, and speculation of a most unsatisfying sort, too. He got the stone, at any rate; and here we have another instance of the man's peculiar disposition.

Whatever he did with the ruby nobody knew. There were many connoisseurs and jewelers on this side of the water who were naturally curious to see a gem of such renown; but with characteristic selfishness the new owner refused one and all, not only a glimpse of his costly prize, but would not even impart any information about it. His was a dog-in-the-manger attitude; with no appreciation whatever of his possession, he refused bluntly to allow anybody else to enjoy it. The ruby was kept hid away.

Such, briefly, were the data I had neatly pasted in my scrapbook and which memory had been all the morning trying to recall.

I paused in my promenade to survey Burke: what new adjustment must be made of the bare facts so far gathered; what now, in view of this new element injected into the case, was the attitude of this strange being toward it – my regard shifted to Maillot – and his?

Just at this juncture my cogitations were broken in upon by the door being unceremoniously thrown open. Stodger, much excited, darted in, closing the door after him. He handed me an envelope, accompanying it with a look of suppressed eagerness which suggested certain details pertinent to the missive which were being reserved – with difficulty – for my private hearing.

"Note for Maillot," announced he, his eyes fixed curiously upon the young man.

Maillot, apparently dumfounded, rose slowly to his feet.

"A note – for me!" he faltered. Then, quietly: "Give it to me, Swift."

Our glances met – and stayed. I had the envelope before me pinned to the table with the outspread fingers of my right hand. Maillot was unmistakably in great distress of mind, and his expression was that of a man desperate but determined. Only for a moment I hesitated; then without raising my hand, I slid the envelope across the table to him.

"It's a question of confidence, Mr. Maillot," said I, calmly, endeavoring to convey my earnestness in the look which had not for an instant swayed from his. "I reserve the right, should the occasion arise, to read it; understand?"

With a curt nod of acquiescence, he snatched it up from the table. A glimpse of the handwriting brought a flush to his face and a glad sparkle to his eyes; but the missive troubled him. It was short, and as he slowly returned it to its envelope his hand shook and his countenance grew more and more harassed and perplexed.

I glanced at Burke's pallid features and found them as impassive as any Indian's. It was impossible to determine whether he was watching me or Maillot.

Evidently assuming the incident to be closed, Stodger saw his opportunity to speak again.

"Chap's out here that brought it," said he; "coachman, he looks like; waiting for an answer." Then he turned to me, continuing:

"Four reporters out there, too; what shall I do with 'em?"

Maillot suddenly startled us by smiting the table violently with his fist. He was white, trembling, and apprehensive; but his determination was by no means broken.

"Swift," said he, in a hushed, strained voice, "step aside with me; let me have a word with you."

He seized my arm, and fairly dragged me off toward the curtained alcove.

"Swift," he whispered, not releasing his grip on my arm, "I'm in a devil of a position. For God's sake, show some sign of humanity! That note was from a young lady – "

"I surmised as much."

"Damn it, man! Don't laugh! I'm more dead in earnest than I ever was before in my life. This means more to me – to her – than you can by any possibility conceive, astute officer of the law though you may be."

My expression must have contained something of surprise at his vehemence, for with an effort he abruptly checked himself and at once went on more calmly.

"Swift, it's the young lady I expect some day to marry; she's heard a rumor of the tragedy, and is worried about me. The note was brought by her coachman, and she's waiting on the corner a block from here for me to come to her."

I tried hard to consider what was best to do. Enter a woman into a case like this, and assured conduct becomes an impossibility. Maillot was searching my face eagerly; in a moment he laid more of the matter before me.

"She's a sensitive, high-strung girl whom the slightest breath of scandal would fairly kill. I can't let her name be dragged into this mess; I can't answer her note, and send the reply away from under your very nose without a word to you. And the reporters! Gracious heavens! Swift, Stodger wanted to know what to do with 'em: for pity's sake, tell him to kill 'em!"

Again I interrupted. I trust that I may in all modesty record that I have more than a spark of the feelings to which the young fellow made such a passionate appeal.

"Look here, Maillot, has the young lady a companion?"

"Yes – usually; a young lady cousin who lives with her."

"Very well. If they happen to be together now, we can settle the matter quite easily. Answer her note; request the two of them to come here in a half-hour. Within that time we can get rid of the reporters, and you can – well, you can collect yourself. If your present expression is an index to what you are likely to say, this will be no place for a young lady – for the next thirty minutes, anyhow."

He caught and wrung my hand.

"Swift, you're a damn good fellow!" he said impulsively, and hurried back to his seat.

However, I did not forget that I had not heard this young man's story; nor did I fail to consider that he was a lawyer, and hence possessed of advantages for appreciating and intelligently weighing all the chances for and against his sweetheart becoming involved.

As Maillot dropped into his chair, Stodger could no longer contain himself. Drawing me into the hall, though the door was left wide open, he said, in a whisper that was heavy with importance:

"You'd never guess whose coachman it was."

I made no attempt to, and my stout friend impressively announced: "Fluette's."

"What!" Surprise jerked the exclamation from me; but I kept my voice subdued.

"Fact," – Stodger nodded his round head impressively, – "Alfred Fluette."

Here indeed was the promise of a pretty state of affairs!

5
THE HIDDEN SAFE

I left the four reporters to Stodger's tender mercies – his instructions did not include any such extreme measures as Maillot had suggested – confident that he was the proper person to relieve me of this unwelcome intrusion. It has always been hard for me to talk to these sharp-eyed, alert young chaps of the press, without saying something I had no business to say. Even if I didn't say it, some one of them would be sure to make a pretty shrewd guess, sometimes causing me no end of trouble. Stodger knew nothing of my intentions; therefore he could let nothing slip that might in any way affect my future movements.

Maillot's note dispatched, I directed my attention to ascertaining just what Alexander Burke meant by his reference to the ruby.

His explanation in itself was simple enough. He had heard of the ruby, of course – who hadn't? – and during his wanderings through the house the previous night, while he waited for Maillot to finish his business with Mr. Page, he had paused now and then in the vicinity of the library door. Twice he had heard the gem mentioned by those within.

Maillot accepted this statement with an offensive incredulity which was plainly deliberate.

"The house was very quiet," Burke made haste to add.

"Perhaps," Maillot spoke with sneering emphasis, his look frankly hostile, "perhaps you could have heard us; I'm ignorant of the degree of acuteness to which your hearing has been developed; *but*" – turning to me – "I want to say, Swift, that during the whole time Mr. Page and I were engaged in this room, our voices were not once raised so that a person beyond the closed door could have heard us intelligibly. I think, Burke, I see the imprint of a keyhole on your ear."

"Temper your language, Maillot," said the other, with a touch of asperity. Instantly Maillot was upon his feet.

"Shut up!" he thundered. "Don't you talk to me, you scamp!"

"Here, don't quarrel," I interposed pacifically, pressing the angry, glaring lawyer back into his chair with a persuasive hand upon his shoulder. I then said to him:

"You might appropriately relate what your business last night with Mr. Page was."

"I will" – bluntly – "to you."

The proposal being a reasonable one, I agreed to defer the matter. "However," continued I, "while you two are together there are some points upon which I want enlightenment. Reserve your personalities for another time. Is it positive that there was no one else in the house besides yourselves and Mr. Page?"

Neither spoke, each waiting, as it seemed, for the other to reply. My glance travelled between the two, and finally settled upon the secretary, whose long, nervous fingers were beating a silent tattoo upon the table.

"How about it, Mr. Burke?" I pressed him. "Your familiarity with the house entitles you to answer."

"I can take oath there was not," he now said. Stodger had already assured me that when he arrived every door and window was fast on the inside. So I next asked:

"When you went to notify the police, did you depart by way of the front door?"

"I did," he replied in a subdued voice.

And Maillot immediately added: "It was fast, Swift – bolt and spring-latch, both. I remember because the fact made me think there might be somebody else in the house. As soon as Burke left I went over the whole place, methodically and painstakingly, and I can now swear, if anybody was secreted in here anywhere, why, he's here yet. I inspected every door and window, upstairs and down; all were fast."

The unbroken, spotless mantle of snow outside limited the possibility of ingress or egress without leaving betraying footprints, to either the front or the rear door, where the paths had been kept clear.

Dismissing this nonplussing phase, I turned to the subject of the gem once more.

"Regarding the ruby, Mr. Burke," said I, "do you know where Mr. Page kept it?"

Maillot fixed a scowling look – not at all relieved by his discolored eye – upon the secretary, while that young man thoughtfully shook his head.

"No," Burke said at length; "not certainly. I never heard Mr. Page mention it; but I have an idea that it is in a small concealed safe in his bedroom, because there is where he keeps those things which no eye but his own ever sees."

Was it possible that Felix Page had any hidden treasures of sentiment? If so, here, in all truth, was a surprising side-light thrown into an unsuspected recess of his character. I was to have a hint presently of what was tucked away there.

But Burke had something more to say. "Perhaps," – slowly – "you would like to see that safe, Mr. Swift. I know where it is located, and can save you a needless search. It will have to be opened later on, I imagine."

"All right," I said, with much interest. "Lead the way."

Burke rose, with a queer glance at Maillot, and – turned toward the curtained alcove.

If he had any intention of moving in that direction, however, he quickly changed his mind; for Maillot and I followed him through the doorway, down the length of the roomy panelled hall, to another door on the same side of the house as the one we had just quitted. I could hear a

murmur of voices across the hall, where Stodger was
entertaining the reporters.

"The safe," said Burke, as we entered a large,
handsome, but very disordered sleeping-chamber, "is
what decided Mr. Page on selecting this room in
preference to one on the second floor. It was placed here,
I suppose, at the time the house was built; it is very
artfully hidden."

The bed betrayed the fact that it had not been slept in
recently, and the room that it was unused to a cleansing
supervision. Some soiled clothing lay in a heap in one
corner; a pair of trousers were collapsed over the back of
a chair; the dresser-top held a lot of linen and cravats,
both clean and soiled; half-closed drawers overflowed
with garments that had been thrust in any way, and an
over-turned ink bottle on a handsome mahogany stand
had never been righted. Even a careless housewife would
have been driven insane by such deliberate untidiness.

Our guide picked up a half-burned candle, lighted it,
and then opened a closet door. Next instant he started
back with a queer cry.

Maillot and I crowded forward and saw – nothing, at
first, to explain Burke's conduct. But in a moment I
comprehended.

A section of the closet floor was up, and now stood on
edge leaning against a wall; beneath it was a shallow,
cemented hollow, with four wooden steps leading down to
the bottom, where, obviously, one might stand to get
conveniently at the small safe thus disclosed.

It was also manifest that somebody had been doing
that very thing. For the safe door stood open, as well as
the inner door; and a flash of the candle, a single brief
glimpse, assured me that – whatever it might have held –
it was now as empty as on the day it left the maker's
hands.

But, stay – there *was* something, though not in the
safe. I took the candle from Burke, and went down the
steps. On the cement floor, in the shadow of the open

safe door, was a visiting-card, yellowed by age. I thought
it blank at first; but on turning it over I saw some
writing, faint and faded but legible, which had been
penned by a feminine hand:

*"I pray that you be showered with all the blessings of
the season. With love from*

"CLARA."

And in the lower left-hand corner, a date was written
– an old, old date: "Xmas, 1857."

Next I satisfied myself that the doors had not been
forced, and that every compartment was indeed empty.
Then I looked back over my shoulder, to be puzzled by the
baffling, indecipherable stare of Burke's tawny eyes. Was
he looking at me, at the reaved safe, or at the pathetic
little reminder, which I was holding in my hand, of that
long-ago Christmas present? Though I could not be
certain, I somehow felt that his interest was, at the
moment, intense, and that I had been mistaken in
thinking him a young man.

As I slipped the time-worn card into a pocket,
Maillot's voice broke in harshly upon my meditations.

"So – we have a thief to deal with, as well as an
assassin," he observed, his glance roving casually over the
secretary. "Burke, how would you, now, account for the
safe being open?"

And for the first time I detected a sign of emotion in
the yellow eyes: they darted a look toward Maillot, and
away again; but it flickered with a spark of malice –
gleamed for an instant with a light of malevolent
contempt – which made me feel that the fellow had all
along been keeping something in reserve, something
which must inevitably come to light presently, to
Maillot's utter discomfiture and undoing. It suggested
that Burke was patiently biding his time until some
sudden turn of events should permit him to triumph over
the other. Clearly, there was no goodwill lost between
these two men.

At once the eyes were again the same blank windows whose scrutiny was so indeterminate. Burke let down the trap-door in the closet floor, and I paused a while to admire how cunningly it had been designed. Although knowing it to be there, I could discern no trace of the aperture. We then reentered the bedroom.

I observed a door in the wall nearest the front of the house, and, seized with a sudden fancy to ascertain upon what it opened, went and laid my hand upon the handle. Burke's steady progress toward the hall door seemed to be aimed at diverting my purpose; realizing that he had failed, he turned and called aloud, staying my hand while it was in the very act of turning the knob.

"That's only the conservatory," his voice rang out; "it's empty – save for dust and cobwebs, there's nothing in it."

"Nevertheless I have a fancy to explore it," returned I; and I opened the door.

A narrow passage was disclosed, across which was another door. Both swung open noiselessly, a circumstance which struck me, in view of the fact that the conservatory was empty and unused, as being rather odd; and as I closed the second door behind me, I turned round as if to make sure the latch had caught.

The hinges had been freshly oiled.

A bay of glass, semi-opaque with dirt, occupied the space of the outer wall, and the glare from the dazzling snow outside brought out the whole interior with a sort of brutal vividness. A number of water-stained shelves; a few shallow boxes disintegrating and distributing their contents of earth over the floor; one or two crisp, brown, desiccated plant-stalks: such was the interior of this apartment set aside and dedicated to flowers and bright growing things.

And it had been used infrequently as a passageway, too. In the dust on the floor were footprints; some of them old, where later dust had settled, without quite obliterating them; some fresh, as if made but an hour ago.

As I came up to the next door I observed that its hinges had also been freshly lubricated, and was not surprised when it opened without a sound. When I stepped through it, I was in the curtained alcove off the library. Truly, there had been some secret, surreptitious flittings in this old mansion.

At that moment, in my abstraction, I was humming a little tune. I heard Stodger jovially speeding the departing reporters; and after the outside door closed behind the last of them, I shouted for him to enter the library. Our eyes met, and I indicated the secretary by the faintest of signs.

"Mr. Burke," said I, quietly, "will you please wait with Mr. Stodger while I have a few words with Mr. Maillot?"

The blank, pale face was turned briefly toward me – or Maillot – then the man bowed without a word, and followed Stodger. He paused an instant at the door, and looked across his shoulder at Maillot; enigma that he was, I nevertheless again caught a triumphant gleam in the tawny eyes. Then he passed on.

The fire on the wide hearth had been replenished during our round of the rooms; it was now blazing cheerily and doing its best to drive out the chill and the damp from the library; and it was a relief to get back to the easy leather chairs once more. I rested my forearms upon the back of one; but the instant the door closed on Stodger and Burke, young Maillot sank with a groan into a chair by the table.

"The devil! I'm glad you got rid of that fellow," he muttered. "He wears on one like the very deuce."

Now, during the last hour I had been sensible of a growing change in this young man; of a gradually increasing nervousness and apprehension, – as if I had all the time been pointing out little details, which he had previously overlooked and which were forming together, link by link, into a chain that would connect him with the tragedy. Up to the present he had concealed his thoughts only with an effort; but now his expression was become frankly worried and anxious; and as I stood silently regarding him, his agitation measurably increased. At last –

"For God's sake, Swift, don't look at me in that way!" came in a sudden outburst from his tightened lips. "I know – I can see – now that I've had time to think it over – that the facts are damning. If I close my lips and refuse to make any statement at all, it will be equivalent to a confession. On the other hand – "

I waited, silent, motionless, without removing my eyes from his face. Some moments elapsed before he went on, during which he was patently exerting an effort at self-control.

"Swift," he at last continued, more calmly, "I'm well aware what your conclusions must be; the responsibility for that old man's death lies between – between that secretary fellow and me; any fool can see that. It's downright devilish to be one of two such alternatives; but if I tell you what brought me here last night – Swift, I just simply can't contemplate doing it!"

Again he paused.

"Take time, Maillot," I admonished, "but choose wisely."

He lifted his head with a little jerk.

"Give me a moment to think. I must decide, and decide irrevocably, whether to become as dumb as a graven image, or else take you into my confidence."

At this unfortuitous instant there came a loud rap upon the door, which immediately opened to disclose the rotund form of Stodger, and behind him two slight figures in furs and veils, bearing into this desolate and gloomy old mansion a delicious flavor of young, dainty, pretty femininity.

"Miss Belle Fluette and Miss Genevieve Cooper – to see Mr. Maillot," announced Stodger, with all the absurd importance of a conscientious flunkey.

One, a tall girl in brown furs and with truly wonderful hazel eyes, came rapidly, gracefully, into the room, her companion following more sedately, and then stopped suddenly, as if petrified. She stood a moment – this haughty, handsome maid – a lovely picture of bewildered astonishment.

"Royal Maillot!" she cried, "whatever in the world has happened to your eye?"

6
AN EXTRAORDINARY ERRAND

I fancy that in ordinary circumstances Mr. Maillot would have betrayed some discomposure at the unintentional ridicule of this remarkably pretty girl's *naivete*, and furthermore, that the fact of his not having done so at once perplexed and alarmed her. For a moment she contemplated his worried countenance in round-eyed bewilderment, and then glanced inquiringly at me.

Maillot, in a sober manner, presented me. The handsome brown-eyed girl was Miss Belle Fluette; the other was her cousin, Miss Genevieve Cooper. She, too, was strikingly pretty, but instead of brown, her eyes were a deep and wonderful blue. Her hair was wavy and had many of the bronze lights and shadows that lurked in her cousin's reddish tresses, although it approached nearer a chestnut shade than auburn. She was not so tall as Miss Belle, and was more reserved in her demeanor.

Yet, in her sidewise regard of Maillot, there was a humorous, shrewd appreciation of his damaged appearance, connoting worldly knowledge sufficient to ascribe it to causes not precisely complimentary to his sobriety. Both, however, were very lovely, and very jaunty in their turbans and veils and long fur coats, while their cheeks glowed and their eyes sparkled from the crisp wintry air.

Miss Fluette acknowledged the mention of my name a little distantly. She made me feel that she had already surmised trouble, and that she was disposed to hold me accountable for it.

Miss Cooper was more cordial. She was very gracious, in a quiet, reserved way, and the expression of her blue eyes was so congenial that I caught myself more than once attempting to steal a glimpse of her countenance without her observing me, only to be disconcerted by a candid and not at all shy regard.

"Can we not go at once, Royal?" queried Miss Fluette, doubtfully. "It is dreadfully warm and stuffy in here. Jepson is waiting with the carriage."

I understood clearly, of course, that my presence accounted for her constraint. More than likely she would have given much to have got Maillot away immediately; but he replied, with a gravity that did not ease her mind:

"I'm afraid not, Bell – not for some minutes. Mr. Swift and I have to discuss Mr. Page's death."

Instantly her countenance reflected a deep concern. "It is true, then, is it, that your uncle is dead?" she asked in a hushed voice.

His uncle! For the second time that morning I was staggered. Felix Page's nephew and Alfred Fluette's daughter sweethearts! The two men themselves bitter enemies! One lying cold in death – murdered! Is it any wonder that I was stricken speechless?

"Don't look so astonished, Swift," Maillot was saying. "That is only a part of what I have to tell."

"But – Felix Page your uncle!" I marveled, as soon as I recovered my breath. "Look here, Maillot, it's not often that I'm so thunderstruck; why haven't you told me this?"

"It's true," he said slowly; "he was my mother's brother. Neither of us was particularly proud of the connection – not enough to brag of it. I was meaning to tell you, though, Swift; it is an essential part of my story."

He wheeled a chair up to one side of the table for Miss Fluette, and I made haste to perform a like service for Miss Genevieve Cooper; an act which she recognized with a slight smile and one of her friendly looks.

"Perhaps you and Genevieve had better get out of your wraps," the young man suggested to Miss Fluette, "because I want you to hear all I have to say to Mr. Swift; it will take some time."

She was now genuinely alarmed, and the handsome hazel eyes searched his face with an apprehension and dread that made her love for him only too apparent. Most young fellows, I hazard, would court any peril for such a look from a girl as beautiful as Miss Belle Fluette.

And the blue eyes, too, mirrored anxiety; they turned to me in a quick, questioning glance. I tried to disregard them – to ignore the presence of these two pretty girls – and confine myself strictly to what Maillot had to relate. It was not easy to do, since Miss Fluette's attitude toward me had become not only openly accusatory, but more than a little scornful; and I feared, moreover, that I should shortly lose the support of Miss Cooper's sympathetic interest.

First of all, though, both young ladies were anxious for an account of the tragedy – a task of which I relieved Maillot by relating briefly the details as I understood them, but, of course, adding no comment that might be construed as an expression of my opinion as to who might be responsible. They listened attentively; but when I had finished, Miss Fluette turned to Maillot as if I were no longer in the room. I noticed that Miss Cooper's brow was gathered in a little frown – whether of perplexity or disapprobation I could not determine – and that she was looking fixedly at her cousin.

"Royal," said Miss Fluette the instant I was through, "is that – is Mr. Burke here?" Unless I was very much mistaken, the abrupt lowering of her voice which accompanied this question, the sudden narrowing of her eyes, betokened a strong dislike for the secretary. So, then, Miss Fluette was acquainted with him, was she?

"Yes, he's here," Maillot absently replied. Then a swift look – a flash of understanding – passed between the two girls.

Both pairs of eyes, the brown and the blue, avoided mine – in a studied effort, I fancied – when I glanced from one to the other to read further.

After all, I concluded, I was glad these two young ladies happened to be present.

"The object of my coming here last night," the young man at length began, "was known only to myself and Mr. Fluette, although I told Miss Fluette the bare circumstance of my intention. My mission would seem so absurd to any sane man, so utterly hopeless; it would be so impossible to bring any one else to look at the matter from my point of view, that my fear of ridicule stayed me from taking even her into my confidence. It was this."

His voice dropped, and he had every appearance of one who speaks with the utmost reluctance.

"I came to ask my uncle for the Paternoster ruby," he announced.

I merely waited, neither stirring nor speaking; not so the two girls, however, who made no pretence of concealing their amazement.

"You asked him to *give* it to you?" gasped Miss Fluette.

Maillot laughed bitterly, looking straight at me.

"I did," said he, as one convinced that he would not be believed in any event. "I not only asked him to give it to me – after having stated my reasons – but he promised to do so – this morning."

He seemed to measure our incredulity; to determine if its degree would warrant him in proceeding. My own countenance, I know, told him nothing; but it was obvious that the girls were assimilating his startling affirmations only with the greatest difficulty. I watched them curiously. They knew this young man perhaps better than any one else, and their fresh youthful faces were a clear index to their thoughts. Both were deeply troubled.

And now Miss Cooper, after a quick side-glance at me, spoke. Her voice was remarkably sweet and soft, her whole attitude inexpressibly gentle.

"Royal," said she, "you are greatly wrought up; I think I know why; but take your time, and keep nothing back.

The truth is not going to hurt you; lack of candor may be extremely harmful."

He responded to this appeal with a slight gesture and a rather wistful smile; they reflected a certain hopelessness.

"Swift," he bluntly asked me, "have you ever heard of that confounded ruby?"

I told him that I was pretty well acquainted with its history; but did not tell him that I was cognizant of Alfred Fluette's association with it. Neither did I say anything about my knowledge of the long-standing enmity between the two men. I had already received more than one hint that the causes of the tragedy were deep and powerful, whatever their nature – I would have to find this out for myself – and I was extremely curious to hear his story.

"Then you know of the contest several years ago in London for its possession," Maillot pursued; "how Mr. Fluette coveted it for his collection, and how my uncle thwarted his efforts to obtain it. Mr. Fluette is very determined, and when his purpose is once set, it is not an easy matter to change or sway it. He was bitterly disappointed, though he never ceased hoping that some day he should acquire the jewel; but knowing Mr. Page as he did, I believe he was in a measure reconciled to a conviction that he would have to wait until the owner died.

"As I have said, his failure to get the stone was a great blow – perhaps more so than you can imagine; and, besides, my uncle stepping in in the way he did and outbidding him seemed so like a bit of petty spite-work – dog-in-the-manger, you know – that he couldn't get over it. The stone cost my uncle a cool five hundred thousand: a pretty big price to pay for the indulgence of a personal grudge, isn't it?

"And now, Swift, knowing all this as I did – the strong aversion which each felt for the other – if I should come to you and tell you that I intended asking my uncle to give me his precious ruby for the purpose of passing it on to Mr. Fluette, wouldn't you think I had become a fit subject for a lunatic asylum?"

"Yet," returned I, calmly, "you say that you did this, and that your uncle assured you he would give you the stone this morning – promised after he had heard your reasons. I must admit that your present declarations are very extraordinary; perhaps they will not seem so after you've recounted all the circumstances." And I added a bit grimly: "I'm growing impatient to hear what moved you to come here last night at all."

Once more the friendly blue eyes met mine, and I felt better for their encouragement. But Maillot's look became momentarily apprehensive.

"You already know what my most cherished hope and ambition is," he went on, with a glance at Miss Fluette. Their frequent frank exchange of ardent looks would have made that ambition plain, had I not already been apprised of it. "I'm fairly well off by reason of a small inheritance from my father, and I'm just beginning to make certain my foothold in my profession: prospects as good as most young men can boast of, I don't hesitate to say.

"Our engagement, though, has never met the approval of Belle's father. But that fails to express it: he has been actively opposed to me from the very start. We had the support of Mrs. Fluette, however, and so remained hopeful – until one week ago to-night."

He paused, staring gloomily at the table; and both the young ladies now sat with downcast eyes and sober expressions clouding their pretty faces, fairly enveloping the young fellow in their silent sympathy. Lucky chap! Maillot should have stood a good deal, uncomplainingly, too, for their deep interest in his welfare. He looked up in a moment, and proceeded.

"At that time matters reached a crisis. Last Wednesday evening I called, as I had been in the habit of doing whenever I found an opportunity; and just as I was departing Mr. Fluette sent word to me to come to his study before I left. For a bit we thought he had relented, but on reflection I couldn't entertain the idea; so, much dispirited, I went at once to see him.

"He was walking up and down before the fire, and, further than to nod his head toward a chair in a curt invitation for me to be seated, he said nothing for several minutes, but continued to pace thoughtfully back and forth between me and the hearth, as if pondering the best means of opening his mind to me.

"At last he wheeled about midway in his promenade, and bluntly fired his first question.

"'Why do you continue coming here?'" said he.

"The question stung me – of course it did; but I determined to keep my temper at any cost, and before I left, to find out at least one specific, definite reason why he didn't want me. I did, all right.

"Well, I laid my claims before him, pointing out that I was neither a pauper nor a criminal; I told him that Belle and I sincerely loved each other, and concluded by asking him whether he utterly disregarded his daughter's preferences in her choice of friends.

"'Far from it,' he replied. 'But I certainly interfere when I think she is exercising bad judgment in such a choice.'

"All at once he leaned forward and rapped sharply with his knuckles upon the table-desk, before which I was sitting.

"'One thing you fail to take into consideration,' he said, 'whether wilfully or not, I don't know, of course; but – to me – it is the most important factor of all.'

"And now, for the first time, I could see that he was not only possessed by a deep-stirring anger, but that he had been in a white-lipped fury during the whole of our conference. He went on: "'You are Felix Page's nephew. I would rather see my daughter in her coffin – yes, a thousand times rather – than allied with a man who has a drop of that hound's blood in his veins. That, Mr. Maillot, is my final word.'

"These amazing words, spoken in a voice which trembled with passion, left me speechless. But presently I rose and bowed stiffly, utterly dumfounded by the intensity of his hate for my uncle, but nevertheless keenly incensed and mortified at the injustice he was doing me.

"What had I in common with Felix Page that I should meekly bow my head before the wrath of his enemies? Nothing whatever but that bond of kinship, to which neither of the persons most interested attached the slightest importance. Mr. Page had ignored my very existence – not that I had ever looked to him for anything, because I hadn't; but during all my struggles – through school, college, my efforts at establishing a practice – he never by so much as a word or sign acknowledged that he was aware that there lived anywhere on the face of the earth such a person as Royal Maillot. He had quarreled with my mother shortly after my father's death – when I was only a kid – because she would not take charge of his household on conditions which would have been intolerable; and then he washed his hands of his sister and her child, I fancy.

"'Mr. Fluette,' said I at last, 'since your objections are not worthy of a man of your intelligence and ideals, I choose to think, therefore, that you don't sincerely entertain them; they are grossly unjust to Belle and me alike.' But he wouldn't let me go on.

"'Young man,' said he, in another wrathful outburst, 'I certainly admire your cheek – advising me – in my own house, too – as to my treatment of my own family!'

"For a second or two I returned his infuriated look; and then, resolved not to stand there bandying words nor to be led into a quarrel with him, I said: "'I'm sorry, Mr. Fluette – more than I can express – that you feel towards me as you do. Nobody could be more ignorant than I am concerning the nature of your feud with Felix Page – unless it is that you are visiting upon me the consequences of his opposition to you in the Board of Trade.'

"He spurned this supposition with a scornful gesture. So I continued: "'I am glad to know it is not that; I couldn't conceive of you doing anything so outrageously unjust. Could anything be more unfair,' I asked him, 'than to make me share all the animosities that Felix Page has engendered? Why, he is scarcely better than a stranger to me; my profound ignorance of his affairs is the best testimony that I can offer in my behalf.'"

He paused a moment and tried to drive the distressed look from Miss Belle's face with a cheering smile. He failed to do so, however, and immediately proceeded with his recital.

"Well, I failed utterly to move him; but you will be more than merely interested in what presently followed. Said he:

"'Admitting all that you say, you have brought forward nothing that is to the point; the one over-shadowing, unalterable fact remains that you *are* Felix Page's nephew. Prove the contrary to be true – satisfy me that you are free of that detestable blood taint – and you remove the last of my objections to you as a son-in-law.'

"He fell to pacing the floor again, and then presently he stopped and eyed me with a curious expression; I knew that he was turning something over in his mind. When he spoke, his words surprised and puzzled me not a little.

"'If you are so bent upon having Belle,' he said, there's just one way you may go about getting her.'

"Considering what he had already said, it is no wonder that I didn't know what to say to this. I waited, and his next words betrayed the real cause – at least, I took it to be the real cause – of his bitterness and ill will. There was a sneer in every word.

"'Bring me the Paternoster ruby,' he said, 'and if, in the meantime, she hasn't acquired some of the intelligence with which I have always credited her, why, you may take Belle.'

"After I got over being stupefied at the amazing effrontery of the thing – if accepted seriously – I began to do some pretty tall thinking, and I thought rapidly, too.

"'Is that a bargain?' I said at length. "I spoke quite calmly and seriously, and he favored me with a surprised stare. But he snapped out a curt reply.

"'It is,' said he. 'And I don't give a rap how you get it, either. I wish you success.'

"Was I cast-down and disheartened? Swift – good Lord! – words can't define my feelings. Sly disposition is sanguine enough, but when the blue devils once do get hold of me – well, I'm all in. I believe I suffer more in the dumps than any other living mortal.

"But somehow or other, that mad proposal stuck by me; it followed me persistently into the depths of my misery and colored all my hopeless cogitations – if only I could get my hands upon that bit of crimson glass! Great Scott, Swift! I believe, had I known where it was and could have gotten at it, I would have stolen it. Yes, sir, sardonically as it was advanced, the proposal to obtain the Paternoster ruby was not to be banished from my mind, and in a day or two I found myself weighing the chances of success.

"Well, the results in favor of accomplishing an undertaking so foolhardy were, even when contemplated in the most favorable light, exactly *nil*. And then there flashed into my mind a number of questions which – and I trust you'll believe me when I assert it – had never come to me before: Who was my uncle's heir? To whom, when he died, would the ruby go? Who, or what, was to benefit by all that vast wealth he was so laboriously piling up?

"Now I had – and still have, for that matter – good reasons for believing that I was the only living relative, and of course knew that if he were to die intestate the whole of his property would pass to me simply by operation of law.

"But suppose he *had* made a will – was it likely that I had been entirely ignored? The drawing of a will is a solemn matter to the party most concerned, and at such a time the tie of blood is apt to urge its claims in a still small voice – a mere whisper, maybe, but astonishingly pertinacious. Therefore, was Mr. Page so indifferent to his only living kin – had all the common feelings of humanity so far evaporated from his heart – that he would remain deaf to that feeble plea?

"The end of this line of thought was a resolution to call upon my uncle, bare my heart to him, and then appeal to him on the strength of our relationship and his loneliness, to aid me. Without presuming that I entertained any expectations from him, still, if he meant to remember me at all, I intended to urge my present necessities as out-weighing every desire and hope of the future.

"Hopeless? Crazy? Of course it was! But I never would have been satisfied until I made the effort. . . . Belle, I want to smoke."

He paused, and producing a cigarette, lighted it. But as it was plain that he had not finished, his hearers were far too absorbed in his surprising recital to break in upon the silence. Miss Fluette had followed his every word with a light of love and sympathy shining in her hazel eyes, which was undoubtedly exerting an encouraging influence over the narrator; but Miss Cooper, I observed – and not without some inward satisfaction – was covertly watching me, as if she would fathom my thoughts and read the effect which the story was producing there.

And right here let me say that at the moment I would have been hard put to it if suddenly called upon to define that effect.

First of all, Maillot had shown that he was keenly sensible of the seriousness of his position, and in looking forward to the incredible story he would have to tell, had realized that its entire trend would mean self-incrimination. As he himself might have phrased it, he was supplying me not only with a motive for the crime, but, from the time of his conversation with Mr. Fluette forward, with evidence which cumulatively inculpated himself.

So far, I had felt like one listening to a confession; as if all that I had already harkened to was but a preamble to the tragedy which was yet to follow. I may go still farther: the thought occurred to me that he might be paving the way for justification for a deed of blood. Convinced that the responsibility for Page's death lay between himself and Burke, it would appear that he was adopting the only means of getting out of a bad hole.

Still I knew in my heart that the denouement of his recital had at best been only hinted at. Had he been under arrest, it would have been my duty to warn him that whatever he might say could be used against him as evidence. Yet I was bound to listen, to encourage him to talk, if he would; but I could not help considering the effect this story would produce upon the minds of a jury. I caught a wistful look in the blue eyes; and then I told Maillot something of what was in my own mind.

"I know it, Swift," he at once returned. "But I believe my only hope lies in placing myself unreservedly in your hands. I'm going to trust myself to your – "

A queer little sound from Miss Fluette – between a gasp and a sob – checked him. She got abruptly to her feet, and fixed such a look of aversion upon me, that I hope I may never again be the object of its like. It is decidedly unpleasant not to be in the good graces of so handsome a girl. The color ebbed quickly from her cheeks, her eyes widened and her lips trembled.

"Royal," she said brokenly, but with an effort at self-control, "does this – this man mean that you are suspected of – of your uncle's *murder?*" And all her feelings were compressed into the emphasis of that last word. "Belle!" came in gentle chiding from Miss Cooper, "Don't! Can't you see that Royal is trusting to Mr. Swift?"

Then she too rose; she passed round to her cousin's side of the table, drew a chair close up to her and sat down. She took Miss Fluette's hand into her own, and sought to draw her back into her seat, just as Maillot spoke up with a confidence and assurance for which I could not help but admire him.

"Suspect me!" he cried amazedly, dashing the remnant of his cigarette into the fire. "Oh, figs! Of course he doesn't, Belle; but — look here: there are plenty who will. I want to make it plain that, in a way wholly unintentional on my part, I have got myself mixed up in a pretty bad mess, and then I want to make sure of Mr. Swift's cooperation in my efforts to extricate myself.

"My dear Belle," — a gentle note crept into his voice, — "please consider the circumstances under which I came here last night; think of the tragedy which followed so swiftly; consider the story I have to tell, and then ask yourself, Who is going to believe it? God help us both, dear girl, but this thing has all got to be brought out and aired in public!"

The fine brown eyes searched my face.

"Do you believe that Royal Maillot is guilty of this monstrous crime?" she asked me point-blank.

Before I had time to frame a reply, she once more sprang impetuously from her chair, her face flushed and her eyes sparkling with anger.

"Answer me, sir, do you believe that?"

I replied, then, calmly, if non-committally:

"As Mr. Maillot has said, I am of a disposition to help him out of a tight place, and I trust that his friends will not put unnecessary obstacles in the way of working to that end."

She said no more. Poor Belle Fluette! She was to have my sympathy more than once during the days that were to follow. Miss Cooper looked at me a little apprehensively, but I read confidence in her eyes.

"Let Mr. Maillot proceed," I now said. "It is not fair to him to fail at this stage to hear all that he has to say, providing he really desires to continue. I want to ask one question, though, before you proceed."

"Well?"

I glanced meaningly at Miss Fluette. "Considering all the circumstances, can you confide in me with propriety – just now?"

"To be sure," he replied, promptly and earnestly; "as well now as any time. You may readily imagine that to sit here and unfold affairs so intimately personal is a matter of expediency and not of choice."

He had missed my point altogether; I wanted to spare the girl.   But it wasn't for me to warn him of the complications which were likely to arise from his disclosures.

"I can well believe that," said I. "Go on."

7
HOW THE ERRAND ENDED

"Don't you know, Swift," Maillot resumed, after a meditative pause, "that it's a mighty easy matter to misjudge a man? Certain reports concerning a person become current, for example, and before we know it – perhaps without giving the matter a thought – we gradually grow to accept them as accurately descriptive of his personality.

"I have wondered more than once during the past week whether we haven't an entirely erroneous conception of every prominent man whom we don't know intimately. 'By your actions be ye judged' – if we were, most of us would be condemned out of hand.

"No, sir; it's not by a man's actions that he may be accurately appraised, but the motives that lie behind those actions; and those motives are exceedingly difficult to define. The incentive that impels us to a given act may be all right, the intention to perform it the best in the world, and then the act itself may be all wrong. Who's to blame then? Who more than any other can set himself up to censure our conduct, or lay down a code of ethics and morals for his neighbor to follow? I am assuming that you have heard a good deal about my uncle, and I know the reports concerning him are anything but flattering."

This speech fell in so harmoniously with my own train of reasoning, that I gave the young man's words the closest attention. Assuming that he was in fact guilty, as I had already tentatively theorized, then would not his present utterances appear very like a plea in vindication of his deed? – or, at least, as an apology? If he were guilty, he was supplying me the support of a sound argument.

His analysis of motives, at any rate, made me exceedingly regardful of every shifting light and shade of his really remarkable narrative. I remained keenly alert not to miss a phase of it, but carefully to ponder and weigh every one.

However, that narrative must not be retarded.

"Before I came here last night," he took it up once more, "I thought I had imagined every possible combination of emotions with which my uncle would receive my brazen offer; but his amazement when he heard me was as nothing to mine at the way in which he took it.

"First of all, in a gruff, glum sort of way, the old gentleman seemed really glad to see me; but he was in a hurry to warn me that I had better get my errand over quickly, as he was contemplating catching a nine-thirty train for Duluth – for what purpose he didn't say. As the evening wore on, however, and after I had once or twice hinted that I could wait till a more opportune time to make known my business, he impatiently commanded me to proceed; whereupon I naturally concluded that he had, since my coming, given over the projected trip.

"That fellow Burke was in the hall when I entered; and while there was nothing in his manner that I could have picked out as hostile, still I felt vaguely that he resented my intrusion. But why should he? Blamed if *I* know. As my uncle and I entered the library, Burke had the nerve to butt in with a reference to some papers and a reminder that the Duluth train left at nine-thirty. Maybe you think the old gentleman didn't turn him down cold – didn't bother Burke in the least, though, or interrupt the cool, unwavering inspection that he continued to bestow upon me. The fellow was fairly burning up with curiosity to find out what my business was.

"Well, after Mr. Page and I got in here, he put it to me bluntly: Did I want money? If so, how much and what for? Now wasn't that an encouraging beginning in view of what I was after? Nevertheless I was resolved to do or die; to be heard to the end, or else kicked out of the house forthwith. That last is what I had coming to me, all right – it's what I was looking for.

"I began by saying that I simply wanted him to listen to me for a few minutes – to hear me till I got through – and then he would know well enough what I was after. I could see that my manner, if not my words, had aroused his curiosity; thus emboldened, I plunged right in. I told him of my love for Belle."

The two of them then and there verified this all-absorbing fact by another interchange of ardent glances. Heaven knows, neither of them was in the least self-conscious or at all shy over the matter. Miss Belle seemed to glory in it; to accept his unspoken professions of devotion with a joyous sort of triumph which crowned her haughty beauty with the shining mien of a conqueror.

I thought of Mr. Fluette, financier, speculator, man of affairs that he was, and concluded that I did not at all envy him his self-imposed task of keeping asunder these two lovers. I wondered, too, in the event he could be brought to appreciate the depth and sincerity of their attachment, whether his opposition would still remain obdurate. If so, the future must be dark and stormy – if not tragic – for him. Here was a woman, if I read aright, capable of great sacrifices; she was ready to rush headlong into them, too, if need be.

Ah, well! When did a parent and a lover ever see things from the same point of view?

Maillot did not pause long.

"When I first mentioned her name, – for as I had to do so, I did it boldly, – his interest quickened, and I was positive that his attention became more respectful. He seemed to think quite suddenly that what I had to say might be of some importance, after all.

"Mr. Page was not given to betraying his mind and emotions; indeed, I believe he was usually credited with possessing an abundance of the former to the exclusion of the latter. Nevertheless I knew that he was interested, for it was at this stage that he irritably silenced my references to the nine-thirty train.

"Swift, I don't know whether I can make you see it in the way I do. It is all so marvelous and strange; the canvas is so big, and I can't handle my colors very well. During the course of my narrative he would smile now and then, or even chuckle, as though hugely delighted over some aspect of the subject which did not appear to me as being at all funny; but the instant I paused, he would promptly command me to proceed.

"Candidly, his attitude was very mystifying; but since he was not only harkening to me, but doing so with a marked, if peculiar, attention, I made the best of an extremely disagreeable task, and pleaded my cause with all the ardor of which I was capable."

I here caught Miss Cooper indulging in a furtive little smile. "When I concluded by bluntly asking him for the ruby, his face was a study." Maillot drew a long breath, and shook his head over the recollection.

"I wouldn't again undergo the ordeal of the succeeding minutes for a whole bushel-basketful of rubies, every one as large and priceless as the blessed stone I was after. It was a question whether I'd have to defend myself from a sudden assault, or be treated as a dangerous lunatic. And all the time he sat there twiddling his thumbs, apparently oblivious of my presence.

"I can see the old gentleman now. He was sitting there where Miss Cooper is, his chin on his breast, and from time to time he would take me in with a look from beneath his gathered brows, which, for sheer, downright hyperborean iciness, had a Dakota blizzard backed away down to the equator and stewing in its own perspiration. I was afraid to say anything more, and at the same time I was wild with impatience to get some inkling of what was going on behind his impassive crust.

"And, Swift, you never, never could guess how that silence was broken. He suddenly tossed his head back, and burst out with a great guffaw of laughter. I jumped clear out of my chair.

"'What a nephew!' he cried, while I stood staring at him in dumb astonishment. 'Good Lord, what I've missed by not knowing you all these years! A chip off of the old block!' He abruptly squared round on me, and paid me a compliment very similar to one I had heard a few nights before.

"'See here, my boy,' said he, admiringly, 'for pure and unlimited cheek, you're in a class by yourself. Why, the very audacity of your impudence is not without its attraction! Here you come into my house and ask me to stand and deliver a fortune, with all the light and airy assurance of a bill-collector. And the best of it is that you are dead in earnest, too – oh, Lord!' And he went off into another gale of laughter.

"I here timidly mentioned the fact that I had never in my life been more dead in earnest.

"'Earnest!' he barked at me. 'D' ye suppose I can't tell when a man means what he says? Humph!

"'But see here, my lad, it's a pity we weren't drawn together years ago,' he broke off to snap at me. 'Sit down! I'm not going to bite – if I am a "hound."'

"Well! I dropped back into my chair, where I sat blinking, a good deal bewildered, realizing only dimly that I had not been thrown bodily from the house, and, after a while, that he was not even angry.

"On the contrary, he seemed to be in the best of spirits. Presently he began to put me through a cross-examination, which I can recommend as a model for any one to follow who wants to elicit the minutiae of detail of another fellow's life.

"Before he finished, he had dragged out everything that had ever occurred to me with which anybody bearing the name of Fluette was even remotely associated – a complete history of Belle's and my acquaintance, everything I knew or had ever heard about Mrs. Fluette, all about Genevieve, and every word that I could remember that had ever passed between Mr. Fluette and myself.

"He took me through my talk with Mr. Fluette last Wednesday night I don't how many times – anyhow, until he must have had it pretty well photographed upon his mind. For some mysterious reason, he seemed to relish the epithet by which Mr. Fluette had referred to him. I'll bet I repeated that part of our conversation a score of times; and every time I uttered the word 'hound' Mr. Page chuckled.

"But by and by I came to observe that each mention of either Belle or Mrs. Fluette was received with a courtesy and respect for which I could not account. I was at last moved to ask him whether he was acquainted with them; but he testily shook his head, and bade me with some asperity not to ask questions. He dropped into a brown study pretty soon, so I shut up.

"When he spoke again his words effectively banished all speculation from my mind; in fact, they left me speechless. Of a sudden he looked at me with a sly smile.

"'My boy,' he said, almost in a whisper, 'the ruby's yours.'"

Thereupon, Maillot declared, Mr. Page inquired whether he had ever seen the ruby; to which the young man replied in the negative. The fire on the hearth had by that time sunk to a glowing bed of coals, and, save for the dim ruddy glow, the illumination was afforded by means of a single candle – just sufficient to make of the commodious library a place of ghostly shadows, and failing to relieve its farther reaches from utter gloom and darkness.

"It's a bonny bit of glass," the old gentleman had next said. "It's as compact a package, I daresay, as one can crowd a fortune into. I'll get it." With a brusque injunction to his nephew to remain where he was, he took the candle and disappeared behind the curtains of the alcove, which, as the reader will remember, concealed the passageway extending thence, through the conservatory, and into the bedroom.

Maillot could not say how long his uncle was gone; he was still too full of awe and wonder to note the passage of time; but by and by Mr. Page returned, bearing the lighted candle in one hand and a small, worn, leather box in the other.

The first he placed upon the table immediately, and then, after resuming his chair, laid the little leather box in front of himself. He sat absently tapping it with his fingers, and from time to time regarding his nephew with the same secret, indecipherable smile which the young man had already observed and wondered at.

And now we approach the most startling, the most mystifying, stage of this amazing conference.

"Before giving you this ruby," said Mr. Page, after a while, "I'm going to bind you to a few conditions – for your own protection," he had hastily added, with a grin, when the young man's face suddenly lengthened at this unexpected contingency. "You'll agree fast enough after you've heard me. If you don't, you don't get the Paternoster ruby" – and with a peculiar little laugh – "most people would agree to anything for that, my lad."

Maillot's interest was now centered upon the conditions; and they at once became a part of the fairy tale of which he was the beggar-transformed-into-a-prince hero – so much were they of a nature to add to his elation, rather than provoke objections.

Therefore he promptly acquiesced in their terms, binding himself upon his honor as a gentleman to fulfill them to the letter.

"Take this little box to Fluette," were the words with which his uncle charged him; "show him the contents, but" – and here Maillot said the old gentleman probed him through and through with a look – "on no account allow the ruby to go out of your possession – not even for the briefest instant. Whatever else he may be, Alfred

Fluette is no fool. Once he gets his fingers on this ruby, there's no telling what he'll try to put over on you. Of course he has no idea that you took him at his word, but I reckon he'll have to believe the evidence of his own senses."

Mr. Page had here rubbed his hands together in secret delight, and Maillot said that his eyes sparkled as he proceeded.

"Then you can make him come to terms. We'll see which he wants to keep the worst – his daughter, or the ruby he's sweat blood to get. . . . Won't let his daughter marry a man that has a drop of this 'hound's' blood in his veins, hey?" Page had snarled. "Well, you just watch the old 'hound' close his jaws." Suddenly he became the masterful, domineering man the world knew; he addressed Maillot in the curt, incisive tones which never failed to exact obedience.

"You tell him this, young man, exactly as I am telling it to you. Tell him you have performed your part of the bargain; tell him that the second Miss Belle is yours, the ruby shall be his; tell him he shall never get his hands on it one tick of the clock before.

"He won't hesitate; I know Alfred Fluette. If you follow my instructions explicitly, the young lady will be Mrs. Royal Maillot by this time tomorrow night. If I'm not very much mistaken, he'll be the most astounded man in the world when you open the box. You want to do it, too – open it under his nose; dazzle his eyes – hypnotize him with its blood-red flame." He had been working himself slowly into a passion; now it ended in a violent outburst. "Make the old dog get down on his hunkers and beg, d'ye hear? Make him whine! Then close the box and put it in your pocket. . . . A 'hound,' am I?"

He sat silent for a while, then went on quite calmly, in his former concise manner.

"I'll give you a line over my signature – he has mighty good reasons for recognizing it on sight – so he can't dispute your right to bargain with him. Then – "

Maillot's eagerness and impatience were so intense that he had been unable to restrain himself when the old gentleman lapsed most vexatiously into a reverie.

"Well?" Maillot had urged.

"Marry the girl. Then give Fluette the Paternoster ruby. Bring your wife to me – for after all is said and done, Royal, I'm a lonely old man. I'll see you started on a honeymoon that will make old Fluette open his eyes still wider. You never heard that I was stingy when I wanted to gratify a whim, did you? Well, it's my whim that this thing be done in the best style. I'll have to leave that part of it to you. You just go ahead and do the proper thing – and send me the bills. . . . *Hound*? Bah!"

Mr. Page sat toying with the jewel-box many minutes before he expressed himself as confident that Maillot would carry out his instructions to the letter; then, without warning, he pressed the spring and the lid flew open.

The gem lay between them like a splash of crimson flame..

8
Maillot's Experience

"We must have made a Rembrandt-like picture" – to quote the young man again – "the two of us bending over this table by the light of a solitary candle. There was a wan reflection of the flame from the polished table-top, but elsewhere all was darkness and the shadows crowded in close. The most brilliant thing in the room was that wonderful jewel, glowing and scintillating like blood-red fire.

"It was considerably larger than the end of my thumb – as large as a big hickory-nut and, my uncle averred, flawless. Rubies of such a size and without a flaw are extremely rare, I believe; in fact, there are only one or two known to be in existence. The old gentleman declared that one of five carats was worth five times as much as a diamond of equal weight, and that the value increased proportionately with each additional carat.

"But I could only sit and stare at it and wonder, and now and then pinch myself to see whether I was in reality awake and not the victim of a fantastic Arabian Nights sort of dream."

After a while the conference between uncle and nephew ended. Mr. Page would not allow the young man to depart from the house at that hour of the night with the gem, pointing out (reasonably enough) that nobody but a fool would be abroad at such a time with five hundred thousand dollars on his person; though, in his anxiety to secure the ruby and be away before his uncle had an opportunity to change his mind, Maillot might have retorted that a fool would not have had it at all.

"There are men who have left no stone unturned to discover where I have kept *this* stone," Mr. Page had concluded, with another chuckle, "and they have by no means given it up yet." Then, with grim significance in view of the tragedy which so swiftly followed, – "I'd have been murdered long ago, if it would have helped 'em to finding where I keep the stone hid."

The leather jewel-box – shabby, according to Maillot's description, and plainly showing the marks of age – was at last closed, and shortly the young man was shown to his room by Mr. Page.

Maillot declared that, ascribing the circumstance to reaction from the evening's powerful excitement, he almost immediately sank into a deep sleep.

"I was as exhausted," he amplified, "as if I had been all day digging ditches or shoveling coal. I could scarcely realize that my mission had succeeded; I feared the entire proceeding was only a stupendous, ghastly hoax, which my uncle had in mind, but to what end, or who the intended victim, I could not in the least conceive.

"And then came a crash that made me think the house had collapsed, and I knew I had been asleep. I was only dimly sensible that the noise, whatever its source, had been loud and decidedly out of place in this household at such an hour.

"I sprang from bed, and first thing banged against the door of a wardrobe, which had swung open. It nearly knocked my brains out, and hurt something awful. So I straightway forgot all about the noise, and after groping a while for matches, presently found one and lighted the candle. Then I filled the basin on the wash-stand and bathed my eye."

What followed was something more than corroborative of Burke's statement. After the secretary had rapped and Maillot thrown open the door, the latter was considerably surprised at Burke's very patent fright.

"The plain truth of the matter is that the fellow was in a condition of cowering terror," was Maillot's language, "and when I learned that he hadn't made the first move toward ascertaining the cause of the disturbance, why, I simply pushed him to one side and went to see about it myself.

"Burke disgusted me. He would neither approach the body nor allow me to get very far away from him; and when I broached the matter of going after help, he even went so far as to argue with me that there was no necessity for either of us leaving the house until daylight. The mere suggestion that he should wait here alone threw him into a blue funk; so I was finally obliged to tell him flatly, that if he didn't go, I would, and that he shouldn't follow me, either.

"Well, apparently he chose the lesser of two evils, and went to fetch the police."

I remembered Burke's reluctance to come down the front stairs, after I had sent Stodger to conduct him to me, together with my colleague's remark to the effect that "Burke didn't have much sand"; clearly, the secretary was a coward.

And now, too, I recalled the triumphant light in his pale eyes, while we were inspecting the concealed safe – the only time I had detected any expression in them – as if he had already anticipated the predicament Maillot would be in after relating his story of what had brought him to this house, and the occurrences of last night. How could he have had an inkling of all this?

However, at the time I didn't waste many minutes over an unprofitable mental catechism; there were other and more vital matters requiring immediate attention. I asked Maillot a good many questions, but elicited no further information germane to the tragedy. So I presently said:

"Have you any idea what your uncle did with the ruby after having shown it to you?"

"Well," he returned, with thoughtful deliberation, "there's the safe. I suppose, when he disappeared through the curtained alcove last night, he went at once to his bedroom, got the box from the safe, and when we separated for the night – well, I don't know; I can't guess. When he left me in my room, he was still carrying the box in his hand."

"You are positive of that?"

"Yes, positive; for after all that had happened between us, and knowing as I did what the box contained, I remember very distinctly that I looked oftener at it than I did at him. The little leather box in his left hand is more vivid in my memory than any other detail of his appearance."

"But you can remember how he was dressed?"

"Oh, yes; just as we found him. After bidding me good-night, he certainly didn't go to bed as he announced he should; he couldn't even have started to undress."

I glanced in Miss Cooper's direction. Her blue eyes were regarding me with an expression of deep and interested attention, but they also yielded a faint light of some emotion which materially aided me to a decision. I can make my position clear only by briefly sketching what was going on in my own mind.

Why did I hesitate to decide between Maillot and Burke in charging one or the other of them with the perpetration of this crime? – for crime it was, beyond a shadow of doubt. Well, there were several reasons, any one of which was sufficient, to indicate what my attitude toward these two men should be.

In the first place, both had frankly and without the least hint of reserve respecting each other's attitude that I had been able to detect, told stories which they must have known beforehand would tend strongly to incriminate them; but notwithstanding this fact, they had given their accounts with a knowledge that if they maintained a strict silence, I must have remained unable to find this information otherwise. The hostility between the two – and I could not account for it – did not explain this willingness, because neither had made an open attempt to direct suspicion toward the other.

I make a possible exception here: Burke's enigmatic conduct while we were examining the hidden safe might be construed as innuendo deliberately planned. On the other hand, if he were innocent, and considering that the two had been alone, then he might honestly have believed Maillot to be guilty, but was reluctant to make a charge which he was unable to defend with tangible proof. The circumstance of their stories agreeing in all essentials verified my conclusion that both had told the truth; still it was possible that either of them might not have told all the truth.

Again, I was convinced by the manners of both that there was more behind the tragedy than had been made to appear, excepting by the haziest sort of allusion; a potential factor whose existence had been barely suggested, whose nature remained entirely obscure. On the surface it looked as if somebody had slain Felix Page and stolen the ruby. Simple enough. But was this all? I was sure not.

The point, though, that I wish to make is this: whatever the prime motive for the murder might have been, Maillot had not the slightest idea respecting it, nor did he even suspect that such a motive existed. He was still too dazed from the whirl of events of the past twenty-four hours to consider the matter in any other light than the way in which it most nearly affected himself.

As for Burke, I was pretty much in doubt. I felt that he knew something that he was keeping in reserve, but what it might be or how to get hold of him and force the information from him I did not at this stage know.

If anything at all about the puzzle was clear, it was that the two had not and were not working together. Individually, the evidence – such as it was – more strongly indicated Maillot. It was at this moment that I looked toward Miss Cooper and decided.

"Maillot," said I, tersely, "it's up to you and Burke to submit to a personal search."

He flushed hotly, but maintained his attitude of calm. I did not dare a glance in Miss Fluette's direction.

"Candidly," I added, "I don't think you have the ruby – for that matter, I don't think Burke has either. But such a proceeding is only fair to me, for if I turn you two chaps loose I'm taking all the chances. I ought to be bundling you both off to jail; I don't want to do that, you see, and I deserve some sort of – "

"Enough," Maillot cut in. "I believe you're a good fellow, Swift; I have no objection to you going over me with a microscope."

He rose at once, extended his arms above his head to facilitate my task, and even essayed a bit of banter at my hesitating to begin.

In truth, it was hard enough to do; the presence of the two girls made the operation not only doubly disagreeable, but extremely embarrassing as well. Miss Fluette's cheeks were hot with indignation, her hazel eyes snapped. She made no comment – thank goodness! – but it was plain to be seen that she restrained herself only with the greatest of efforts. I am pretty adept at "going through" a man; and while in the present instance it required but a few moments to satisfy myself that Maillot could not have the gem, I was all the while acutely sensible of a little foot tapping nervously beneath the table and an angry look searing my offending back.

"There!" I ejaculated at last, with an attempt at making light of the matter and at including Miss Cooper and Miss Fluette as recipients of my apology. "If you'll only lose sight of the man in the instrument, you'll forgive the liberty, Maillot.

"You may go; but let me tell you" – I eyed them all seriously – "prepare for a grilling at the inquest. I would advise you to be frank, as you have been with me; the instant a jury feels that answers are being dragged from a witness they straightway receive a bad impression. I'm sure Miss Fluette would far rather put up with unwelcome publicity, than that you should suffer through any quixotic ideas of shielding her name."

He took it all as I intended he should, but never a sign of approval did I get from the two pretty girls. With my concluding words Miss Fluette thrust a hand under Maillot's arm and gave it an affectionate little squeeze.

Before the door closed, Miss Cooper's head bent and she glanced back at me across her shoulder. She was much the more beautiful of the two.

9
TRACKS IN THE SNOW

I knew that Royal Maillot appreciated his position as well as I did myself; and I felt perfectly secure in granting him his liberty. In truth, I had a certain policy in doing so. He might possibly have slain his uncle; if so, however, the act had not been premeditated, but the result of a sudden uncontrollable outburst of passion, and he was not the sort of fellow who would run away from the consequences, however severe they might be. The effects of my friendliness and my willingness to take him at his word were plainly demonstrated by a gratitude which was the more convincing and trustworthy by reason of its not being outspoken. If he was keeping anything back, I was adopting the surest means of forcing his confidence.

And I meant, too, before I was through in this house of death, to send Alexander Burke about his business. My plans concerning that gentleman, however, included an espionage that would record every detail of his conduct for some days to come. During the time I was with Maillot in the library, a number of Mr. Page's business associates had gathered at the house for the purpose of performing such offices as they could. Among these was Mr. Ulysses White – of White, Stonebreaker & White – Mr. Page's attorney. This gentleman informed me that he was quite certain the millionaire had never made any testamentary disposition of his property, in which event Maillot would inherit the whole estate. This was a contingency which the young man had already mentioned, and for a few minutes its reiteration made me grave.

After spending some unprofitable time with the assembled gentlemen – all men of affairs who were impatient to be off – I sought out Stodger, finding him engaged in conversation with the coroner's deputy, a talented and ambitious young physician of the name of Wentworth De Breen.   Later on Dr. De Breen and I became warm personal friends, and I shall have much to say of him before concluding these "Reminiscences".

He and I went together to the landing to inspect the body, for there were one or two matters concerning which I was desirous of his opinion. Dr. De Breen was a blunt, abrupt young fellow, not given much to conversation upon topics outside his profession, and even then his remarks were invariably terse and much to the point.

He was very near-sighted, and while he persisted in wearing nose-glasses, it seemed impossible for him to obtain a pair that would remain on his nose for more than a minute at a time. They were saved from destruction by a black silk cord; and there was something in the way with which he would adjust them and fix his attention upon a person or thing, which made you feel that whatever escaped his scrutiny must be surpassingly minute. And such, indeed, was the fact.

He examined the crushed skull, silently and methodically, touching it here and there with fingers as light and refined as any woman's.   Not a word did he utter until of a sudden he bent a scowling look of comprehension upon the iron candlestick.   The only cranial wound or contusion was on the right temple.

"Who did this, Swift?" he asked.

"That's the problem, Doctor," was my reply.   "There are two chaps, though, who are in a devil of a ticklish position.   Since you're here now, it will probably be you who will conduct the inquest, and I'm a little curious to see how the evidence strikes you."

He nodded, and after deftly recovering his glasses, emptied the pockets.   They yielded up nothing of the slightest consequence to either of us, and in a moment Dr. De Breen hesitated and frowned over the body's left hand.

He presently took it in his own hand, and scrutinized it intently, I watching him interestedly, for he had stumbled upon one of the very points concerning which I wanted his opinion. Next he turned quickly to the right hand. Both members were bruised and discolored in spots, and bore a number of abrasions.

Dr. De Breen now darted one of his quick, penetrating looks at me.

"Carrying something," he said concisely. "They couldn't break his grip – rapped him over the head."

"So that's what you make of those scratches and bruises, is it?" – for I wanted to be convinced.

"Sure. . . . What was it?"

"I think I know," was my reply: "an oblong, leather box, about four inches by three or three and a half."

"Humph!" – as he filled in the blanks of a removal permit – "not much to kill a man for."

"Ever hear of the Paternoster ruby?" said I, casually.

Dr. De Breen turned to me with uplifted brows, and his glasses at once shot to the end of their tether. He blinked a moment.

"The devil!" he then muttered. "You don't say!" From which I gathered that he had heard of it, and also that he had already drawn his own inference as to the contents of the leather box.

"I'll wait till after the inquest, Swift," he informed me at parting, with a very direct and authoritative manner; "but if this case turns up any promising features, I'm in; get that?"

I grinned cheerfully. "Very well, Doc."

And the last I saw of him, as he went away, he was still feeling aimlessly for the silken cord, the while his mind was intent upon something else. A queer, congenial chap was Wentworth De Breen, and as keen and fine-strung, despite his absent-mindedness, as is said to be the bridge leading across to Mahomet's paradise. He had a whim for dabbling in such puzzles as my calling now and then brought me face to face with; and before I got through with Mr. Page and his ruby, this hobby of the doctor's was to supply me with an invaluable bit of evidence.

I carried the removal permit to Mr. Ulysses White, and then betook myself to a more thorough examination of the tragedy's surroundings.

First of all, I went again to the untidy bedroom and the closet above the concealed safe.

A careful and methodical search brought very little to light which I thought might subsequently be of use to me. I examined the safe carefully with an idea of discovering a secret compartment; but there was none. The position of the safe itself, evidently, had been considered sufficiently private by the builders.

I paused for a moment beside an old-fashioned walnut table which stood close by the bed's head. Its top had been covered at some remote period with artificial leather, which was held around the edges by a strip or braid of similar material, the whole made secure by ornamental brass-headed tacks placed at intervals of two or three inches.

In the dust on the imitation leather cover was an oblong imprint which, the instant I perceived it, I was seized with a caprice to measure. Its dimensions proved to be just four by three and one-half inches.

Now, this mark in the dust was so manifestly fresh, and its size and shape so suggestive, that before I was well aware of the mental operation, my mind had already accounted for its presence there.

After Mr. Page had obtained the ruby from the safe last night, he had, for some reason, paused by this table before returning to Maillot in the library, and had laid the box thereon. Why? He had retained the candle, which he was at the time carrying, for there was no indication in the dust that he had temporarily relieved himself of that object. Had he turned aside to get something from the bed? – or maybe from the table?

The first mentioned, though unmade since it had last been slept in, was not disarranged in the way one would be obliged to disturb it in getting at the usual places of concealment, and it was hardly likely that Mr. Page would have taken the pains to obliterate any such indications.

As for the table, it had no drawer.

Pondering the matter, perhaps more than it warranted, I turned to the dresser. The only detail here worth a passing notice was a small pasteboard box containing a number of .38 caliber cartridges. Originally there had been fifty in the box. I counted them. Six were missing; just the number required to charge the cylinder of most revolvers of the same caliber. However, there was no revolver; nor did my entire examination of the apartment avail to bring one to light.

At last, – just as I was turning to leave the room, – I received a shock which, for the time being, fairly paralyzed me.

As I have already recorded, the room in which I now was occupied that portion of the ground floor immediately behind the conservatory, and in the wing containing the library – that is, the eastern wing, as the house fronted south. Two large windows, small-paned and opening on hinges, afforded light and ventilation. It was through one of these that my surprise came.

On entering the room I had drawn aside one of the blinds, and had done so without more than the most casual glance outward, because I had already thoroughly inspected the premises contiguous to the house.

But now, as I lifted my hand to draw the blind over the window again, I happened to look at the snow beneath the window. In a flash I froze, my outstretched hand remaining suspended in mid-air.

When Burke, Maillot, and I had been in this room an hour or so earlier, the snow was then like an unsullied tablet upon which no character had been written; but since that time – during the very minutes I had been busy in this room, perhaps – it had received a record. Somebody with unusually small feet – small enough to be a woman's – had walked around from the front of the house to the window. After looking in – possibly at me intent upon my investigation – the mysterious prowler had departed again, but not as he had come. The retreating footsteps extended away at a right angle from the house, and at a short distance disappeared among some shrubbery.

A moment's reflection made me feel sure that only my presence in the room had forestalled a rather perilous undertaking. Why should anybody want to look in, simply, and why adopt such a compromising means of entering, if the temptation had not been extraordinarily powerful?

My hesitation was but momentary. I flung open the window, leaped out and commenced running along the trail of the daring, unknown visitor. The visit had been so recent that I was spurred by a faint hope of overtaking the fellow.

I had not proceeded far before I heard a shout from the house. I glanced back without slacking, and saw Stodger staring at me in amazement from an up-stairs window. Motioning to him to remain where he was, I continued to follow the footprints.

As soon as the bushes screened me from the house, I arrived at a point where the trail presented a new aspect: the distance between the impresses measurably widened, signifying that my unknown caller had broken into a run the instant the shrubbery concealed him from the house. I quickened my pace.

The chase led me to a low stone wall marking the boundary of the premises, across some vacant lots, to the intersection of two streets, where the presence of a trolley line discouraged further pursuit.

On one of the corners, however, stood a grocery of the suburban variety; and when I arrived hatless and without an overcoat, the grocer came out, and eyed me curiously.

"Did you see anybody just ahead of me come this way?" I panted.

"Yep," returned the grocer. "Fellow came running across those lots not five minutes ago. Three other fellows waiting for him on the corner here."

"Three others!" I exclaimed. I hadn't the least idea what it all meant.

"Yep," said the grocer. "When he came there were four. The whole bunch caught a down car. They was Chinymen."

I could do no more than vent my bewilderment in ejaculations. "Chinamen!" I cried.

"Or Japs," remarked the grocer. "Come to think of it, they must've been Japs; they didn't have no pigtails."

Well, there was nothing else for me to do but turn round and go back the way I had come. The grocer could tell me no more, and I was completely stumped. Why four Chinese – or Japs – should be interested in my movements in the Page house I could not in the least imagine.

But one thing was certain. I had skirted the border of some secret, desperate enterprise. It challenged directly all my powers and capabilities. I was irritated, nettled, not at my inability to fathom the mystery at once, but at a species of mental numbness which prevented me from even conjecturing a plausible theory to account for the strange episode.

I strode along in a deep, moody revery, unconsciously scanning each in turn of the absurdly small footprints. I vaulted the low wall into the Page premises, and before I had fairly recovered my balance, I pounced upon a folded sheet of paper which lay in the snow on one side of the trail.

I unfolded it. The sheet bore a roughly sketched floor plan of some house's interior. There was a wide hall, a square stair-well, and three or four rooms. One of the rooms – the smallest – had been designated by a cross.

All at once I uttered a little cry. This was a second-floor plan of the very house I had been exploring. Although I had not been up-stairs yet, I had seen enough of the relative positions of the different rooms to recognize the one indicated by the cross.

It was the bath room.

10
THE SECOND STORY

The reader will have observed, very likely, that up to the present I have made no mention of a close examination of the second story, nor, moreover, of having ascended the stairs above the balcony-like landing with its gruesome burden.

Such was indeed the case; and while my failure in this regard might argue neglect, or at least a strange lack of system, I can only point out that the entire sequence of events, from the moment of my arrival at the house, had been most unusual.

It is rare that so many divagations become inevitable. I was obliged to acquaint myself with the circumstances as they forced themselves upon me, and not as if I had been free to ferret them out in accordance with any customary course of procedure. All along I had been impatient to get up-stairs; but first one thing and then another had arisen, demanding immediate attention. We shall soon learn, however, how my search in the second story was rewarded. While the results may appear not very significant, they were nevertheless of vast importance in pointing a way to the riddle's answer.

For, mind, although I was reasonably sure that the ruby represented the motive for the murder, I had been given a number of reasons for believing that this motive involved a plot infinitely farther-reaching than the determination of some common thief or housebreaker to secure the gem. If I wanted to fix responsibility for Mr. Page's cruel death, I would be obliged to lay bare the controlling cause in all its ramifications. Whether Maillot or Burke was the guilty man, it was at this stage of vital consequence that the State's Attorney be given light upon every factor in the tragedy; and as this was my business, it is not surprising that I was animated with an ambition to make a thorough job of the matter.

And furthermore, I was satisfied that the Paternoster ruby had not yet been removed from the house, wherever the murderer might be – a belief which I was very shortly to have strengthened by certain seemingly unimportant incidents.   The trail in the snow was one of these confirmatory incidents, although I had no occasion yet to so regard it.

While it was my first duty, therefore, to discover the murderer, I saw no reason why I should not at the same time find the well-nigh priceless gem, inasmuch as I hoped that the latter would point definitely to the former.

The ruby had disappeared between eleven o'clock last night and the time of Stodger's arrival – shortly before three in the morning.   One of the two men who had passed the night in the house might have secreted it. Their presence offered the most plausible explanation.

Was Maillot the one?   His fantastic story was certainly a strain upon one's credulity, I must confess; yet, I had sat face to face with him, and I am not without skill – nor was I at the time – in penetrating a man's outward aspect and discerning the sincerity of his purpose.   In justice to him, I can not emphasize too strongly how convincing had been every utterance of his, the which I have been at some pains to record. And then, I could not attribute the freshly oiled hinges nor the rifled safe to Maillot. Consequently the next step was to turn to Burke: when I did so I was met only by a mental image of his inscrutable tawny eyes; the baffling, impassive visage which showed no mark of age.

Well, Maillot did not have the ruby. And now, if a search of Burke's person and belongings resulted as the former search had, why, I must look to some hiding-place near at hand. And this was a task after my own heart. I cast ahead in pleased anticipation to some delightful hours after nightfall in this dreary old mansion, when I would be alone and at liberty to pursue my quest with the least likelihood of being disturbed.

If the ruby were really here, I meant to remain pretty close to it until it came to light, or else have a dependable substitute take my place when it should become necessary for me to go abroad. It was this determination which led to the scar that will disfigure my face as long as I live.

The erstwhile secretary submitted without demur to an examination of his clothing, and without any change of expression that I could perceive. The pale eyes followed my movements with a blank, incurious stare (though Stodger maintains that they did not cease for an instant regarding him), and I was glad enough to see the fellow depart, after I had privately passed word to Stodger not to lose Burke until another man could relieve him.

The flight of stairs above the landing gave upon a hall which – excepting in the front, where there was a large diamond-paned window – entirely surrounded the stair-well, and was continued by a lateral passage connecting the gables or wings.

One leaning over the balustrade at the top looked down upon the ascending stairs, the balcony midway up, and a good portion of the spacious hall below. The lateral hall gave access to all the rooms on the second floor.

An examination of the appended plan, although drawn from memory and by fingers to which such a task is strange, will give a better idea of the *locus criminis* than any amount of verbal description alone can accomplish. So the reader, if he will consult the chart from time to time as the narrative proceeds, will escape much confusion in his attempts to follow the movements of the different actors.

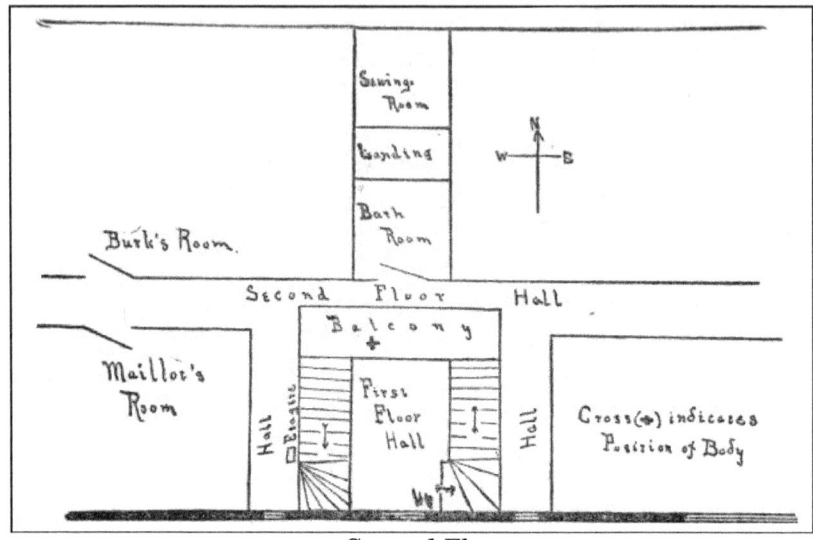

Second Floor

Arriving at the head of the stairs, I first gave my attention to the *etagere*. This piece of furniture was simply a pedestal of shelves, without sides, front, or back, so that to tilt it in any direction far out of the perpendicular would mean to spill its burden of old newspapers and periodicals.

Maybe it would have been convenient in a music-room, but situated where it was it was certainly in the way of anybody using the stairs. If a person unfamiliar with the house should ascend the stairs in the dark, the instant he turned at the top he must almost inevitably collide with it – a circumstance which I was to have brought home to me a few nights later, with consequences which missed being fatal by only the slenderest of margins. But after all, I concluded, if a stranger missed it only by a miracle it might have served a double purpose here; no one slept in the second story, ordinarily, and it would make a good burglar alarm, as well as a repository for the iron candlestick and the sea-shell match receptacle.

From the point where it now leaned against the balusters back to the lateral corridor or hall, there were many little details to arrest and stimulate my curiosity. The carpet between these two points plainly showed signs of a recent struggle, and at the western vortex of the angle formed by the balustrade surrounding the stair-well, innumerable drops of congealed paraffin were scattered widely over the floor.

And the railing itself also held a record. Stout as were the uprights sustaining it, it had received the impact of a body sufficiently heavy to throw it askew. At this point on the railing there was a deep triangular dent, destined to assume a high place in solving the problem of Felix Page's murder.

When I stood directly in front of the bath room door, I could look down over the balustrade to the landing – the body had been removed to a more suitable place – and I could also see the front door and most of the first-floor hall.

A dozen or so feet west of the stair-well two doors opened upon the lateral passage. They were directly opposite each other; the front room having been the one occupied by Maillot the previous night, while the other was Burke's.

Now as I allowed my glance to rove along the dim-lighted hall in the direction of the two bed-chambers, it was at once arrested by some small – and at the distance, indistinguishable – object lying in the centre of the floor a few feet beyond the two doors. I went and picked it up.

It was the shabby leather jewel-case.

But now it bore many indications of extremely rough usage. It was not only open, but empty; the lid was bent, twisted out of shape, and hanging precariously by one damaged hinge. The leather was freshly torn and scratched, while the inner lining of faded blue satin had been slit in a number of places. I contrived after some manipulation to get the box into a semblance of its former shape, and then slipped it into a pocket of my coat.

Neither Maillot's room nor Burke's revealed anything of much consequence. In the former I noted the open wardrobe door, and, owing to its position relative to the bed, was obliged to admit the likelihood of Maillot's accident. In the other room, in a small leather satchel, were the papers by which Burke accounted for his presence. They were of no interest to me. I turned them over to Mr. White, who, with the other gentlemen, was just departing.

With a feeling of lively anticipation, I entered the bath room. I had not forgotten that this room alone had been designated by a distinguishing mark on the chart which I had found while following the mysterious footprints. But I discovered nothing to justify my hopes. The place was monotonously like other bath rooms in which I had been. I gave it an exceptionally thorough overhauling, then went carefully over it once more – even resorting to my magnifying-glass from time to time – but all to no purpose; the room was discouragingly wanting in anything that might be regarded as a clew.

In the end I fell to musing over a bar of common laundry soap on the stationary wash-stand. It was impossible not to contrast this humble detergent – for it was of a bigness and coarse yellowness to suggest the largest possible quantity for the smallest possible price – with the dead man's wealth, and to wonder a little at such petty economies as were signified by it, by the paraffin candles, the absence of servants, and by some other details of the *menage* which perhaps I have already mentioned.

I recalled, with a smile, that Burke had smelled of laundry soap, and that on the wash-stand in Maillot's room there had been no soap at all. Well, there are some queer ways of utilizing wealth; but I contend that, of all of them, to deny oneself the commonest comforts of existence is the queerest and the hardest to understand.

A philosophy of living is involved utterly incomprehensible to me.

Passing through the bath room, I emerged upon the landing of the rear stairs. Across the landing was another small room, which contained, besides a dust-mantled sewing-machine, nothing but some broken and worn-out furniture.

I followed the stairway to the bottom, and about half-way down found a bit of flattened paraffin about the size of my thumb nail.

After re-ascending these stairs I stood once more looking idly down over the balustrade, going over in my mind the parts of the puzzle which had been set for me to bring together into an intelligible and perfectly rounded whole, and wondering what I would succeed in making of it all. For a while I was aware of a strange lack of confidence in myself, of a feeling of uncertainty. Had I been negligent in not arresting both Maillot and Burke? It seemed the simplest and most direct method of proceeding; it would be no difficult matter to fasten the crime on one or the other, or both of them; why should I go behind the few plain details which lay so invitingly before me?

Perhaps the intrusion of a pair of blue eyes into the midst of my cogitations had much to do with my irresolution. Somehow I was extremely desirous of winning their approval. The possibility that I might win more did not enter my thoughts, because, I reflected rather dismally, the owner of the blue eyes moved in a sphere in which I had neither part nor parcel.

Still, my determination to solve the mystery of Felix Page's death was inextricably interwoven with another determination to win one final friendly, commendatory look – perhaps a word or two, or even a warm hand-clasp – from Miss Genevieve Cooper.

How was I to do that? By fastening an odious crime upon her cousin's lover? I shrank from such an alternative. Heaven grant that so far I had not reasoned falsely.

It may seem a poor business thus to mix sentiment with one's humdrum daily affairs; but – well, and so it is. After mature reflection, I can think of but one extenuating plea: I was only twenty-six at the time.

Up to the present it had been difficult to ascribe to each circumstance its own proper value; but now they were beginning to shape themselves into some semblance of order, and for the first time a fairly complete concept of the tragedy's enactment irresistibly presented itself to me.

The antecedent circumstances leading up to the crime, however, were largely conjectural, although they were pretty strongly suggested by the details of the struggle itself. I was thus enabled to supply the missing portions with more or less plausibility. Here, then, is the way I reconstructed the night's occurrences in this house – the fatal sequence of events which began when Felix Page bade Maillot good-night, culminated in the older man's death, and ended with the flight of the murderer. You will perceive that the four "Chinese" had no place in it; I could find none for them.

After Mr. Page and Maillot separated, for some reason the former had not retired. I took it as being more than likely that he had returned to the library, where presently he fell into a doze before the dying fire. But, no, first of all he went to the safe to dispose of the box containing the ruby; after that he returned to the library. While he nodded over the fire the thief stole to the safe, opened it *with the combination*, and took not only the ruby, but everything else the strong-box contained.

But cautious as the thief is, some disturbing noise penetrates to the sleeper's consciousness; in fancy we may see the old man – fox, pirate of the pit, as he had been called – starting broad awake, fearless, every faculty alert and strained to catch the betraying sounds.

In a moment he bestirs himself to ascertain what is afoot in his house at so unseemly an hour. Noiselessly he enters the hall from the library, in time to behold the marauder – by the latter's own candle flame, I was positive – ascending the front stairs.

And here the tragic episode departs from all precedent; at this stage it assumes its baffling aspects. If the thief had not been a member of the household – even but a temporary member – why should he have gone up the stairs instead of leaving the house by the nearest way? And again, why should Mr. Page have followed the thief so stealthily if he had not recognized him?

But the master of the house steals on up the stairs behind the other. At about the time he arrives at the head of the stairs the thief vanishes: else why did Mr. Page pause to light the candle in the iron candlestick which stood upon the *etagere*?

Fatal move, that! In some manner the *etagere* is knocked forward against the balustrade; the thief is alarmed, although some door must have closed behind him. And now the old gentleman is facing no longer a thief merely, but a man with murder in his heart.

Which door had it been: Maillot's, or Burke's, or yet some other door?

Once more we are given a strong indication that Felix Page knew the man, for he and the assassin *in limine* do not immediately close in combat. Not yet. Some words certainly pass. The taper in the heavy iron candlestick must burn long enough to account not only for the drops of paraffin scattered about over the floor, but those that ran like congealing tears down the side.

I could fancy the outraged and mystified old gentleman demanding an explanation, and before long exploding with wrath, the thief standing hopelessly convicted – caught "with the goods."

Suddenly the struggle is precipitated by the infuriated householder endeavoring to recover his property. We may safely assume that it was by no gentle means that he sought to do this, and at once the battle wages to and fro between the head of the stairs and the lateral passage, quite up to the bath room door. The thief is striving to retain the leather box, the other to wrest it from him.

It is pretty certain, too, that the old gentleman hastily put down the iron candlestick before he grasped the box – on the floor, somewhere near the western angle of the balustrade – and in the end, as the combat in one of its uncertain revolutions sweeps past it, the thief frees himself with a desperate effort, snatches it from the floor, and becomes an assassin *in actu.*

The dull impact of the blow, as the scene is blinded by sudden darkness; the crash of the body against the railing; the dominant jar when the body strikes upon the landing below – and the dark deed is accomplished.

What next follows?

Panic on the part of the murderer, we may be sure, as he stands one second in a stupor of horror at what he has done; then he must have flown – whither?

It is at this juncture that Alexander Burke steps into the hall, and beholds nothing in the light of his own candle. It is at this point that Royal Maillot springs from his bed, collides with the open wardrobe door, and straightway forgets the tumult in his own physical suffering, until Burke raps upon his door. And it is at this point that, unless there was some third person in the house, either one or the other of these two young men has deliberately lied. In turning them both loose I trusted to convict the guilty man by his own conduct. It will develop how far my course was justified.

The mute but vivid testimony would seem to lead, step by step and with irresistible logic, straight to the private secretary – had it not been for two circumstances which placed him once for all beyond the possibility of having been the person who struck the blow.

First, he would have been but as a babe in Felix Page's powerful grasp; there would have been no struggle at all.

Second, the fellow was an arrant coward, and he would never have offered the least resistance unless convinced that he was in imminent peril of his life — which was improbable.

The rear stairway was associated with the thought of Burke's cowardice, for he had chosen that way to accompany Stodger: whose shoe-sole had left the flattened fragment of paraffin there?

For some time I had been alone in the house — save, of course, for the still, sheeted form. The place was as silent as any tomb. Then of a sudden a sound smote upon my ear that brought me in a flash to attention.

There is a certain fascination about a door slowly opening in a house which you suppose to be empty. Until you have found out the cause you ascribe it to anything from ghosts to Bengal tigers, and even then may be sure of a surprise. The invisible agency may turn out to be only the wind or a wandering cat. But it makes no difference what starts the door to swinging open; the bald fact of its doing so when by all known laws it should remain firmly shut, is *per se* potent enough, or hypnotic enough, — or whatever influence it is that it exerts, — to root you at once to the spot until the Unseen declares itself. In truth, an opening door is pregnant with such infinite possibilities.

It was with some such sort of suspended animation that I stared down over the balustrade and waited, my look glued upon the front door. It swung inward with a slowness inexpressibly aggravating. And then I recoiled with a little cry.

Miss Genevieve Cooper was standing in the lower hall, pale and trembling, and darting quick nervous glances in every direction.

11
A PACT

At my involuntary expression of amazement, Miss Cooper looked up, and our eyes met. Her charming face immediately broke into a smile; her fears seemed to fall away from her like the dissolving of a sun-smitten mist.

"Mr. Swift!" she exclaimed under her breath. Her voice expressed relief. And, too, she spoke as if there might be others in the house whom her errand did not in the least concern. "I'm so glad! I was afraid I should not find you here."

The idea of her wanting to find me for *any* reason was distinctly pleasing. I'm afraid I appeared for the moment a trifle foolish; I was tongue-tied, at any rate.

"May I come up?" she went on brightly. "Or will you come down?"

She was so pretty standing there and looking up at me, so everything that a dainty, refined little lady should be, that I could have remained indefinitely watching her.

But I'm glad to say that I did not. I found my tongue by and by, and voiced some inane remark to the effect that she might most assuredly "come up," if she had the least inclination to do so, but, on the other hand, that I was more than willing to "come down." Which I did, when she made known her choice by sitting down in the settle Stodger and I had occupied some hours earlier.

But I moved down the steps deep in meditation. Great as had been my surprise when the opening front door disclosed Miss Cooper, I was not long in surmising why she had come, and I was more than a trifle reluctant to discuss the brutal details of the tragedy with a lady so obviously gentle and refined. The subject was so utterly foreign to anything within her experience that I felt she could harken to and review the different aspects of the crime only with shuddering aversion. But, dear me, how incapable is any man of estimating a woman's fortitude!

While I descended to her, she continued to talk – the merest bit flurried, perhaps, but with a direct, fearless glance which the dullest comprehension must have understood.

"I suppose I should have rapped," she was saying; "but who was here to open the door? Poor Mr. Page! Poor man! How terrible it is!"

She was a little awed, and seemed glad when at last I stood confronting her.

As if it were the most natural thing in the world to do, she made room on the settle for me to sit beside her. I did so, awkwardly enough. There was not the slightest trace of coquetry in her conduct, she was entirely free from the least indication of affectation, and I could not do otherwise than meet her in the same spirit, although I apprehended some difficult moments before our colloquy should be finished. Her errand must indeed be urgent that she should alone brave this house of death.

After a minute of hesitation on her part, during which she sat with downcast eyes while I took a base advantage of the opportunity to drink in her loveliness, she abruptly faced me. Her countenance reflected an expression of determination, tempered by the wistfulness of uncertainty and doubt.

"Mr. Swift," she began, in a straightforward manner, "it was simply impossible for me not to have sought you out – if not here, then at the police station, or wherever it is you make your headquarters."

I remarked that a message would have brought me speedily to her.

"Oh, no!" in quick protestation. "There is no place where we could have been private – to-day. And, besides, I wouldn't have put you to so much trouble."

"Trouble!" I interrupted. "I would have been only too glad."

She smiled at my warmth, proceeding:

"Anyhow, I succeeded in finding you alone; now tell me – truly – am I bothering you?"

"Truly, you are not bothering me in the least. I can fancy nothing nicer than sitting just like this and talking – with you. It's so – so – "

"Comfy?" – archly.

"Exactly. But that's a woman's word; I never would have thought of it."

The handsome eyes flashed a look at me which made me hastily revise my opinion that she was entirely free from any trace of coquetry.

"I didn't come here to listen to nice things," she said, smiling into my eyes; "I'm awfully serious."

And, in very truth, she straightway grew grave. She drew a long breath, and sat suddenly more upright, questioning me with a look. Such fine, honest eyes!

Her first spoken interrogation was direct enough, in all conscience; while I was expecting some such inquisition, I was by no means prepared with an immediate answer.

"I want to know, Mr. Swift, – is it going to appear that Royal Maillot murdered his uncle?"

She spoke very quietly, but, too, very earnestly. Murder is an ugly word; I marvelled that she did not shrink from it.

"Why are you so anxious to know, Miss Cooper?" I temporized – "out of friendship for Mr. Maillot?"

"No," frankly meeting my intent look, "though that would be a sufficient reason." She paused a moment, biting her under lip in the intensity of her musing. Then,
–

"Mr. Swift, I'm going to be perfectly candid with you; I'm going to lay bare my mind – and my feelings. I pray that you will do the same by me. Am I presuming too much?"

Lay bare my feelings – great heavens! She would have thought me crazy. In a sense, Torquemada himself could scarcely have made me more uncomfortable; but I would not have had that delightful *tete-a-tete* broken in upon for anything in the world.

"I realized this morning," she proceeded, after I had clumsily begged her to, "that Royal is in a desperate plight, though why or how he came to be I can't understand.

"I realized, too, that the story he told will appear incredible – even ridiculous – to anybody who does not know him. I do know him" – I could well believe that! – "and for that reason, nothing short of an admission of guilt from him would cause me to consider him as a participant – in any capacity, Mr. Swift – in last night's tragedy."

"Your loyalty does you credit," I murmured, for lack of anything better to say.

"Loyalty?" she cried, with emotion. "Oh, Mr. Swift! That's not the word! It's not loyalty that moves me to speak in Royal's behalf, although I would do much for him in any case. But – Belle – "

She was stopped by a sudden accession of feeling, and I tried to inject into my demeanor the encouragement she quite plainly needed.

"Before you go on," I quietly observed, "I will say that Mr. Maillot impressed me very favorably."

"Yes," quickly; "I also perceived that. It was that circumstance which finally overcame my reluctance to intrude upon you. You were greatly puzzled, though, baffled, by his extraordinary story."

"Not baffled, I trust," I said.

"Well, no; perhaps not baffled. But the extravagant recital that fell from his lips must have seemed to you fantastically improbable.

"It is chiefly for Belle Fluette's sake, however," she pursued, "that I want to learn – oh, everything about this dreadful affair – all the little details. I want to enlist your sympathies for Royal; not against him."

It was a relief when she grouped her desire for information into this vague generalization; I could see my way as long as she was not too specific. But some further intimate knowledge respecting this pretty young lady was imminently in store for me.

"Miss Cooper," said I, "I am against no man – except the guilty one; and even he, in a measure, has my sympathy."

"Then" – she was suddenly breathless – "in your estimation. Royal is *not* the – the – not the guilty – "

My smile checked her. Alas, I was not to escape.

"You read a meaning into my speech that was not in my mind," I said – and immediately regretted it. Her countenance at once reflected a deep concern.

"Please, please, Mr. Swift, don't be inscrutable with me," she pleaded.

I thrilled at the wistful light in her handsome blue eyes, and I looked longingly at the wavy brown tresses and at the scarlet lips, now eagerly parted and revealing a glimpse of pearly perfection beyond. Such delectable realities were quite unknown in my lonely life, and before them the image of Miss Fluette's more highly colored and aggressive beauty faded away to a mere blur.

"Miss Cooper," I rejoined, with perhaps unnecessary warmth, "heaven forbid that I should not be frank with you. The truth is, I'm sorely perplexed. It did not require this appeal from you to spur me on to find a way for Mr. Maillot out of his predicament, for undeniably – whether by his own fault or by accident – he's in a very serious one. Maybe, if you will state more definitely just what you want to know, I can then tell you."

The expressive eyes thanked me, then suddenly twinkled with a gleam of humor.

"Even a mere man," she sagely remarked, "could not have remained blind to the fact that Belle and Royal – foolish children! – are awfully fond of each other."

"Your assumption of mature wisdom is eminently becoming," said I, "because it is so apparent."

"My!" she retorted. "I really believe you improve with acquaintance."

"Thanks," I said; "I need encouragement."

"On the contrary," she said coolly, "I think a snubbing is what you need."

I dodged. "Yes," said I, "I could not help noticing that their affection is – er – rather immoderate."

Instantly a tiny line appeared between her brows; she was all seriousness again.

"There you have my interest in this matter – my reason for meddling," she informed me. "Belle's welfare means a great deal to me; just how much you can perhaps best understand after hearing a bit of my history. Have you the patience?"

What a question! Lucky it was for me this day that I could combine business with the delight of reveling in this agreeable *tete-a-tete*. It was lucky, in truth, for all who were being drawn into the web of the Page affair. For if the two had not fitted so smoothly together, the interests of the Central Office would have been forgotten.

She colored prettily at the ardor of my gaze – it was of no use; I couldn't help it – but save for the circumstance that she temporarily averted her look from mine, went steadily ahead with what she had to say.

"I have been an orphan ever since I can remember, though my father and mother are not even memories. They fell victims to yellow fever in New Orleans before I was two years old. Uncle Alfred took me at once into his household, which has been my home all of my life that I know anything about.

"I am two years older than Belle, but reared together as we have been, we are more nearly sisters than cousins.

Indeed, I even believe that we are closer together than most sisters; we love each other very, very dearly.

"You can see, then, how anything affecting her will equally affect me. Belle has been gently nurtured; she is a proud, high-spirited, intrepid girl, but of a delicate organism that would break beneath the shock of Royal Maillot being stigmatized by such a crime. I tremble to think of it!"

Her look was again bent upon me, with utmost gravity now, and her voice broke a little as she concluded:

"Can you comprehend my anxiety, Mr. Swift? Can't you see that I would make any sacrifice to forestall such a dreadful chance?"

In spite of her reserved nature and admirable habit of self-control, it was easy to see that she was deeply affected; she was, indeed, torn by conflicting doubts and anxieties; and I became meditative and, for her sake, exceedingly desirous of lightening the burden of her worry.

That very beautiful and very wilful young lady, her cousin, would never have made such an appeal to me. I did not care to conjecture the way in which she, long before this stage of the conversation, would have been expressing her indignation and withering me with her scorn and contempt.

"Miss Cooper," said I at length, "assume for just a moment that Mr. Maillot *is* guilty: would you counsel me, for the reasons you have stated, to turn aside from my duty and permit him to go unpunished?"

She caught her breath sharply. Her lips went suddenly white, and her look became a trifle wild. I watched her keenly.

"Mr. Swift!" she presently whispered, in dismay. "How unfair!"

"I do not mean to be unfair," I tried to make clear; but she cut me short.

"Are you trying to prepare me for – for the worst?"

"Gracious, no!" I expostulated, with an embarrassed laugh.   "But I should like to have you answer my question."

"It is hideous even to assume such a thing," she very soberly made answer; "but if such were actually the case, I – I – "

"Well?" I prompted curiously, when she paused and pressed a hand to her throat.

Of a sudden the lovely eyes were brimming with tears. She timidly laid a hand upon my arm.

"You *don't* think he's guilty, do you?" she murmured distressfully. It wrung my heart.

"Don't – please don't," I said hastily. "Here is my honest opinion, Miss Cooper: whatever that young man has done to involve himself in this affair, I am sure that he is no deliberate, cold-blooded assassin; my judgment of his character could not be so far at fault.

"For the same reason I am strongly inclined to believe his story, preposterous as it appears standing alone.   I don't mind admitting – to you, Miss Cooper – that I'm looking beyond him for the guilty man."

She drew a long breath of relief and clasped her hands in her lap. But how little did either of us realize that we had disposed of one difficult situation only to turn round and find ourselves face to face with another. My candor, to which she had made such a powerful appeal, soon led to an impasse; one that neither of us was in the least prepared for.

"Of course," she said presently, in a low voice, "I would not utter a word or lift a finger to influence you from what you regard as your duty. If your assumption were true, why, I would be with Belle, doing all that lies within my humble power to comfort her."

She leaned toward me impulsively, her face all at once bright and animated.

"Mr. Swift," she began, and stopped amid sudden confusion.

"Tell me, Miss Cooper," I encouraged her.

"Oh, I can't – I should not," she said, blushing.

Her blushes signified a deal to me, for I harbored an idea that she was not given to betraying her feelings so vividly. I was curious.

"The first impulse was the best, I'm sure," I urged.

"It was merely a flitting thought," she responded, her repose still shaken; "it was purely out of absent-mindedness that I came so near to voicing it. It was nothing, believe me. There – it is gone!"

"Which is to be deplored," I soberly returned. "I attach considerable importance to your thoughts. Besides, you opened this conversation with an assurance of frankness. Perhaps – so far – I haven't been as frank as I might; but it's simply because I have not yet found words to tell you all you want to know."

At once she stripped the occasion of its seriousness.

"Dear me!" she laughed, "you are a diplomat, too; how alluringly you persuade one to talk! Very well. If the impertinence of my poor little idea will not drive you to changing your opinion, I will put it into words."

I waited.

"I wondered," she continued shyly, "supposing I knew every detail of this crime that you know – if I could aid you any. Only in this one particular case," she made haste to add, "because it means so much to me."

My pulses leaped. The idea of having this lovely girl as a coadjutor, to give her sharp wits free play with the harassing minutiae which had not only arisen but were bound to continue to arise as I went deeper into the mystery, was one that filled me with joy.

After all, doubtless I had been unnecessarily considerate of her feelings. Miss Cooper was a gentlewoman, to be sure; but it did not inevitably follow that she was too sensitive to harken to a distasteful topic. I know that my features must have reflected my feelings at this moment, for the color began to grow deeper and deeper in her pretty face, and at last she sprang nervously to her feet.

"It was only a silly impulse," she deplored, in a flustered rejection of the scheme; "it was very stupid of me to express it. Pray forget it. . . . I – I must go." She darted an uncomfortable glance toward the door.

I did not stir. She was so lovely in her discomposure, so inexpressibly winning, that I sat there with my heart throbbing as it had never throbbed before.

Make her my confidante? Every nerve of my body thrilled at the thought. And the incentive that had prompted the proposal left it shorn of all forwardness or presumption. I appreciated the cause of her agitation; and at last, with an effort, I hid my own emotions behind an appearance of calmness.

"Please sit down again," I entreated. "It is a bargain."

She stood irresolute, poised for flight, yet constrained by a desire to return again to the settle. Her color was still high, her eyes were sparkling, she was breathing fast.

"You would be an invaluable aid," I said simply. "The idea, instead of being impertinent, gratifies me more than I can express; I'm sometimes very blind, Miss Cooper. And think: you may be the instrument of freeing Mr. Maillot from all suspicion or blame."

Slowly, her eyes shining, she resumed her seat. It was manifest that my regarding the matter so favorably pleased her immensely – doubtless because the potentialities appealed strongly to her curiosity and imagination, aside from any faith she might have entertained in her ability really to assist me. She was collected once more, but alive with enthusiasm.

"Such an alliance," I went on, "will entail many demands upon your time; from now on I shall make no move that we have not threshed out together."

"How lovely!" she murmured, joyfully. "And you will always find me ready."

And then I told her everything there was to tell. I recounted every incident that had befallen me since coming to the house, every fragment of possible evidence that my search had brought to light; to all of which she listened with the closest attention, interrupting only occasionally to elicit more comprehensive information. Verily, how I had misjudged her!

Next I strove to prepare her against the inquest. "It will try your strength to the utmost," said I. "What with Mr. Maillot's injured eye, coupled with the struggle preceding the fight and Burke's inability to have delivered the death-blow himself, you must anticipate the worst."

"Royal may have to go to jail?" she interrupted, in a troubled voice.

"It's not unlikely. If the coroner's jury fastens the crime upon him, the coroner will have no alternative except to hold him for the grand jury. If we could show that a third person was in the house last night, it would help him tremendously.

"But bear in mind, Miss Cooper," I strove earnestly to allay her fears, "that the inquest will be merely a preliminary hearing, of no consequence further than the extent to which it will excite comment and influence public opinion; that's the worst feature of it for an innocent man. Whatever we may succeed in accomplishing will in all probability come after the inquest."

Last of all, I produced the small leather jewel-case, and the visiting-card I had found lying before the concealed safe. She examined the card first, reading aloud the inscription thereon:

"'I pray that you be showered with all the blessings of the season. With love' – "

Her face went suddenly white. The hand holding the card dropped to her lap. She sat bolt upright, and directed at me a look of surprised bewilderment.

"Clara!" she gasped. "Why, that's – "

We both started and looked at the front door.

"Listen!" Miss Cooper whispered.

Light, stealthy footsteps sounded upon the porch. Next instant the knob was being slowly turned by a cautious hand.

12
THE CIPHER

We sat rigid and breathless, with our eyes glued to the slowly revolving door-knob. At last a faint click announced that the latch was released. Then the door opened a few inches, to reveal the slender figure of Alexander Burke.

Manifestly he was ignorant of our presence. Neither I nor Miss Cooper stirred, and Burke was for the time being blinded by having come so abruptly from the snow glare into the comparative dimness of the hall.

I regretted that we were not in a position to follow his movements unobserved, for of course he must be attracted to us the instant either of us stirred. I was exceedingly curious to learn what had brought him back to his employer's house.

And now he did a singular thing. His hand was still on the knob, and only his head and the upper part of his body projected through the doorway. His attitude was that of a strained listener; and had I not been there to testify to the contrary, one might have sworn that he received a warning not to enter. The silence, however, remained absolutely unbroken.

All at once a shudder convulsed his frame. He slowly withdrew his head, as if fearful of disturbing the house's lifeless occupant. Next he deliberately closed the door, without entering at all.

Miss Cooper turned to me in blank amazement, and for a moment I confess that I was nonplussed myself by such singular conduct. But in a second I comprehended: the fellow was afraid.

I laughed quietly, and explained to my companion: "He expected to find the house thronged with people, and the undisturbed stillness dismayed him. . . . Careful! He's still on the porch, hesitating between desire to enter and fear to make the attempt.

Slip quietly into the library; I mean to find out what he's after, if I can. He doesn't need to know of your being here."

She colored, and nodded in comprehension, and at once tripped across the hall, carrying with her the card and jewel-box.

"Mind, I shall be close at hand," I whispered after her; which she acknowledged, before the door hid her from me, with one of her bright, friendly smiles.

I then went and threw the front door wide open. Burke jumped as if I had unexpectedly fired a shot at him.

"Come in," said I, dryly.

He stared unblinkingly at me for a moment, but during that moment he recovered his equanimity, and became again his customary inscrutable self. It would perhaps be too much to say that the color returned to his face, for it was colorless at all times. However, I knew that for once I had caught the man off his guard.

I surveyed him with derisive contempt.

"I didn't expect to find you here," he said at length.

"And all whom you did expect to find have gone," returned I. "But that's no reason why we should stand holding the door open and filling the house with cold. Come in."

"I don't understand you," said he, hesitating a second longer; "I was looking for no one."

I glanced out for some sign of Stodger, but saw nothing of him. Then I closed the door and placed my back against it.

"Perhaps no one in particular," I observed. "Neither did you anticipate encountering such a forbiddingly empty house. Look here, Burke, what *did* you come back for?"

His eyes might have been actually sightless, his pallid features a lifeless mask, for all the expression they conveyed; there was absolutely no facial sign by which I could even determine whether I commanded his attention; but his hands were never quiet, the slender, nervous fingers twitched unceasingly.

Was his mind occupied by the crack in the library door? For an instant I imagined that he detected Miss Cooper's presence, and my look hardened with a sudden gust of anger; but he immediately answered my question.

"I came for the papers I brought here last evening; they should be returned to the file-case."

"Is Mr. Page wanting them?" I inquired ironically.

"It's not a joking matter, Mr. Swift; it would be decidedly awkward for me to have them misplaced."

"Then I can set your mind at ease: I gave them to Mr. Ulysses White" – naming Mr. Page's lawyer.

Burke elevated the blank expanse where his eyebrows should have been. "Don't you think," said he, in a tone of hurt surprise, "that you might properly have consulted me before making any disposition of them? I feel, in a way, responsible for all the business affairs which Mr. Page ordinarily entrusted to me."

"I daresay I might have done so," returned I, indifferently, "if you had been present when I handed them to Mr. White. Don't you regard them as being safe with him?"

"To be sure – they couldn't be in safer hands. But it is the implication that I no longer command or deserve the confidence – "

"Pooh!" I unceremoniously cut in. "Burke, if I were you, I'd be a little careful how I emphasized an attitude of innocence toward this affair. There's no implication or innuendo about; I'm only too willing to tell you frankly that I am something more than suspicious of you. I *know* that you haven't told everything you might about this murder. You're lucky that I haven't run you in before this. Is that plain enough?"

He recoiled a step, with a queer, hissing intake of breath.

"Swift," he muttered, "I have half a mind to make you prove your words."

"Do," said I, grimly. "I would like nothing better."

He stared at me so long that it gave me an uncanny feeling. I broke the silence with a blunt demand.

"Burke, where's that ruby?"

"Don't try to browbeat me," he said through his teeth. "Please understand that you are not dealing with a criminal, and I don't propose to be bulldozed by any fat-witted sleuths."

I laughed in his face.

"Maybe it will interest you to know that I have wit enough to contrast your secretive manner with Maillot's willingness to talk, and to draw the one consistent inference therefrom."

There is a nervous affliction of the eyes, called by pathologists nystagmus, which is characterized by a perpetual weaving to and fro of the eyeballs; it is impossible for the unfortunate victim to fix his look upon a given point without the greatest effort. When the attention of such a one is not centered the swaying of his eyes goes on incessantly.

So it was now with Burke's pale orbs and his lean death's head. He seemed to be searching, forever feverishly searching, for something that he could not find. There was something positively repulsive about the man in this new guise, although the change was so subtle that I was unable to define it. At last he spoke.

"Swift," he said, scarcely above a whisper, "I'm a peaceable man; nevertheless I resent your aspersions. I can't do it openly in the circumstances; this murder ties my hands; but – damn you!" he suddenly spat at me, "if my silence would hang Royal Maillot, I'd bite my tongue out before I'd ever utter another word. There you have it."

I stared at him in astonishment. Was it possible that this cold-blooded creature could harbor an emotion as fiery as hatred?

"What have you against Maillot?" I sternly asked, after a pause.

His bloodless upper lip, thin and flexible, curled in a smile; there was a momentary flash of his teeth.

"You're a detective," he said; "find out."

I pondered, still regarding him.

"So," said I at last, "it's to be warfare between you and me, is it? Very well. Take care, Burke, for I do mean to find out. And I promise you that when I do you'll get all you have coming to you."

He knew that I was more or less at sea; he had divined that in my own mind I had already cleared him of the actual murder.

"Thank you," he now had the impudence to say suavely. "Forewarned is forearmed, you know."

"You get out of here, Burke," I said, without heat, eying him steadily.

"Do you mean," he asked quickly, "that I'm not to have an opportunity to ascertain whether I left any of my possessions here?" I fancied that he was disconcerted.

"I mean that I haven't any time to waste on you," I replied, evenly. "I'm busy now; but I'll take care of you when the time comes. If you want to go to any other part of the house, be quick about it."

Again his voice dropped.

"You intend to go with me – I see. I'm not to be trusted. I'll submit to no such indignity."

"Just as you choose."

He moved over to the door. There was no use questioning him further, because all his defenses were up. But I watched him steadily – as I would have watched any other dangerous animal that I was not at liberty to crush.

At the door he paused and looked back; for the briefest instant his restless glance lingered upon an indefinable point up the stair-well.

So thereabouts lay the centre of interest, did it?

The door was open; he turned again to me.

"I'll go," he said, "and – "

"And you need not come back," I broke in curtly. "This house will not be unguarded for one second until the ruby is found."

I felt, rather than saw, that the blank eyes flashed venomously.

"You devil!" he hissed, slipping hastily through the narrow aperture – "you devil!"

Next instant he was gone. And I drew a great breath of relief.

When I turned round Miss Cooper was advancing from the library, her eyes bright with suppressed excitement.

"What a horrid creature!" exclaimed she. "I heard all, Mr. Swift; no wonder Uncle Alfred despises the man."

I looked sharply at her: what earthly reason should Alfred Fluette have for despising Felix Page's private secretary? But of this later. If I was not much mistaken, Miss Cooper held in her hand the cause of her present pleased agitation.

"What have you discovered?"

"This." She handed me a small slip of paper. "I found it inside the lining of the little leather box."

"A cipher!" I cried, sharing some of her excitement.

The bit of paper, perhaps three inches long by an inch wide, was of almost parchment-like fineness and bore a number of peculiar characters written in black ink. At the first glance it suggested a safe combination; but after a minute's intent examination, during which the girl could scarcely restrain her eager impatience, I was obliged to forego that idea.

"Good for you!" was my admiring tribute. The color heightened in her cheeks. "I wonder, now, since you were keen enough to find it, whether you can make anything of it? Honestly – do you know – when I examined that box I never thought to look under the lining."

With her head on one side, she stared regretfully at the bit of paper.

"It's Greek to me," she said.

"To me, too. I'd give a good deal to know what those hieroglyphs mean."

She clapped her hands with sudden delight.

"My!" she exclaimed, "it's just like a story! Isn't this what you call a cryptograph? It tells where a hidden treasure is, does it not?"

Glancing at her beautiful, animated countenance, I answered truthfully, "Yes"; but added, "It at least points me to a treasure that is unattainable."

For an instant she was puzzled, then she bent suddenly over the cipher and asked no more questions.

We had gone in to the big library table, where, with heads pleasantly close together, we studied in silence the seemingly meaningless characters. But after some minutes devoted to this exercise, we were constrained to give it up as hopeless. This is what the paper bore:

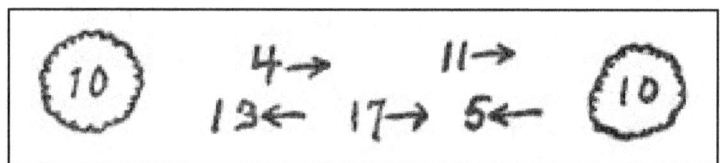

The Cipher

"I'm afraid I shall prove to be a very indifferent assistant," she lamented, with a rueful little laugh. "I didn't deserve your commendation even for finding the cipher, because, while I was examining the box I was too intent on listening to you and that dreadful Burke creature to heed what I was doing. I felt the paper crackle, and then saw a corner of it through one of the rents in the faded blue satin."

"Never mind now. Maybe we shall understand it later. Some ciphers, you know, are to be read only in connection with something else; I think this is such a one. Let's put it away and take up something that I know you can help me with.

"That faded card" – I pointed to it lying upon the table, and noted that her face instantly grew grave – "why did you start so when you first looked at it – just as we heard Burke on the porch?"

She regarded me steadily.

"Mr. Swift, that is my aunt's handwriting – her name."

"Do you mean Mrs. Fluette?" I was in truth unprepared for this blunt announcement.

"Yes," she replied simply.

I believe the first effect of this disclosure was no more than an uneasy, apprehensive feeling; but in a flash the possibilities entailed began to occur to me, and I was left groping for words.

During the silence that followed I vainly tried to arrange my thoughts; the color slowly faded from Miss Cooper's face, and by and by she averted it from mine. I knew that our minds were working in parallel currents; I knew without looking at her that she was anxious and trembling.

At last I secured a grip upon myself, and I addressed her with decision.

"You believe I will do what is right, do you not?"

"Yes," she murmured, without looking up.

"Then I fear that our pact is to be short-lived, after all. This cursed tragedy is twining its tentacles nearer home than either of us dreamt of."

What, in the bitterness of my own reflections, was I allowing myself to say! I silently cursed myself for a blundering fool. The girl's gray face, the pinched look of it, frightened me. I started from my chair.

"Miss Cooper!"

For her head had dropped forward upon one curved arm, and she was shaken by a storm of tears.

13
DISCLOSURES

After some minutes of miserable waiting on my part, the storm spent itself; she sat upright again, dried her eyes upon a bit of handkerchief, and spoke – quite calmly, but terribly in earnest.

"Mr. Swift, I know what your inference is – that Uncle Alfred must be in some way involved – but you don't know all the significance of the flash of understanding that so overwhelmed me. The idea that there could ever have been a love affair between Aunt Clara and Mr. Page is astounding enough" – she glanced at the card – "eighteen fifty-seven: why, she was only a mere slip of a girl then; much younger than I am now!"

It was patent that the revelation had startled and thrilled her; however, there was a more insistent, underlying trouble struggling for expression.

"But – Mr. Swift – do you think that this wheat deal has hurt Uncle Alfred financially?"

Poor child! One could not smile at the simplicity of such a question. I now thought I knew the foundation of this new fear that was gripping at her heart. But I didn't – not entirely; there was another surprise in store for me.

"It is very likely," I soberly made answer.

For all I knew to the contrary, his entire fortune might have been wiped out in the crash; he might have been beggared, stripped utterly; although, since he had not engineered the corner single-handed, he would be obliged to meet only his proportion of the total loss, whatever that might be. An outsider might only guess.

"It is not charitable to think or speak ill of the dead," she was saying, "but, oh! what a cruel, pitiless man Mr.

Page was. Think of the long years of persecution Uncle Alfred has had to endure."

But I was regarding the matter from quite a different point of view. I was thinking rather of that broken wheat corner as the culminating stroke of an implacable enemy; of the probability that the rifled safe contained more love-tokens similar to the card – so many more, in fact, that the thief did not miss the one he had lost. I was thinking that the warfare between the two men had its inception much farther back in the past than anybody had ever imagined, and that it was no longer strange why Page had wrested the ruby from his rival. One must consider Fluette's passion for collecting rare gems to appreciate to the full the consummate malice of that coup.

This disturbed pondering, however, carried me round in a circle. If there had been love-tokens in the safe from Clara Cooper, Alfred Fluette was the only man living who would have any interest in getting them from Page. Again, if Page's hatred of Fluette was so intense that he would part with a fortune merely to deprive his rival of a coveted jewel, would he give this same jewel to a nephew for whom he entertained no liking, knowing that the jewel was destined for his enemy, simply upon that nephew's demand? Why, the bare grouping of the facts discredited Maillot's story; he was left in a worse plight than before.

I trust it is at least clear how heterogeneous were the elements of this crime.

And then – to start swinging round the circle once more – if Alfred Fluette was entirely blameless of Felix Page's murder, the tragedy could not have occurred at a more unfortunate time for him. Considering all the circumstances, it would be no great strain upon the credulity to picture Fluette, driven to desperation, ridding himself of the foe that had hounded him to ruin.

There was nothing else for me to do except follow all these avenues to the end; but whichever was the right one, that end must be bitter. I met the piteous look in

Genevieve Cooper's eyes, and my heart sank. I have often been told that when I want it to be my countenance is illegible; assuredly, at this moment it was not my desire that she should glimpse the tumult of thought and emotion to which I was a prey; but I have reasons, numberless as the sands of the sea, for knowing that it never was indecipherable to the bright blue eyes now searching it so earnestly.

All at once Miss Cooper was on her feet, the shadow of a great dread darkening her countenance; her voice trembled like the voice of a little child that is afraid. Her next words supplied more definite knowledge respecting her uncle's financial condition.

"I told you that both my parents died when I was an infant, Mr. Swift; they did not leave me entirely penniless. Uncle Alfred is the guardian of my estate – my personal guardian, too – and he – my God, I can't say it!"

"Perhaps," said I, gently, "I can surmise what you can't bring yourself to put into words: is it that he may be unable to strictly account for his trust?"

She winced at the question, and sank back into her chair.

"No – that's not it – not exactly," she said, With manifest effort. "But it is almost as bad.

"I was of age the fifth of last month – December – and on that day Uncle Alfred came to me in great distress. He told me that he was expecting any day – almost any hour – that a demand would be made upon him for an enormous sum of money; a demand that he would have to meet promptly or go down in utter ruin. He told me that his own affairs were in such shape that he couldn't raise near the amount of the demand, and that he would be obliged to eke it out with my patrimony.

"I don't know whether or not the demand has ever been made; I don't know whether or not he has used any of my fortune – it isn't much; but he is welcome to every penny of it, for he has always been good and kind and generous. I have never asked him for an accounting, nor has he volunteered one. I simply don't know what to think. If he is in such desperate straits it is inevitable that his name will be linked with this crime. Poor Belle! Poor Aunt Clara!"

I could not dispute the reasonableness of her conclusion; her own mind had already linked the man with the crime. But what was the nature of the demand he was expecting? Her disclosure was mystifying. It was not probable that he had anticipated failure for his Board of Trade operations at such an early date.

"It was a foolish step, my coming here to see you," Miss Cooper complained heartbrokenly; "it places me in a bitterly cruel position. Knowing what I do now, if I remain silent I may be to blame for Belle suffering through Royal's unjust accusation; if I speak I will be treacherous to the very hearth that has fostered me."

I am glad that my chief's cold, unfeeling eye did not rest upon me at that moment. Her distress was mine. And I could not turn aside from the way which was opening so plainly before me.

Here, now, I had two motives for the murder: Fluette's mad desire for the ruby and, since the ashes of old romance had been so ruthlessly stirred, the most powerful of all human motives – jealousy.

It was possible, too, that a third person had been in the house last night; but if so, one of the two men had lied. The bit of candle found by me on the rear stairs had adhered to somebody's shoe while still plastic; if either Burke or Maillot had used these stairs at or about the time of the murder, then both had studiously kept the fact from me. It was possible that one of the two could have made fast the front door behind a fugitive, without the other's knowledge; Burke, for example, before he summoned Maillot.

But my chief concern now was for this sorely distressed girl. She had told but the bare truth; her position could scarcely be more cruel. Her eyes followed me with an expression of such tragic helplessness that I knew the issue was left for me to decide. I sprang up and commenced walking the floor. It was a long time before I could make up my mind just what to say, and during my troubled cogitation there was not an interruption, not a sound, from her.

By and by I paused, and stood looking down into the wistful face.

"Miss Cooper," I began, "it seems that you trust me, and, believe me, I'm keenly sensible of the responsibility. I shall ask nothing of you which I think you can't freely perform; nothing that is not for the best interests of all concerned – all for whom you care, I mean."

She interrupted me.

"Sit down – here where you were before; it will not seem so much like your talking to me from a distance."

I obeyed. The chairs were quite close together.

"It seems to me," I went on, "that we should continue in the direction that has been pointed out for us; follow the light, however dim. There is a mystery here, and we are just now only skimming the surface of it; let's plunge below and see if we can't bring up at least a part of the truth.

"It is hard to believe that Alfred Fluette has been instrumental in Felix Page's death, even indirectly, but harder, more unjust to him, to pause without dissipating the cloud we have unexpectedly cast over him. The temptation to scrutinize his conduct and bearing is irresistible. Is it not better to lay bare all the facts, than to leave matters in the equivocal condition they now are?"

"You mean," she murmured brokenly, "you mean that – now – after what has happened between us – the duty of pressing forward at whatever cost is far more imperative than any other obligation that I may be under; that the innocent must not be sacrificed to shield the guilty."

That was precisely what I meant, but I lacked the courage to tell her.

"My dear Miss Cooper!" I said, in a voice as tremulous with emotion as her own.

"I trust you," she said simply.

I knew not what to say; her faith in me was manifestly so boundless that I was humbled to the earth. And yesterday we were ignorant of each other's very existence!   Stressful circumstance can level the conventions with amazing swiftness.

"You are trembling," she whispered presently.   "I am making what would be a commonplace matter very difficult for you."

"No – no!" I protested.   "I feel for you; I can't tell you how much."

"Don't think of me," she again whispered, her look averted.

"I can think of nothing else," said I.   My teeth suddenly clenched, and I bent toward her.

"I'll not allow this thing!" I undertoned in a savage outburst, recognizing the futility of my anger even as I spoke.   "I shall not allow you to become further involved in this thing.   Whatever the cost, *I* shall shield *you*."

A pitiful smile stirred her lips.

"You have shown me my duty," she said, with gentle firmness; "you can't dissuade me now."

What do words avail at such a time?   I loved this splendid girl, and my heart ached for her.   I was almost swept from my balance by a sudden mad yearning to take her in my arms and try to comfort her.

Yes, I loved her; there is no use in holding back the confession; else where would be my great personal interest and concern in the death of Felix Page?

Yet I did not protest further; remonstrance would avail me nothing.   Gently as she had spoken, it was driven home to me that she had expressed a determination which no power in heaven or on the earth below could change.

Another long silence followed, during which I as well as she was stirred by the most conflicting emotions. At last, though, I too began to see my way clear. Matters could not be helped any by either of us shirking the least part of a responsibility which had, within the last few minutes, become sweetly mutual. How anxious I was to spare her!

The silence was broken by Genevieve abruptly rising.

"I must really go," she announced, hurriedly. She was the least bit flurried, and there was a wonderful soft light in the handsome eyes that had not been there when she came. As she passed me she lightly brushed my shoulder with the gloved tips of one hand.

"I am no longer cast-down," I heard her murmur; "I know you will do – what is right."

I caught the fingers, detaining her.

"Don't go – not yet."

She lingered, expectant and more cheerful.

"I can't let you go like this" – I was steady enough now. She moved again to the chair she had just vacated, and I released the slim, soft fingers.

"There is one thing we haven't considered," I pursued, "and that is Mr. Alexander Burke. You say Mr. Fluette despises him: if he does, it is not without warrant, I'd be willing to swear. What that fellow's game is I can't just at this time conceive, but I'm confident that he's playing one of some kind – a deep one, too. If he is, the potentialities are endless with such a cunning, unscrupulous rascal.

"I'm satisfied, moreover, that he has lied to me. According to his statement, no one was in this house last night besides himself, Mr. Page, and Royal Maillot. Between him and Maillot I give the latter the preference, for, if the stories of both are true on any one point, it is that Burke was up and about before and during the time the murder was committed. Burke is consequently in the best position to know who was or was not in the house.

"Now I have a particular reason for thinking that this is one phase of the matter about which he has lied. Should it be that some one else was here – some one that we know nothing about – why, that would put an entirely different complexion upon the affair."

"Suppose," she propounded evenly, "that it was Uncle Alfred?"

I looked at her earnestly.

"You don't know that he was here," was my sober comment.

"No."

"Well, then, what's the use of borrowing trouble?"

"It's very silly – especially as I have trouble enough as it is."

With an impulsive movement, she thrust one little gloved hand into mine.

"I am still your assistant," she affirmed, striving hard to be gay, "if you will have me now. Together we will drive the trouble away."

I caught the other hand, and held the two of them together. She permitted the caress for a moment – for caress it was – then drew her hands away.

"Good-bye," she said faintly, without looking up.

But I got my hat and coat and walked down to the gate with her. Of a sudden, after we reached the walk, she moved a pace or two away from me and halted. Her pretty face dimpled in a smile, and there was a gleam of mischief in the blue eyes. One can't be always melancholy.

"I suppose I'm a big goose," she said, "to have any faith in you; I'm thinking it's a case of misplaced confidence."

She waved a hand, gathered her skirts closely about her slender figure and tripped away through the snow.

I could not realize any portion of the past when she had not been near and dear to me.

14
RIDDLES

I returned to the library and heaped the fireplace with coal. For an hour after Genevieve's departure I was utterly unable to concentrate my mind upon any congeries of fact that might be of the least possible use in unravelling the badly tangled skein presented by Felix Page's death; I could see nothing but the fine blue eyes clouded with trouble, and the sweet face under the shadow of her gnawing anxiety.

I fished up the cipher, flattened it upon the library table, and strove manfully to hold my vagrant attention to the task of interpreting its secret message. My thoughts straightway wandered back to Genevieve again.

Now that I was alone, it was inevitable that I should sum up the results of our conference. I did not blink the truth; the facts were plain, not susceptible of argument.

No matter what the future might have in store for Genevieve and me, whether it was replete with delicious promise, or whether the useless iron gate marked the parting of our ways, her intrusion must ever remain a cherished memory. But it would have been better for her peace of mind not to have sought me out. If she had not, she would have remained ignorant of the circumstance that she possessed any knowledge hurtful to her uncle; if she had remained away, the accusation that he had come to harm through her could never reproach her in after years.

Her errand had been impelled by a conviction that I would appreciate her more intimate knowledge of her cousin's lover. She knew that she could lay before me no tangible testimony in his behalf, but hoped that I could be made to sympathize with her estimate of his character.

During her first visit to the house, with Belle, she had clearly recognized the seriousness of the young man's predicament, and that I would be governed only by the facts as I read them. Notwithstanding he was somewhat fiery and headstrong, if she could influence me to see that he was honest, sincere and straightforward, she felt hopeful that I would continue my investigation with a strong leaning in his favor.

Was ever a cipher so empty of all meaning! What addle-pate had conceived it? Why should he want to perpetrate anything so idiotic?

By her simplicity and singleness of purpose, however, she had innocently drawn my attention to her uncle; then, in a measure, she had verified my awakened suspicions. While Maillot and Felix Page were in the library, engrossed in their own affairs, could Alfred Fluette have been in the house?

Highly improbable as such a contingency might appear, still it was by no means impossible. "Suppose," Genevieve had asked me, "that it was Uncle Alfred?" Never, unless she herself had some reason to doubt and mistrust, would she have propounded that question. Had he been absent from home until an unwontedly late hour last night? Was his manner in the morning of a nature to draw attention to himself, so that, in the light of later developments, it had provoked her suspicions? I had purposely refrained from asking her any questions touching upon this possibility.

In a flash the image of Genevieve Cooper swam out of my thoughts. My whole attention became glued to the cipher. At each end of the two rows of numerals and arrows was a peculiar crenellated design; it had struck me with a sudden sense of familiarity. Where had I ever seen anything similar or identical, that this odd symbol should penetrate into the midst of my absorption and force me unwittingly to try to recall the circumstance? Quite recently, I was sure – to-day – in this very house. My glance skirted the spacious library, darting from one object to another, but encountered nothing at all that in any way resembled it. Here was a subliminal reminder which my perception was dull to read.

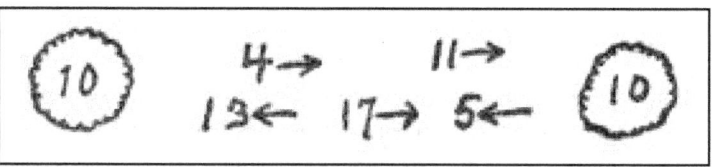

The Cipher

Filled with the idea, I thrust the strip of parchment like paper back into my pocketbook, and started eagerly upon another tour of the entire establishment. I paused in one room after another, examined each article in turn, but ended not a whit wiser than when I began.

Yet my belief in the correctness of the veiled mental impulse remained unshaken. The design was a facsimile of some object in this house; something my eyes had rested upon, albeit without the existence at the time of any occasion to fix it upon my mind; but conjure my brain as I would, I could not recall where or when.

When Stodger returned, I determined at last, I would set him at work searching for the odd symbol, or whatever it might be. When I made this resolve I was standing beside the old walnut table at the head of Mr. Page's bed; with a forefinger I idly traced the design in the dust on the artificial leather cover, beside the impress made by the jewel-box.

My preoccupation was broken in upon by the arrival of the undertaker's men. It would not do — if the ruby was really beneath this roof — to grant any strangers unrestricted privileges of the house; at least not without keeping a heedful eye upon their movements. Alexander Burke, I shrewdly suspected, was equal to any subterfuge or ruse to obtain the jewel, and I did not mean to be caught napping.

No small responsibility is involved in safeguarding $500,000 – the amount Maillot declared his uncle had paid for the ruby – particularly when the guardian himself does not know precisely where the treasure lies. It would not do to take any chances. Otherwise, if the amount had been materially less, or had been in a form not so easily disposed of about the person or by thrusting it into a convenient cranny, or, perhaps, even tossing it unseen through a window to a waiting confederate on the outside, my wisest course might have been to permit Burke, or whoever knew where the jewel was, to lead me to its hiding-place. But I must be vigilant, always alert; there would be little sleep for me until I had this extraordinary gem safe in my hands.

So I remained with the undertaker's men until they departed with the body.

As I turned to reenter the house Stodger's portly form hove into view. He dropped into one of the library's big easy-chairs.

"Whew!" he gasped. "I'm a peach of a shadow, ain't I? Nice work for one of my build. Say! That fellow Burke – Alexander Stilwell – he's the – you know – most restless party I ever saw. If Fanshawe hadn't relieved me when he did I'd be worked down to about middle-weight by this time."

"Anything particular?" I inquired.

"Er – no. You know he came back here. Rest o' the time he spent dodging in and out of old Page's offices at the Drovers' National. Walk like a house afire for – m'm-m – maybe a block; next time maybe six blocks."

"Well?"

"Then he'd – ah – he'd turn round and walk back again."

"Not very interesting for you. But we know one thing for certain: he's uneasy. I have a far lighter task for you, though, than following the erratic movements of Mr. Alexander Burke."

And then I recounted for his benefit all that I knew respecting the ruby, declared my belief that it lay somewhere in the house, and, finally, outlined my plans for the immediate future.

"We'll divide the vigil between us, Stodger; you and I shall camp right here until that costly bauble comes to light. We'll have to keep our eyes open and our wits about us, too; I wouldn't be surprised at some tricky attempt to recover it at any time – especially during darkness."

After showing him the cipher and requesting that he be observant to find the counterpart of the two peculiar designs, I left him in charge of the house. Next I arranged that our meals be brought to us, after which I returned to town and held a long conference with my chief. This proved to be eminently satisfactory, inasmuch as he left the Page affair entirely in my hands.

Although I hoped that some new development would require another interview with Miss Cooper, absolutely nothing transpired until the next morning. During the rest of Wednesday afternoon – perhaps I forgot to mention that the murder was committed at about midnight Tuesday – and until late Wednesday night, Stodger and I prosecuted a diligent and systematic search for the ruby, the original of the design on the cipher, and for anything else that might bear upon the crime, but found nothing to reward our efforts. At a late hour we knocked off and sought the library's easy-chairs. After a while Stodger asked me for the cipher. When I dropped off to sleep he was industriously digging away at it, with many gasps and inarticulate exclamations.

Concerning the cipher, it is perhaps well to mention that I applied it to the door of the hidden safe on the chance that the opposed arrows indicated the different movements of the dial; but I discovered the combination to be much simpler. In fact, there were not sufficient tumblers in the dial to allow for so complicated a combination at all.

There remained the possibility that the numerals belonged to some other safe, though I did not think so: those two odd crenellated figures could have nothing in common with any permutation-lock. I had seen them; they were tantalizingly familiar; but where? And what meaning did those two figure "10's" bear? Here was a riddle for Oedipus.

The next morning – Thursday – Dr. De Breen conducted the inquest in the library. I mention this hearing solely because of a number of circumstances which occurred during the proceedings – although unrelated to them – and which have a bearing upon the story. As for the testimony itself, it was about as satisfactory as in most instances where little respecting the crime is definitely known.

Stodger and I had the burden of additional watchfulness imposed upon us; a number of people would be brought upon the scene, and each of us had to be present at some time during the hearing without leaving the house unguarded for a second.

"Looky here, Swift," Dr. De Breen buttonholed me, grabbing at his glasses, "what's in this case, anyhow? Have you got the man? 'T isn't a woman, is it?" He cocked his head on one side, and favored me with a squinting regard.

"No, I haven't," I emphatically returned. "And what's more, I don't think you're going to hit upon him to-day. It isn't a woman, either."

"Don't say! But what have you?"

I displayed the cipher, at which he scowled ferociously for a second.

"It's a combination," he announced decisively; "bet the cigars it's a combination – or direction of some sort."

"Sure thing. Perhaps, too, you'll tell me where I can try it out."

Holding his glasses with one hand, he stared through them at the bit of paper.

"What are those fluted affairs at each end with figure '10's' in 'em?"

I shook my head. "You can search me. I thought you might tell me something; I can ask more questions about it myself right now than I can answer."

But I added my conviction that they were facsimiles of some detail of ornamentation I had seen in the house. I also told him where the cipher had been discovered – but not who had discovered it – and, in short, gave him a summary of the entire case. Before I was through he was grinning at me in a very superior and knowing way.

"Nice, bright sleuth, you," commented he, mockingly; "can't you see through a grindstone when there's a hole in it? Now looky here, Swift: old Page kept the replica in the box as a blind; this cryptogram tells where the real ruby is."

I shrugged my shoulders; the idea was by no means novel. But it did not make matters any clearer.

"It must have been the ruby which he showed Maillot," I insisted. "That young man may not be much of a gem expert, but I don't think any mere paste imitation of a ruby would have inspired him to such a flight of vivid description as he indulged in when he talked with me yesterday morning. Guess again."

He jammed his glasses down combatively astride his hawk-like nose, and squared his shoulders.

"I won't guess at all. Looky here: old Page switched 'em. That's what he did – switched 'em to show Maillot the real thing. Every time I converse with you, Swift, my theory about the equality of mind and matter receives a jolt: you have more brawn than brain, old sport."

Squinting at each newcomer, he bustled away before I had time to get back at him. I was rather touchy about my size; I couldn't help being a giant, and the little ferret of a sawbones knew it. I had only one means of revenge.

He was a great stickler for maintaining the dignity of his profession, and I always called him "Doc."

While De Breen was getting his jurors in line, I disposed the two patrolmen who had accompanied him – one in the hall, to direct those who had business here this morning straight to the library, and to allow nobody, under whatever pretext, to wander to any other part of the house; the second was stationed just inside the library door. Stodger was to remain up-stairs until called for, when I would relieve him during the brief period required for his testimony.

Burke and Maillot arrived while I was thus engaged, and before I had time to enter the library the front door opened to admit a party of three – Miss Cooper and Miss Fluette, who were accompanied by a handsome, dignified man with white hair and a closely trimmed beard which he wore parted in the middle and brushed straight back.

Instinctively I knew this man to be Alfred Fluette. And as soon would I have expected the attendance of the Caliph of Bagdad. I fell to watching him narrowly.

His features were not familiar to me, but certain details of his appearance were so striking that I could scarcely do otherwise than conclude that his bearing and countenance had quite recently undergone a marked change. He was a man, I imagined, who could hide his feelings with eminent success; yet, his upstanding figure, without being precisely bent, expressed an idea of drooping. The lines of his face gave it a haggard expression, while his eyes wore a furtive, hunted look at certain periods when he forgot to keep himself in hand. All these details taken together gave me food for sober reflection.

With the wax impression on the iron candlestick in mind, I bent my glance to his hands – to the right hand – but he wore gloves, and moreover, the long sleeves of his heavy overcoat came well down over his knuckles. A stirring of the library fire might persuade him to remove his wraps later on.

But something happened that banished everything else temporarily from my mind. The instant he stepped across the front door-sill his eyes sought the upper regions of the house – the balcony or the second story hall. The glance was feverishly eager. He looked away again quickly; but I could not help associating this brief episode with Burke's wistful look in the same direction the afternoon before.

15
A Woman's Scream

I turned from Alfred Fluette to encounter a sober, questioning look from Genevieve. Her sweet face was pale and still troubled, and while nothing would have pleased me better than to hasten to her side, I was obliged – for the present only, I made mental qualification – to content myself with a smile and a reassuring nod. Her cousin Belle's demeanor was haughty, even supercilious, and she quite frankly ignored everybody excepting her father, her cousin, and Maillot.

Nothing occurred to retard the inquest, which I shall refer to only as is necessary to keep bound together the thread of my narrative.

After Stodger had given his brief testimony and returned to his post in the upper hall, I descended to the library and took a seat beside Dr. De Breen at one end of the big library table. As I did so I observed that Mr. Fluette was taking stock of me with a keen sidewise look. I recognized in his regard, surreptitious as it was, that quality which is accustomed to estimating and judging the characters of other men, – usually with unerring exactness, I fancied, – but I affected to appear unconscious of the fact that he was noticing me at all.

Alexander Burke was the second witness. His testimony did not vary from his already familiar story, and after the deputy-coroner had put all the interrogations he could think of, I began to prompt the energetic and shrewd examiner. Thenceforward the whilom secretary's examination proceeded as follows:

"Did Mr. Page have a revolver?" "Yes. But it is now in my possession. More than a week ago I was engaged with Mr. Page here until a late hour. It was necessary for me to go to his office to procure some papers; it was past eleven, and he handed me his pistol. I forgot to return it."

So much for the pistol. The weapon was immaterial.

"In pursuance of your duties as Mr. Page's confidential clerk, Mr. Burke, you had occasion quite frequently to come here to the house, did you not?"

"Not frequently – sometimes."

"Were you familiar with his habits about the house?"

"I suppose so – yes."

"Which rooms did Mr. Page use the oftenest?"

"This one – and his bedroom. He scarcely ever entered any of the other rooms – seldom ascended the stairs."

"How would you account for the door-hinges on all three doors between the alcove and the bedroom having been freshly oiled?"

He didn't attempt to account for it; he merely evinced a mild surprise that such should have been the case. So, impatiently, I requested Dr. De Breen to dismiss him.

I was anxious to have over with the real ordeal of the day, for I knew that I thus correctly characterized to myself Maillot's session in the witness-chair, and, if I was not much mistaken, whatever was to follow after he was through with his remarkable story. Correct as I was in a part of my assumption, everybody present was far from being prepared for the startling denouement.

Maillot began his account of Tuesday night's happenings in a straightforward way, and told it at length as convincingly as such an improbable story could be told at all. His injured eye was even worse discolored than it had been the previous day, and I – watching closely the half-dozen honest citizens with whom lay his immediate fate – observed that they noticed and commented upon it among themselves.

And my anticipations presently began to be realized. As the young man made plain the purpose of his errand to Mr. Page, as he again went over all the extraordinary particulars of his uncle producing the ruby and promising to give it to him to convey to Mr. Fluette, I saw the jurors exchange questioning glances with one another; and then, as the enmity and ill feeling between the two men became more and more apparent, the six faces gradually came to assume expressions of open incredulity.

If the young lawyer remarked the effect of his testimony, which he could scarcely help doing, the circumstance seemed not to dismay him in the least. But the worst was yet to come: plainly, whatever doubts may have lingered in the minds of the jury during this stage of his examination, they were definitely dispelled when the witness frankly admitted that according to the best of his belief he was Felix Page's sole heir.

But to me Maillot's testimony was scarcely more than a running accompaniment to Alfred Fluette's strange behavior. It was impossible to interpret the seething conflict of thought and emotion which his haggard visage hid only indifferently; he stared at the young man, fascinated; but dominating every influence, gripping his very heart and biting like acid, I could discern the evidence of a horror which must inevitably drive him, sooner or later, to some violent outburst. It was manifestly more than human nature could endure.

Why? – I asked myself – why? Why should he be so profoundly stirred by the experience of one against whom he entertained such a strong antipathy? And so promptly that it took me by surprise, he supplied the potential answer to my unspoken question.

With a sudden movement, as if to sit longer inactive had become an unendurable torment, he stood upright, flung off his heavy overcoat and then whipped off his gloves.

On the middle finger of his right hand gleamed a broad band of gold!

I glanced at the sweet, concerned face of Genevieve Cooper. From the intentness with which she hung upon my every action and change of expression, I knew that she was trying to plumb the farther depths and learn the trend of the hidden currents of this drama, which was of such vital moment to her. I was glad that I could still offer her the encouragement of a smile.

My attention was directed to Maillot when one of the jurors began interrogating him.

"While Mr. Burke was absent," inquired the juror, "did you see the ruby?" His reference was to Burke's absence when he went to notify the police of the crime.

"I did not," was the reply. "I saw it no more after Mr. Page returned it to the jewel-case; I never even thought of it during the time of which you speak."

"Were you near the concealed safe?"

"Yes, sir – although at the time I didn't know that the open trap-door in the closet led to a safe. I saw that the small cavity was empty, and that was all I did observe about it."

"When did you first learn about the safe?"

"When Burke showed it to Mr. Swift yesterday morning."

"Why, then, in your testimony, did you say the deceased went to the safe after the ruby for the purpose of showing it to you?"

Maillot frowned and considered a moment.

"I did not make the assertion from knowledge of the act co-existent with the performance of the act itself," said Maillot at length, with a great show of deliberation. A man can't be utterly hardened who can quiz another at such a time. "I advanced it as the most likely theory by which to account for all of his actions during the time I waited here in the library, explaining the antecedent occurrence with knowledge subsequently acquired. Do I make myself perfectly clear?"

The inquisitive juror stared a moment, then subsided. Dr. De Breen turned to me with a broad grin.

"That all?" he whispered.

I nodded. "Let the axe fall; I'm curious to see what effect it will have."

Everybody's attention was abruptly diverted by Genevieve Cooper. Without a word to any one, she rose precipitately, glided noiselessly across the room to the alcove, and disappeared behind the curtains. Blank bewilderment brought me to my feet. What could have impelled her to this extraordinary move at such a critical stage? I started to follow her, but at that very instant the foreman started to announce the verdict.

Silence fell instantly. Maillot sat plucking aimlessly at the margin of a newspaper, the tiny fragments floating unheeded to the floor; while Miss Fluette, strikingly handsome with her transparent complexion, her red-brown hair, and clear hazel eyes, sat imperiously beside him, alone in her assurance as to the outcome.

The young man seemed to have forgotten her presence, so deep was his abstraction. In a little while he pushed the paper to one side, and began feeling idly in a pocket of his vest. His mood was distrait, and in a moment he produced something that glittered; something that made me start and rivet my attention upon him.

The something was a broad gold ring. He toyed with it for a moment, apparently wholly absorbed. Then he slipped it upon the *middle finger of his right hand*!

The ring seemed to fit perfectly. He turned the hand over and back a number of times, inspecting the ornament from different angles of vision. After which, seemingly satisfied with his critical survey, he removed it from the finger and returned it to his pocket.

I studied the young man in perplexity. Here I had two rings on two different right hands: what was I to conclude from –

But events were moving swiftly, almost to the verge of confusion.

"We, the jury," read the foreman, with the tremulous, irresolute air of a man unaccustomed to forensic exercises, "find that Felix Page came to his death from a blow on the head, administered with some blunt instrument in the hands of – "

He got no further. At that instant a piercing feminine shriek rose in some remote part of the house. Coming as it did at such a juncture, when all present were hanging in suspense upon the words as they fell from the foreman's lips, it produced much the same effect as might have followed the explosion of a bomb in the company's midst. Miss Fluette gasped, and her face went as white as ashes. Maillot and Fluette were both instantly upon their feet, startled and tense.

The scream was a thrilling, prolonged note of horror. For one electric second my blood seemed to chill in my veins. The cry swelled in a quavering crescendo, lingered with the persistence of terror, then abruptly ceased, like the cutting off of a shrieking steam-jet.

For one awful moment everybody sat or stood as if petrified. If a bomb had exploded it might have passed unnoticed. Then, with a wild, unnerving recollection of Genevieve, I rushed to the door.

"Don't let a soul stir from this room!" I hoarsely shouted to Dr. De Breen.

In the next instant I had plunged into the hall, brushed aside the stupefied policeman there, and was taking the stairs four at a time.

16
THE FACE IN THE ALCOVE

The first thing I noticed as I sped up the stairs was the absence of Stodger from his post in the upper hall, where I had last seen him. Only a few minutes previously I had peeped into the lower hall to satisfy myself that everything was right; at that time he was leaning on the balustrade, engaged in a desultory conversation with Officer Morrison, stationed below. But in a moment I understood.

The bath room door stood wide open, and on the floor lay Miss Cooper – lifeless, was my first horrified thought. Stodger, with the best of intensions and the least possible capacity for carrying them out, knelt helplessly beside her, under the delusion that he was rendering first aid.

Instantly I lifted the still form from the floor and pillowed the sunny brown tresses in the hollow of my arm. How light she was! How soft! How lovely and tender! It was wonderful – a sublime revelation – thus to feel the actual contact of her warm, yielding body.

But Heaven knows, I didn't stop to analyze my feelings at the time. For a while I was shaken, panic-stricken, utterly unable to do more than stare numbly down at the sweet pale face, framed in its nimbus of wavy brown hair. I got a grip on myself, though, and Stodger was sent flying to fetch Miss Fluette.

She came quickly enough, wondering and alarmed; and when she beheld me holding her cousin, would have snatched her from me – with what biting words I can only imagine.

But for once in her life, at least, that proud, willful young lady bowed without a murmur to the tone of authority; for one brief moment she stared at me astounded, and in the next, as comprehension dawned, melted. It is hard to say which of her two attitudes was the more impressive: the flaming anger provoked by the sight of the unconscious girl in my arms, or the tenderly sweet manner with which she presently turned to minister to her. The voice which bade me leave Genevieve to her care was actually gentle. Very reluctantly, I withdrew with Stodger into the hall. Before I closed the door, however, I tersely charged Miss Belle to give me as soon as possible the explanation of the mystery.

The door closed, I turned upon my unoffending associate rather angrily, I'm ashamed to say; but Stodger's good-nature was imperturbable. He could tell me absolutely nothing that threw light upon whatever terrifying experience Miss Cooper had undergone.

He had remained at the spot where I had last seen him, he said; a position he had assumed purposely, because from there he had a view of practically the entire second story. He had opened all the doors so that the slightest sound or movement in any of the chambers could not fail to attract his attention. Immediately behind him, by simply turning his head, he could see through the bath room, across the landing at the top of the rear stairs, and into the small sewing-room beyond. To right and left – east and west – the corridor extended the width of the house, and an intruder could have gained access to any of the rooms only by passing the watcher.

The sudden piercing scream, Stodger protested, had startled and astonished him as much as it had anybody. He wheeled round to find the bath room door so nearly closed that it was impossible to glimpse what lay beyond until he had again opened it; which he had done promptly, he declared, to behold only Miss Cooper. She was lying on the floor in a dead faint.

Miss Belle called to me, after a minute or two of anxious waiting, and I hastened into the bath room. Genevieve was so far recovered that she was able to look wonderingly up at her cousin, a terrified expression yet lingering in her eyes. Her face was white and drawn. Her cousin was upon one knee, supporting her upon the other and holding her tightly.

I knelt upon the other side, taking one of the little hands in mine. Almost at once I was gladdened and relieved by seeing the sweet face break into one of its lovely smiles.

"What was it?" I asked, anxiously enough. "Have you been hurt?"

"No, no," replied she, quickly, "not hurt – not in the least; only frightened within an inch of my life." She shuddered, and made as if to rise.

"Let me up, Belle; I'm all right now – just a wee bit trembly from the shock, maybe, but I can stand."

She tried to laugh and to make light of the matter, but the pale lips and quivering muscles belied the attempt. I lifted her to her feet. Her cousin remained close to her, keeping a supporting arm round her waist and watching the white countenance with a passionate solicitude that made me glance curiously at her.

Every action, almost every word, of this vivid, high-spirited girl seemed to be an echo of her impetuous, wayward temper. Even a concern as natural as that excited by her cousin's present plight, was charged with an intensity which made me wonder what the effect might be if her feelings were ever deeply or ruthlessly stirred. While her affections were stamped with an immoderate fervor, one might readily enough fancy her resentment, fired by a word perhaps, striking with a blind vehemence that recked not at all of consequences. Her emotions, apparently, knew no happy, tranquil, steadfast medium.

As we stepped into the hall, Genevieve was saying, "I'll go with you to the library. I merely got what I deserved, I suppose, for presuming to think that I might accomplish something single-handed. But – oh, it was dreadful!"

"What was?" bluntly demanded Miss Belle. "What silly notion ever made you jump up and sail out of the room that way?"

Genevieve turned to me with a faint smile.

"The face at the curtains," said she.

"Face!" echoed Miss Belle, manifestly believing that her cousin's mind was not normal. "For goodness' sake, Genevieve, what do you mean?"

But the girl continued to address me.

"You didn't see it?"

We had paused at the head of the stairs, two of us nonplussed and very curious. I shook my head.

"When you left the room," said I, "I was too occupied otherwise to be heeding the curtained alcove. I wondered, though, what sudden impulse moved you – why you should have gone into the alcove at all."

"I knew that you could not leave the room right then," she explained, the color coming quickly back to her cheeks; "I remembered our pact, and I thought I saw an opportunity of being really of assistance. It is not to be wondered at that nobody else saw what I did. It all happened so swiftly. By the merest chance I glanced toward the alcove, and at that very instant the curtains parted sufficiently for me to see a face." Again she shuddered.

"Mr. Swift, it was the most hideous face I ever looked upon. Had I been alone in the library doubtless it would have terrified me even then. But instantly it disappeared, and without a thought of being afraid, I hastened to investigate.

"As I got to the conservatory I saw the door at the farther end just closing. It didn't slam – there wasn't a sound – but simply closed quickly before my eyes. Never for a moment did it occur to me that I ought to be cautious; that closing door only made me run the faster to learn who or what had closed it.

"Well, when I opened it, and the next door across the little passage, I saw the same thing repeated in the bedroom beyond – a door closing, apparently from its own volition. The same thing happened with the door opening into the rear hall.

"It was maddening to be just so far behind and unable to gain the fraction of a second which would enable me to find out who was fleeing from me in such haste – maddening to be rewarded with no more than a procession of closing doors.

"The chase continued on up the rear stairs, to the landing between the bath room and the small room at the back; there for the first time I felt a misgiving, and I hesitated. I was out of breath, my heart was pounding until my ears roared; everything else was so deathly still.

"A glance told me that the rear room was empty of any living presence. Cautiously I pushed open the bath room door; but it was too dark to see inside."

"Was the door into the hall shut?" I interrupted quickly, remembering that Stodger believed it to be open.

"Yes. I entered a bit timidly; all my assurance had somehow evaporated. Then – then, before I had time to make another move, two hands seized me.

"I was thrown violently against the wall, and one of the hands tried to grasp my throat. I was fighting as hard as I could; but – I was helpless.

"Then I screamed. I put my whole soul into it. Everything slipped away from me, and I knew nothing more until Belle was holding me in her arms and I felt her dabbing my face with water. . . . Dear girl, don't look so tragic; I'm all right now."

While Genevieve hung close at my side, the inquest waited until I had searched the place from cellar to garret. But never a trace of the mysterious intruder did I find. When I became satisfied that he had safely made his escape I asked Genevieve to describe the face.

"I'm afraid I can't," she returned hesitatingly. "I had such a lightning-like glimpse of it. Still, in a general way, it was very swarthy and wrinkled – quite ape-like. The lower part was covered with a short, curling, sparse black beard; the eyes were like" – she searched for a simile – "like a snake's."

"That's graphic enough," I said; "but the description fits no countenance that I can now call to mind."

"What can it mean?" she asked wonderingly.

"It means," I grimly replied, "that I guessed right: the ruby is in this house. And I'm going to have a time keeping it here, too, until I find it myself."

The one mistake of the intruder, whoever he might be, had been in peeping between the alcove curtains; of course he had been reconnoitring only; but a person who could move through the house so noiselessly might easily have accomplished, without discovery, whatever errand brought him there.

The idea was positively uncanny and far from pleasant to dwell upon. Stodger's hearing may not have been remarkably acute, but if my life depended upon shutting that door so close behind him and not attracting his attention, why, I should have hesitated long before essaying the performance. To have the ruby lifted from under the very noses of the watchers – while they were wide awake, too – would in all truth be a sorry ending of our search for it.

For the nonce, however, the mysterious face introduced only an additional problem; one upon which I had but little time, just at present, to bestow thought. The drama in the library had been interrupted at its most crucial stage. It was all-important that at least one phase of the case be brought to a termination, however unsatisfactory that termination might be, before anything else should be undertaken.

After explanations had been made and order was restored, the foreman did not proceed, as might have been expected, by reading the verdict. Instead he jerked his head sideways toward Miss Cooper.

"Mr. Coroner," he said, "we'd like to ask the young lady some questions."

He was a poor specimen, that foreman; one of your little, officious, meddling busybodies, as aggravating as the buzzing of a persistent fly.

"If they are pertinent to the inquiry," said Dr. de Breen, "it is not only proper, but your duty to ask them. The young lady will be sworn."

At this unexpected demand she darted a startled glance from the foreman to Dr. De Breen, and then looked at me – as I joyfully fancied, for guidance and support.

I nodded – she couldn't avoid the ordeal – and she bowed in acknowledgment of the oath, which the doctor rattled off as if it were all one long word.

And just here I am unable to refrain from pointing out how small an incident will sometimes afford the turning-point for a momentous crisis; such an apt illustration is presently to follow.

When interrupted by Genevieve's shriek of terror the foreman had been in the very midst of pronouncing the concluding phrase of the verdict. Had it not been for the strange face, had the venturesome girl not followed the face's owner, who could say how differently events might not have turned out? For I know now that the first verdict was quite different from the one finally read.

The catechism which Genevieve was required to undergo follows:

"What is your name?"

"Clara Genevieve Cooper."

"How old are you?"

"I was twenty-one in December."

"We would like to know, Miss Cooper, what relation, if any, you bear to the witness Maillot?"

"Merely that of a friend."

"How about him and the other young lady?" – an interrogation which instantly made Miss Belle flush and bridle. But the witness was fully equal to the occasion.

"I wouldn't undertake to speak for them," she replied composedly.

The succeeding questions brought out the relationship between the two girls, and also established Miss Fluette's identity. Something akin to a sensation prevailed in the jury-box for a few seconds after the six good men and true realized that the handsome gentleman with the white hair and dark beard was no other than the celebrated "wheat king."

Their manner toward his niece underwent a sudden transformation; their attitude became more respectful.

Miss Cooper was dismissed, and Maillot was recalled. He denied any formal engagement between himself and Miss Fluette; but it soon became apparent, both from his manner and her growing vexation, pretty precisely what the relations between them really were. The jury learned that the young man's quest of the Paternoster ruby had not been undertaken without the stimulus of a very warm-hearted devotion.

Maillot was left sitting in the witness-chair while a new verdict was made out. It formally charged the young man with the murder of his uncle.

I afterward learned, by questioning the self-important foreman, that the first verdict had been an open one. The demand for Miss Cooper's testimony had been prompted by the "diversion" – I am using his own word – she had occasioned when she left the room, and afterward threw the proceedings into wild disorder by her scream. The interrupted verdict had failed to hold Maillot only by the narrowest margin; Miss Cooper's adventure had served to turn the scale against him.

"Look here," I demanded warmly, "don't you believe what she said?"

He smiled with an air of such superior knowledge that I very nearly cuffed his ears.

"Oh, I don't blame the young lady! – dear me, no!" he said, with a smirk. "Loyalty, you know. What do you think of it?" I had turned to move away, much disgusted; but I lingered long enough to look him over curiously. "What's your name?" I bluntly demanded.

"Griggs – Samuel B. Griggs."

"I think, Mr. Samuel B. Griggs – if you really want to know – that you're a damned idiot."

17
PRISON DOORS

As I recall the scene that brilliant winter morning in the Page library, one detail stands out so much more prominently than all the rest, that the really important aspects are quite overshadowed in my memory, and notwithstanding the surprising nature of Alfred Fluette's deportment, I am obliged to pause and group them in my own mind in order to produce a reasonably correct portrayal of what actually transpired. But one's memory is apt to play strange and unaccountable tricks, and mine is no exception. The best mental image I can recall is distorted, all out of drawing, as the artists say; I can see only Belle Fluette.

After the accusation fell from the foreman's lips, I quite suddenly became aware of the fact that she was standing rigidly erect, one hand strained to her bosom, the other clenched tightly against her cheek. Every vestige of color had flown from her face, leaving it as white as marble.

But her eyes! It is her eyes that still haunt me. They burned with a light of despair so profound that no mere human note could even feebly yield a hint of it; and behind the despair, plucking and tearing at her heart-strings, lay a misery unutterable. She alone had remained serenely confident of the outcome, and now, being the least prepared for it, the shock to her high-strung susceptibilities was more keenly poignant than human flesh could endure. She presented the appearance of one stunned, of one beaten and buffeted to stupefaction, yet through it all still sensible of an anguish that wrenched her very soul.

There was no outcry, no spoken word; but in a moment a tremor ran over her slender form, her knees gave way, and with one last desperate effort she tried to reach Maillot. Even as she turned to him, before a move could be made to sustain her, she tottered and fell prone upon her face. One extended hand clutched once at the young man's foot, then relaxed and grew still. It was as if her last conscious thought had been governed by a flitting impulse to seek the support of even so mean an assurance of his presence.

In a flash the lover was kneeling at his sweetheart's side, pressing her white face to his bosom in a wild embrace. He called to her frantically, coaxed her with endearments, wholly oblivious of his shocked audience. He assured her in choked, incoherent phrases that all was well with him; but he spoke to deaf ears.

Dr. De Breen, direct and practical, brought him to his senses with a sharp command.

Maillot reluctantly yielded Belle to Genevieve and the doctor. Not for a moment did a thought of his own trouble enter his head, I am sure, and he did not remove his tense look of anxiety from her face until Dr. De Breen convincingly declared that she was only in a swoon.

"Best thing for her, just now," said he, crisply; "she can't think. Furthermore, she needs a sedative to keep her from thinking for a while." Then to her father:

"Here, you, you take her home on the double-quick. Have in your physician. Let her cousin get her in bed."

It is likely that Alfred Fluette had not been addressed for many a day with such cavalier brusqueness, and overpowering indeed must have been his emotions now that he did not notice the doctor's abrupt manner. Even his daughter's condition seemed to produce only a momentary impression upon him; for by the time Maillot and Dr. De Breen had conveyed the limp girl to a divan, where Genevieve continued to minister to her, he was excitedly striving to catch the doctor's attention.

"Listen to me, sir," he commanded, his voice trembling, "you are the one in authority here; this young man must *not* be remanded to jail."

Dr. De Breen stopped short and fixed him with a look of surprise. And I was not a little surprised myself. Knowing how bitterly opposed he had been to Maillot's attentions to Miss Belle, what was I to think? Did the manner in which the shock had prostrated her – had literally felled her to the floor – open his eyes to the depth of their attachment, and at the same time touch his heart with pity? His concern could not have been more pronounced if the young fellow had been his own son placed in similar jeopardy. Or – and here was my predominating thought – did he have the best of reasons for *knowing* that Maillot was innocent?

During the brief pause in which Dr. De Breen coolly surveyed him – for once the perverse glasses observing their proper function – he recovered something of his equipoise.

"See here, Doctor," he went on more calmly, "I am not familiar enough with the proper procedure in – er – in criminal cases to know just what I want to say. But is the next step imprisonment for Mr. Maillot?"

"It is," snapped the doctor.

"Then I will go his bond – in any amount; but he must not go to – "

"My dear sir," Dr. De Breen interrupted, with asperity, "a prisoner under charge of first degree murder cannot be admitted to bail; not even by the court having jurisdiction of his case, much less I. The police are now responsible for the young man's movements."

He deliberately turned his back upon the millionaire speculator, and strode away. Years after that scene, Dr. De Breen confided to me that Fluette had given him the impression that he was hinting at a bribe.

The words, however, seemed to strike Mr. Fluette like a physical blow. He winced perceptibly, and his face worked with agitation. But he rose splendidly to the occasion. In a second or so his customary commanding dignity returned, and his keen eyes flashed with resolution and defiance. He wheeled upon Maillot at the instant that much distressed young man was persuaded by Genevieve to leave Belle's side.

"Maillot," said he, in a firm voice, "I sincerely regret any hard feelings I may have entertained for you in the past. You are not only a courageous young man, but an innocent one, and one, therefore, that is being made to suffer a grievous wrong. I wish to say so here publicly; I wish, too, to say publicly that I mean to see that you have at your disposal the best legal talent procurable."

Maillot's reception of this proffer was peculiar. He looked the man of money squarely in the eyes for an instant; then his lips twisted into a mocking smile. He nodded his head ever so slightly, but the movement was unmistakably a curt rejection.

"Thank you," he said dryly, his voice low and even. "But I intend getting out of this scrape myself, Mr. Fluette; I don't wish to occasion you any future embarrassment. Please don't mistake my meaning."

Fluette made no further effort, and it was impossible to determine just how the rebuff – it was no less – affected him; he had himself too well in hand, now. He began preparations for conveying home his still unconscious daughter, and before they departed I contrived to have a private word with Genevieve. Her face was very tragic.

"I must see you alone – as soon as possible," I said hurriedly.

"I can't leave Belle," she whispered. "What is it?"

"My first request from my lieutenant," I chided, smiling down at her.

"Don't!" she pleaded. "I shall come. Where? When?"

"Dear me, no. I'll do the coming; it's only 'when'?"

"To-morrow?" she suggested doubtfully. "You know, we're all so upset. And Belle – " The dear girl nearly broke down. "Yes, do come," she murmured tearfully, "as early as you can; everything depends upon you, now."

I caught her hand. "Please don't worry," I whispered; "everything will come out right. I can't bear to see you suffer. Will eight o'clock be too early?"

"No."

"I'll not say 'Be brave,' for you're the bravest girl in the world; but please, please don't fret and worry. Here's your coachman.

Good-bye."

She smiled wanly. "I shan't," she said. "Good-bye — till to-morrow morning."

She pressed my hand and ran lightly out.

Maillot now came over to where I was standing. He was very pale, his face was drawn with lines of suffering (more for Miss Belle than on his own account, beyond doubt), but his manner was quite composed. In fact, his demeanor was more subdued — chastened, as it were — than I had seen it at any time during our brief acquaintance.

"Well, it's over," he remarked bitterly.

"Don't be an ass," I returned. "If you are innocent, nothing worse can happen."

He smiled whimsically, quickly taking me up.

"And if guilty, the worst is yet to come, eh? Well, at any rate, I'm your prisoner."

"Not necessarily mine," I said.

"By preference. I can't stand for those roughneck cops, and Stodger as a custodian is a joke. I'd be too strongly tempted to dump him into the first handy snow-drift, and cut loose. I don't suppose you'll insist on any rot about handcuffs and all that sort of thing?"

Notwithstanding his pretence of humorous indifference, there was a question in his tone, and he peered at me a bit anxiously. I grinned.

"I don't know," I said. "I won't take any chances on being dumped into a snow-drift."

"Rot! You know I couldn't if I wanted to."

"Mr. Fluette could have helped you, Maillot."

I looked at him narrowly. He shrugged his shoulders, merely, and produced and lighted a cigarette.

"Let's go," he said, flipping the match away.

Stodger was left on guard at the Page place. My prisoner and I walked to a car and proceeded to police headquarters.

His attitude, naturally enough, was one of extreme dejection; nevertheless I tried to cheer him up – vainly – and when opportunity offered I also tried to get some light upon the ring episode.

"It doesn't do for me to express an opinion one way or another as to your probable guilt or innocence, Maillot," I said at one time; "but I can tell you this much for your encouragement.

"Since the murder, several developments have turned up which convince me that there's a deal more in the crime than either you or I can at present conceive. You can keep it in mind that I see more work ahead than I did immediately after quizzing you and Burke Wednesday morning. . . . By the way, that ring you slipped upon your finger this morning, whose is it?"

For a second he frowned with an air of trying to recall the incident. Suddenly his face cleared.

"Did you notice that?" he returned, with perfect composure. "It's mine – was my mother's wedding ring."

I was watching him intently. He met my regard with a level look.

"In the habit of wearing it?" I asked.

"Sometimes."

"See here," I came to the point with abrupt directness. "You appreciate quite as much as I do the significance of that broad band of gold on the middle finger of your right hand. Why did you put it there at such a time?"

He sat silent.

"You've become mighty close-mouthed all at once," I sharply urged.

He gave me a little half-smile, and glanced away.

"By advice of counsel I refuse to talk," said he, quietly.

"If you are the counsel, you have a fool for a client – and *vice versa*," I retorted. "I suppose, too, that you refuse any assistance that I – "

Instantly his assumed indifference vanished.

"By no means," stopping me with considerable warmth. "If there's any way out of this rotten mess it's you that must get me out. My hands are literally tied, now. And – Swift," he hesitated; his face clouded and his voice suddenly dropped, "I – I simply can't say anything more, old chap."

"So," I quietly observed, "you too are worried about Fluette."

He started as if stung.

"My God, Swift!" he began, and stopped. He sat staring at me a moment in utter dismay, then his disturbed look wandered to a window.

"You're too devilish sharp," he muttered.

"Lucky for you that I am," retorted I, cheerfully. "This is a bad tangle that we're caught in, Maillot."

He said nothing more. By the time we reached our destination he was prepared to enter philosophically upon his period of confinement, whether it should prove long or short. As I turned to depart I noticed that he was following me with a wistful look.

"I'll see that you are kept posted about the young lady," I told him; which elicited a deep sigh of relief and a fervent word of thanks.

Again I was preparing to leave him, the turnkey standing by and impatiently jingling the ring of big brass keys which was suspended from his arm, when the prisoner called me back. He searched my eyes earnestly.

"Swift," he began, "as I said before, I'm helpless now to fight for myself. But I want to warn you against that devil Burke. I know nothing further than that he has been in the habit of visiting Mr. Fluette and of being closeted with him for hours at a time. The subject of those long conferences Mr. Fluette has kept strictly to himself, evading all of Belle's inquiries and attempts to make him talk about the fellow. Burke is repulsive to her – for which you can't blame her – and her curiosity over a man like him and a man like her father having anything in common is quite natural. It is odd, you know.

"That's not what I intended saying, though." He paused and eyed me keenly an instant. "If anything turns up that drags Mr. Fluette into this business, you will find that Burke's the one who has tangled him. Watch Burke."

Then the heavy steel door clanged to between us.

18
A Fight In The Dark

After the cell door closed upon Royal Maillot I returned at once to the house of tragedy, whose evil genius was promising to play havoc with the lives of so many of the living; and as I approached the bleak, austere old mansion something in its silent and inanimate exterior seemed to repulse my advance up the gravel walk. My steps lagged, and at last I drew to a halt.

Cold and clear and snappy as the day was, still there was something oppressive in the air that hung about the house of death. I looked at the lifeless windows. Staring vacantly, utterly expressionless of the swift-moving tragic drama that had been enacted behind them, failing to foreshadow what was yet to transpire here, they all at once brought forcibly to my mind Alexander Burke. Thus did his eyes hide, instead of disclose, the workings within.

That the mind of this man was secret and evil I could now no longer doubt. Felix Page had been a powerful man, physically and mentally; yet Alexander Burke, sly and impassive, soft-spoken and soft-footed, ever alert and observant and burrowing, like a mole, in darkness, had undermined him, and − the conviction grew − had brought about his cruel death.

In what way? What far-reaching machination was he so laboriously evolving? What snare was he casting unseen to bring down in ruin the lives of others? And why? Coward that he was, had he at no time worked in the broad light of day?

An unwelcome sense of depression was slowly weighing me down. It was as if the silent house were haunted. At the time, I was convinced that I was merely making a hodge-podge of the hundred and one clews that had come to my hands, though now I know that the whole vast scheme was gradually taking shape in my mind. I was bewildered by the wide diversity of the opposed interests, left powerless by failure to light upon a sure point of common interest defining the attitudes of the different actors. For to say that it was the ruby did not clear the fog any – unless I accepted the growing assurance that Alfred Fluette was the active instrument of death.

Still, every detail I had gathered was necessary to complete the circle. When finally I did have my case all in hand there was no single point that remained obscure.

My brooding inertia was dispelled by a shout from Stodger. He was standing on the front porch, regarding me with considerable curiosity.

"Hi! What you doing down there, Swift? Come here!"

I soon learned that he had something of interest to report.

"D' ye know, Swift," said he, with much seriousness, extending his chubby hands to the welcome warmth of the library fire, "it's an outrage – damme, if it isn't – that I'm so fat. H'm! Believe in ghosts?"

I was instantly all attention. Genevieve's terrifying experience was too recent and real for me to scout any supernatural suggestion of my colleague.

I quickly asked: "Seen anything about the house?"

"Not in here. Outside. Couldn't chase 'em."

"I'm glad you are fat, then; who would have watched the house while you were chasing whatever it was you thought you saw?"

He clapped one hand on top of his bullet of a head, and stared at me in comical surprise.

"Say! You're right, Swift! You are, by George! First time I ever found a – ah – you know – a consolation for my – er m – my stoutness.

"Two shadows. Didn't get to see 'em plain. All the time you were gone I could glimpse 'em now and then –

first one place, then another – slipping and sliding through the bushes, trying to keep hid, y' know."

As may be imagined, I was profoundly interested.

"What did they look like?" I asked.

Stodger shook his head. "Bushes too thick. No leaves; but they wouldn't come close enough for me to get a good look. H'm. Watching the house, all right."

The matter was serious enough, in all conscience. Our incessant vigilance was most certainly justified by the pertinacity of these mysterious prowlers, for as long as they surreptitiously sought to enter the house, my belief that the ruby lay hid somewhere beneath its roof was in a way confirmed.

Stodger was sagely nodding his head at me.

"To-night," he said, with meaning. "Bet anything you like."

"To-night," I thoughtfully echoed. "It would not surprise me in the least."

Although a close watch was maintained throughout the remainder of the day, we saw no more of the elusive "shadows." My arrival, manifestly, had frightened them away.

I put in a portion of the time until nightfall going carefully over the old house again, from cellar to roof. My purpose now was to ascertain whether there were any secret passages or concealed openings whereby we might be surprised; and my labors convinced me that there were none. The face which Genevieve saw at the alcove curtains could be easily accounted for, since, with the exception of Stodger, who was in the second story, and the officer in the lower hall, everybody in the house was assembled in the library, and, of course, completely absorbed in the inquest. It had been an easy matter to open one of the lower windows, or even one of the rear or side doors, and enter the house.

I found that the walls were all of an even, normal thickness, and there were no spaces between floors or walls for which I did not satisfactorily account. I also kept a watchful eye for the prototype of the designs on the cipher, but discovered nothing that was at all like them.

Otherwise the day proved to be wholly uneventful. I spent much time in consideration of my case, naturally; but this exercise yielded nothing more conclusive than that Alfred Fluette's place in it was assuming larger and larger proportions as time went by.

I was much impressed with Maillot's charge to watch Burke. But here again I was offered no new light. It was satisfying to know that another than myself was distrustful of the erstwhile secretary; but as for watching him – well, I knew that he was being subjected to a constant espionage that left nothing to be desired.

It was, doubtless, the emphasis which Maillot had laid upon Burke's secret visits to Fluette that engaged my interest. I would have liked very much to know what they portended. If the slippery secretary had been carrying on negotiations with the millionaire for the Paternoster ruby, then the latter's position relative to the murder stood out quite clearly. With knowledge of those interviews in my possession I would be in a position to lay my case before the State's Attorney, who, beyond question, would procure a warrant for Fluette's immediate arrest.

What a sensation that would create! – Alfred Fluette charged with the murder of his rival and bitter enemy, Felix Page! It would be particularly startling inasmuch as a coroner's jury had already fastened the crime upon another man. I believe the reader will unhesitatingly admit, by this time, that the Page affair presented many remarkable aspects.

There was one discordant element in such a theory, however: namely, how could Fluette hope to retain possession of the gem, once he had secured it? How could he defend his title to it? Although the stone was immensely valuable, any person save the rightful owner would have an exceedingly difficult time disposing of it.

But this objection was in turn offset by the possibility that Page, although he had purchased the ruby openly, *had actually acquired no just title to it.* I admit, considering that Felix Page was never the sort of man to buy a pig in a poke, that the possibility was rather far-fetched; still, it was a possibility, and a very pregnant one, too. For if such were the case, Burke might have obtained, in some underhand manner, authority to dispose of it.

And this brought me to the, as yet, unaccounted-for Japanese – I call them such for lack of a more definite characterization. How otherwise was their obscure connection with the case to be explained? Why, the very word "ruby" instantly calls up a picture of the East. How often have priceless gems been filched from Oriental potentates! How often have mysterious murders been committed to recover some jewel stolen from an Eastern temple, the murderer driven forth by religious zeal – or fanaticism, call it what you will – to a relentless search for the fetich, and to wreak a dire vengeance on the plunderer! Admitting that the present intricate problem involved a similar instance, I could not see how the fact might tend to aid me any.

After supper, which was brought in to us, Stodger and I divided the night into two watches – I taking the first until two o'clock in the morning, and he assuming responsibility from that time on until he chose to awaken me.

I arranged the two watches thus because I imagined that if an attempt should be made to enter the house during the night, it would occur at some time near the hour mentioned when both of us would more than likely be awake. My guess, you will see, was a poor one.

I also wanted to devote the fore part of the night, when my brain is always clearest, to an exhaustive study of the cipher found by Genevieve in the jewel-box. Until Stodger was ready to retire I could concentrate my whole mind upon it, I told myself, without fear of being disturbed. After my companion turned in I would have to remain alert, keeping pretty constantly on the move so that no marauder might steal in upon us unawares, or from an unexpected quarter.

If the place was bleak and dreary in the daytime, what words will describe its dispiriting influence at night? There is a silence that is soothing and restful, which imbues one with a sense of comfort and a pleasant desire for sleep. Then there is another sort of silence; one that magnifies every trifling sound, sounds that could not even be detected during the day; the sort of silence that hints at uneasy stirrings and movements all about one. The distant cockcrow rings clear and high, floors creak, the very timbers of the house complain, and mice scurry in the walls.

It was such a stillness that enveloped us. Even Stodger's irrepressible good-humor failed to cheer. The old mansion was possessed of a thousand voices, strange, indefinable noises that kept our attention constantly divided; yet the night was so still that I could hear our watches ticking in our pockets.

The result was that the cipher received only scant attention from me. I would get only fairly absorbed in my task when Stodger would startle me with a sudden "Ssh!" or a no less startling command to "Listen!"

Whereupon we would both sit straining our ears to hear – nothing.

Every few minutes one or the other of us, or both together, would go over the entire house, examining doors and windows and making sure that no one had entered since the last tour of inspection.

This was repeated so many times that Stodger himself grew glum, and at last signified a determination to turn in. He made himself comfortable on the big library divan, – the same divan which had held Belle Fluette's motionless form only a few hours previous, – wrapped himself in a heavy blanket from Felix Page's bed, and was soon fast asleep; or, at least, he offered audible evidence that he was.

Again I tried to fasten my attention upon the cryptic parchment; but it was of no use. In spite of myself, my head would jerk up to a listening attitude every time a board creaked or I fancied I heard a door somewhere in the house being cautiously opened. Time after time I would be sent stealthily to some remote corridor or chamber, only to return again to the library no wiser than before.

I finally thrust the cipher back into my pocketbook and resigned myself to a lonely vigil. The great library was a place of shadows and dark recesses, as well as of silence; and had it not been for the regular, stertorous breathing of the sleeper, I might have wished myself well out of it.

The hours dragged along – midnight, one o'clock, two, half-past, and still I did not rouse Stodger; I never had less desire to sleep. During one of my excursions through the empty, echoing rooms I set down my lantern – we had provided ourselves with this convenience – and looked out into the night. The pleasant weather of the past few days had ended; it was dark – very dark – and an occasional flake of snow, materializing ghostlike within the square of light from the lantern, scraped along the small diamond panes with a feathery touch.

Presently I entered Felix Page's bedroom. And here, for the first time that night, I was sensible of an absolute stillness. Not even a board creaked. Not a breath stirred the leafless boughs outside, nor rattled the withered vines on the walls. Then of a sudden I grew rigid, tensely alert, and watchful. From somewhere a breath of icy outdoor air struck upon my face and hands.

Now whatever else might be said of this old house, it was not a place of drafts. Its walls were thick and solid, its doors massive, and the doors and windows were snug-fitting; therefore, the fact that I now felt a perceptible rush of air could signify but one thing – that an outside door or window had been opened.

During a brief pause I hesitated over whether I should rouse Stodger; but so slight a warrant decided me not to. A shout from any part of the house, should he be needed, would accomplish the purpose quite as well.

So I merely stood motionless and listened. The circumstance that my straining ears could now hear nothing whatever was in itself ominous. The hush which had fallen upon the place was the sort that heralds an advance through a forest of the most cautious of hunters. Danger might be creeping upon me from every side and in any imaginable guise; if so, here was my warning.

Then it was that I smiled and reached a decision. With infinite caution I sank to the floor, removed my shoes, and draped a rug over the lantern. Only the dimmest points of light showed through the weave of the fabric; merely enough to serve as a guiding beacon in case I wanted to find it in a hurry. Next, with my revolver in hand, I stole to the hall door, which had been left ajar purposely, and peered out.

The darkness was fathomless, the silence complete. The spacious lower hall was the Dionysius' ear of the house; if there was any movement about the place, here if anywhere it would be detected and its source determined.

The floor was of hardwood, and my feet were soon numb with cold. Then, too, bravery is a relative term when all is said and done. A coward may be always a coward, but it is not an inevitable corollary that a brave man is always brave. To know a possible antagonist, to walk boldly up to him in the broad light of day, is one thing; to stand in a hyperborean hall in the dead of the night, surrounded by the darkness of the pit, ignorant alike of the nature of your peril and the point from which an attack may come – that is quite another.

So I freely own that my jaws ached with the effort of keeping my teeth from clicking together like castanets.

In the course of a long and not uneventful career, I have been in a good many tight places and under all sorts of conditions where I had to hold myself to the matter in hand with every grain of will power that I could muster; but never since that night in the old Page hall have I experienced precisely the same unnerving feeling that possessed me then. I came perilously close to an ignominious retreat – and before ever I had an idea of what I was running from!

Fortunately for whatever status I may hold in this chronicle, the movement was checked at its inception. In a flash my momentary panic was forgotten. I caught a sound that I recognized and, moreover, located on the instant. It was the long, unmistakable creak of a loose stair plank such as follows the gradual shifting of a person's weight from one foot to another. Somebody was slowly and cautiously ascending the rear stairs.

I could smile once more and breathe normally. Instead of retreating, I was in the next few seconds stealing up the front stairs. Nor did I move very slowly, either. I knew by experiment that its steps were all solid, and that I need not fear the betrayal of any complaining board.

At the stair head I became cautious again; I didn't want to risk a collision with the *etagere*. What must I do, however, but stumble against the topmost step and plunge head foremost right into the thing.

The ensuing crash that filled the house was like an explosion. It also drowned my comments. To make matters worse, in my efforts to keep from falling, my revolver shot from my hand and through the balusters, and went clattering down to the landing with the noise of a falling brick.

I recovered myself on the instant, however, and with a final malediction, darted toward the bath room. There was a sound of scurrying behind its door; but I paused not for doors. Fortunately it was a trifle ajar, and it went

open before me with a thud. Also from behind it a most
unmistakable human grunt emanated, the sort of
involuntary notice a person gives when he has the wind
suddenly knocked out of him.   Then right in my ears
there sounded the most weird, unearthly cry that I ever
heard; it was positively uncanny.   A cold chill went
through me from head to foot.

Events thereafter moved with such electric swiftness
that the details are all blurred.

I remember that I heard Stodger shouting
encouragement, and his stockinged feet patting the bare
floors as he ran. As the bath room door shot open and the
strange cry shrilled forth, some object fell to the floor
near me. There was also a sound of running feet up the
rear stairs; which would indicate that my enemy was a
host, and that the main body was returning to accomplish
a rescue.

In a flash I had reached forth my arms and grappled
with the unknown behind the door. That struggle would
have been short, for he was like a child in my grasp. But
instantly I was seized from all sides at once, it seemed. It
was as if a dozen hands were feeling over me, to
distinguish friend from foe.

Into what had I rushed so blindly? Who was opposing
me? How many were there?

At least twice I was borne to one knee by sheer weight
and the number of my assailants. Both times I succeeded
in shaking myself free and rising again to my feet. I was
warm enough now, heaven knows, and I had the
satisfaction of knowing that I was inflicting far more
damage than I was receiving.

I knew when Stodger unhesitatingly threw himself
into the thick of the fray. Good old Stodger! And there
we fought, silently, furiously, in the restricted space of
the bath room, enveloped in a darkness that one could
almost feel. Again and again I collided with the porcelain
tub. More than once when I secured a firm grasp upon
one of my unseen adversaries, I picked him up bodily and

hurled him with all the force of which I was capable toward where I fancied the tub to be. But in the riot and frenzied confusion of being jerked first this way and then that, how could mortal distinguish the location of anything!

The struggle ended abruptly. Stodger and I were at a disadvantage, for he dared not shoot on my account, and I had no weapon but my two bare hands.

Not so our antagonist, however. Of a sudden one side of my face felt as if someone had quickly drawn the tip of a red-hot poker from the corner of my eye to my chin. At the same instant a crushing blow caught me above one ear.

The blow did not render me unconscious, but it more than staggered me. For an instant such strength as was left me was needed to keep from tumbling headlong. I was on my knees and one hand, while the other arm was hooked over the rim of the tub.

The fight had ended. I could hear a patter of feet on the rear stairs; I could hear someone near me on the floor, breathing heavily; then fell silence. I tried to yell to Stodger to be up and after them, but the result was only a painful wheezing in my throat. Then the gasping form on the floor groaned, and I managed to get dizzily to my feet.

We received the worst of that fight in more ways than one. When I managed to find a candle and light it, I discovered that Stodger was the one who had groaned. He was sitting up, not badly hurt, and staring dazedly at the candle. His mouth hung ludicrously open. But in a moment he struggled upright.

"Good God, Swift!" he gasped. "You've been butchered!"

Then I recalled the red-hot poker. I put a hand to my cheek; it came away covered with blood. From the shoulder down, my clothes were saturated with it, and I had left a crimson trail to mark each of my movements since the keen-edged blade had laid my face open.

But enough of the wound. The white pucker of scar which to-day disfigures my face will be a life-long memento of that spirited combat in the dark.

After we were in condition to do so, Stodger and I set about an inspection of the scene.

First of all, we didn't find a trace of our adversaries, or how many of them there might have been, until we came to the snow outside. An open dining-room window indicated their method of ingress, the trampled snow beneath their number. There had been five.

"Why the bath room?" Stodger demanded, in deep perplexity. "Why should everything that happens in this house be pulled off there?"

Why indeed?

"Let's go back there and try to find out," I returned, stiffly, for my cheek was paining under the mass of plaster that Stodger had piled upon it.

Carefully and systematically, we went over every inch of space – I don't know how many times I had done so since the murder – but found absolutely nothing that was not already familiar to me. It was miserably aggravating that every search I undertook in this house of mystery should prove fruitless.   Yet, we could find nothing whatever to serve as a reply to Stodger's pertinent question.

It was before the bath room door that Felix Page had met his death; it was the bath room that had been designated on the chart found by me in the snow; it was to this point that both Alexander Burke and Alfred Fluette had turned with a glance of ardent eagerness; it was to the bath room that Genevieve had pursued the mysterious yellow face – always the bath room. It would seem to be the converging point of the tragedy's every moving current.

We were about to give it up in despair, when I started forward with a wordless cry. *The bar of yellow soap was gone!*

On the instant the import of this discovery flashed into my mind. How blind and dull I had been!

During the struggle Tuesday night, between Page and – shall I say Fluette? – in the hall, Burke had in some way secured the ruby, and with diabolical cleverness *had pressed it into the bar of soap*! A bit of manipulation under the water-tap had removed all traces. Think of the brain that could light upon a hiding-place like that in the stress of such a moment! And I had paused by that very bar of soap, philosophizing and moralizing – it made me sick to think of it. No wonder they were all so interested in the bath room!

This revelation left my mind blank for a second. Then came a rush of mingled feelings – bitter chagrin and disappointment, mortification because I had been outwitted, and a blind, hot resentment against those who had bested me.

Recalling the object I had heard drop to the floor at the moment I dashed the door open, I dropped to my hands and knees and began a feverish search for some sign. Yes, there it was – a small smear of soap, where the bar had struck.

For a while Stodger thought I was crazy, and perhaps I was. I fumed and raved at him for not entering into the search with a frenzied zeal equal to mine. At last he too understood.

But our pawing over the floor and the stairs, and even in the snow outdoors, availed nothing. We were beaten, confounded, made a laughing-stock.

The bar of soap was gone.

19
BELLE

It was a very crestfallen detective that presented himself at the Fluette home early Friday morning. I had counted so much upon unearthing the ruby myself, assured that through it I must certainly succeed in drawing some betrayal from the murderer, that its loss amounted to a thwarting of all my efforts. My feeling was that of one who has striven and failed – failed through a solitary act of gross carelessness.

But if I was dejected, I was no less determined. Only a little more than two days had elapsed since Felix Page met his untimely death; the body had not been interred yet; and I knew that I held in my hands the ends of a net which enveloped all the actors. One of them was guilty. My determination was to be no longer considerate through fear of wounding the innocent. I meant to draw in the lines of the net until everybody's position stood clear and unequivocal; but to that end I must be fortified with one more fragment of information. And here it was that I looked to Genevieve.

A neat-appearing maid admitted me, who seemed to be expecting my arrival, for she conducted me at once upstairs, above the second story to the third, and to a room in the rear of the house. I wondered a bit at this; but I was more surprised than ever when the open door disclosed Miss Fluette instead of Genevieve. A good many startling experiences were in store for me that morning.

The maid closed the door and left us immediately. I began muttering some words expressive of my pleasure at seeing Miss Fluette able to be up and about; but something in her manner checked the speech. She had

not even looked at me. In fact, I quite suddenly realized
that she was studiously keeping her eyes averted from
mine.

And again, she presented the appearance of one who
has recently undergone a strenuous exertion. Her rich,
red-gold hair was in disorder; she was breathing deeply,
and her cheeks were flushed, though her movements
were direct and full of purpose. Then, too, if a man may
hazard the guess, I would have said that the lacey,
beribboned dressing gown she wore hid her nightdress.
The situation was most unusual.

When I entered the room she was standing on one
side of the door, precisely as if she had moved aside to
make way for me, meaning to depart as soon as I had
entered. But she did not. Instead, the instant I crossed
the threshold, she advanced quickly to the door. She
turned the key, then withdrew it from the lock, and
hastened to a chair on the side of the room farthest away
from me.

I could not repress a smile – despite my amazement at
these proceedings – when I realized that the chair was
placed between us as an object of defense. She stood,
very erect, behind it, her hand tightly holding the back.
She was prepared with a weapon of offence, also. For now
her right hand appeared, for the first time, from a fold of
her gown; I was startled to see that it held a small,
shining revolver. For the first time, too, her hazel eyes
met mine, and they burned with a light which,
considering the manner of my reception, I was not slow in
ascribing to a state of mind bordering upon
irresponsibility.

"So I am a prisoner," I said.

"You are," she replied. She clipped the words in an
uncompromising way which promised that I was in for a
bad quarter of an hour. Where in the world was
Genevieve? I wondered. But Miss Belle went on at once,
eying me steadily with a hard, stony look.

"I shall get to the point at once. It all depends upon you, whether or not you leave this room alive. It will be for you to choose, and I think you'll choose the wiser course. I'm in dead earnest."

She was, whatever her purpose; there was no gainsaying that. I was profoundly curious to learn what that purpose was.

"May I sit down?" I asked, calmly.

She made an impatient gesture with the hand that clutched the chair-back – the hand that held the door-key. But there were two keys in her grasp, I observed. The flowing sleeve of her dressing-gown disclosed a momentary glimpse of white, rounded arm.

"It's useless – useless for you to play for time. I want to know why you have permitted Royal Maillot to be railroaded to *jail*" – she flung the word at me – "and permitted a *snake* like that creature, Burke, to go scathless.

"But, no, I don't care for your motives. You know Royal to be innocent. Between the two who were in that house Tuesday night – Royal, open, frank, and manly; Alexander Burke, sly, secretive, and a coward if ever there was one. What sort of intellect have you that it should make such a choice between these two? Bah! You're either base – in league with the criminals – or a fool."

She stopped for sheer lack of breath. She stood staring at me with all the dignity of an outraged queen, and for once in my life I was so astounded that I was at an utter loss for words. I sank into a nearby chair – without her permission – and for the second or so of the pause, my thoughts flew like lightning.

When Miss Fluette was carried from the Page library the previous day her condition promised a long siege of illness; Dr. De Breen had confirmed my own surmise with a declaration to that effect. Why, then, was she not at this moment in bed, with Genevieve caring for her? I had an engagement with Genevieve; she was expecting me at eight o'clock. Miss Belle's appearance indicated that she had prepared for this meeting with the utmost haste – she had probably risen and donned dressing-gown and slippers after I rang the doorbell. What, then, had she done with Genevieve?

I was not in the least frightened by her display of the pistol. To tell the truth, it was only with much difficulty that I kept from laughing. Still, I did so. The girl was plainly so overwrought that she was fairly frantic, and it would require the utmost circumspection on my part to keep her from precipitating matters before somebody came. The women folks, I fancied, would then need the assistance of a man; but for the present her condition demanded that I be at least considerate.

So I concluded to humor her.

"What is it you wish me to do?" I inquired, not forgetting my dignity.

She waved the insignificant weapon toward a writing desk.

"There are pens and ink and paper," she said, her voice tremulous with suppressed passion. "I want you to write down a plain, straightforward declaration that Royal Maillot is innocent, and then follow it with the reasons why you know him to be innocent – for you have those reasons. Doubtless it will include an exposure of the guilty; very well, this is the time for such a disclosure."

The amazing effrontery of the proposal made me gasp. Suppose I were to tell her that I believed her father to be the guilty man? Heavens and earth! Here was a pretty pass!

"Miss Fluette," I said at length, very gravely, "such a declaration from me would have no more weight than the sheet of paper itself. The matter is entirely out of my hands. Further than to procure the evidence necessary to convict the guilty, I have no influence whatever."

"So!" Her lip curled and her eyes flashed. "You would weave a rope about Royal's neck!"

"I would not," I emphatically disputed. "If Royal Maillot was instrumental in Felix Page's death, he was so innocently. He don't know now – "

She broke in, leaning with intense eagerness across the chair-back.

"Then *why* is he in prison?" There was a note of triumph in her voice, as if she had me cornered.

"Miss Fluette," I replied earnestly, "will you listen to me for a few minutes? Believe me, there is no occasion for this desperate manner – "

"I *am* desperate."

"Perhaps. I understand your feelings; you and Mr. Maillot have my deepest sympa – "

She cut me short with a rap of the pistol upon the chair-back; I looked to see the thing go off.

"We don't want sympathy," she said through her teeth. "We want justice. And justice we'll have. Go over there and write!"

She imperiously indicated the desk.

Was a man ever caught in such an absurd predicament! I was truly sober now. I was resolved not to commit myself to anything that would only make me ridiculous; but this passionate, high-strung girl had told only the truth when she warned me that she was in dead earnest. My dilemma was most perplexing – and irritating, too. Could she be made to understand that if I exposed my hand now, before the issue was ripe, that the disclosure might work irreparable injury? Would she comprehend that such a course would immediately drive the guilty inside their defenses? Could she be made to see that it was better for her lover to endure a temporary inconvenience, than to be left in a position where he could never be freed from reproach? Perhaps so, but only by showing her where her father stood. I scarcely need point how impossible such a choice was. And in her present mood!

"Where is Miss Cooper?" I asked at last.

She abruptly clutched the hand that held the keys, so that they clicked together.

"Never mind," she flared at me, with a stamp of her foot. "Obey me."

"And if I don't?"

And now she leveled the pistol at me. She threw back her head and her lips curved.

"I'll shoot," she announced, in a tense tone. "So help me, I'll shoot."

For a moment we confronted each other, I utterly nonplussed, every line of the girl's figure breathing relentless determination.

"Miss Fluette," I tried to reason with her, "you are beside yourself. Pray don't do anything you'll regret."

But she stopped me. Her voice was harsh and strained.

"Get up out of that chair. Do as I say."

Should I continue to humor her? — for further parleying was wholly out of the question. And if I wrote anything at all, it would doubtless have to pass her critical inspection — and also into her possession — before she would yield an inch.

I had to decide quickly. I started to shake my head, and *bang*! — the pistol blazed right into my face.

Heaven knows where the bullet went; I only know that it missed me. Next instant I was too busy to think about how narrow had been my escape. I sprang up agilely enough now, and was only just in time to catch the drooping figure before it fell. As I passed a supporting arm round her, her hair tumbled about her face and over her shoulders. Her eyes were closed, her brow was gathered in a frown, her lips were pinched and livid.

I acted rapidly. She had not fainted — was not wholly unconscious — for she was still putting forth a feeble effort to help herself. I eased her into the chair, behind which she had been standing and into which she now sank limp and silent. Her chin fell forward upon her bosom, and now and then her shoulders rose in a racking, gasping sob.

She let the still smoking pistol drop into my hand. Somewhere below I could hear Genevieve calling wildly and someone pounding away upon a door.

Next I got the keys from Miss Belle's yielding fingers, and soon had the door to the room open. The cries and pounding had ceased, and I surmised that the troop of maids and other servants chattering on the lower stairs and in the second story hall had been attracted to their source. Then a hope came to me that the shot had passed unnoticed.

Well, it transpired that Genevieve was locked in a room on the second floor, much to the amazement of the servants, none of whom, I was thankful to learn, had heard the shot. Genevieve had, though, or I was very much mistaken in the cause of her vigorous effort to attract attention and her present frenzied appeals for some one to break down the door.

"Oh, please, please, don't wait for the key," she was importuning them. "Break in the door – only hurry!"

"Everything's all right, Miss Cooper," I called. A little cry of relief came from beyond the closed portal. "I have the key," I added.

The second key which Miss Fluette had held was the one, and I had the bolt shot in a jiffy. Genevieve ran straight to me and threw herself into my arms.

Whatever it was she meant to say in her first overjoyed transport, remained unsaid; for I unceremoniously clapped a hand over her mouth, picked her up and carried her bodily back into the room, and slammed the door upon the gaping servants.

"They don't know," I said. "Go up-stairs to Belle; she has fainted. The explosion was accidental, and no one was hurt." I was still holding her close in my arms. "God bless you!" I whispered at her ear. And then –

Well, even the exigencies of a memoir do not require that I should set down what occurred then. Genevieve, her cheeks aflame, broke from my embrace and ran out of the room. I heard her light steps upon the stairs, and then the door to the room which had come near being the scene of a tragedy, opened and closed.

20
GENEVIEVE'S MISSION

Almost at once a summons came from the up-stairs room for Miss Belle's maid. The rest of the servants were dismissed, and Genevieve signaled over the balusters for me to wait.

A very old man, cheerfully garrulous, who announced that he was the butler, took me downstairs.

"The drawing-room – living-room – or if you're of a mind to smoke, sir, Mr. Fluette's study." He indicated each of the rooms mentioned with a little flourish of the hand.

Although I am not a smoker, the word "study" arrested my attention. I indicated my preference. The old man instantly clapped a hand to one ear, and, leaning toward me, shouted into my face, "Hey?" So I decided the matter for myself by striding down the hall to where a door stood invitingly open.

Now perhaps you may consider it to have been the first duty of a traditional detective to take advantage of this opportunity, and perhaps you may be right. However, I believe I can assert, with some measure of authority, that a man in my profession may be a man of principle and honor and still succeed. I believe I may go even further: honest, straightforward conduct and upright dealing, by winning the confidence and respect of those with whom he holds intercourse, will carry a detective farther along the road to success in a given undertaking than any other means he may adopt. Honesty, in my calling as in all others, is the best policy.

But there are certain subtle impressions, often difficult to define, which are more potent than foot-prints and thumb-marks. A man's words, for example, are often of far less importance than his manner of uttering them. A man's personality is the stamp by which he declares his status among his fellows, and everybody is entitled to scan it that he may weigh and consider and judge. Hence a man's surroundings bear a thousand tokens of his character; for him to try to obliterate them, to keep them hid, is not to be frank and open, and that in itself invites suspicion.

My sole object in entering Alfred Fluette's study, therefore, was prompted by a hope that I might absorb something of its atmosphere. I did not know the man. Here was the place where he spent his leisure hours, where he unbent and became his normal self. It were indeed strange if I failed to gain some concept of his character.

I leaned against a window-casing, and surveyed the room with much interest. From the appearance of the books on the shelves – they were worn from use, but their coating of dust evidenced neglect – I gathered the idea that the master of the house had once been a bookish man, but that of late he had grown away from such pursuits. Here and there on the wide-topped writing-table were letters and papers in neat piles, while other letters and papers were heaped up and scattered about in the most careless disorder. The ink-well and blotting-pad were scrupulously tidy, but he never troubled to clean his pens after using them, or even to place them in the pen receiver.

To me, all this argued a man whose moral forces were undergoing a slow but certain deterioration; and with a man in Alfred Fluette's position, and with his responsibilities, the possibilities were manifold and ominous. His conscience still had a voice to raise in protest against meddling with his niece's heritage; but he remained deaf to the voice. He could stoop to villainy; but he was not so callous to wrongdoing but that the stooping hurt. Alfred Fluette needed a jolt – somebody to bring him up with a short turn – and I resolved, having the means, to be the one to do it.

As my glance roved hither and thither about the room, it was suddenly arrested and held.

On the writing-table, among a thousand and one odds and ends, was a memorandum calendar. It was in nowise different from scores of other calendars; the date displayed was to-day's, and in the blank space below, written in a large, firm handy appeared a notation.

But this memorandum contained a most peculiar word. Somehow, as my eye encountered it, a thrill ran through me. I could not define it; the thrill was without perceptible meaning, but I felt that the odd word should tell me something. The word was so odd, in fact, that I feared I could not remember it. So I copied it upon the back of an envelope, thus:

TSHEN-BYO-YEN.

Immediately under it had been written: "10 o'clock."

Further speculation on the matter was interrupted by Genevieve coming down-stairs. I stepped into the hall when I heard her, and she at once joined me. We went into the living-room.

Her beautiful eyes were round with wonder, her sweet face filled with concern; but before I entered into any explanations, I turned to her and held out my arms.

"First," I whispered, "I want to know whether it is real."

She caught her breath sharply; the color came quickly to her cheeks, a tender light to the blue eyes. She put her hands confidently into mine.

"What has happened to you?" she asked, standing away from me and staring with perplexed solicitude at the testimony of Stodger's barbarous surgery. I had forgotten all about the red-hot poker.

"A mere scratch – a nothing," I made light of it. "I'll tell you all about it when the time comes. There are too many other things to be disposed of first."

"But – you have been wounded," she persisted, now thoroughly alarmed. And so I had to tell her about the night's adventure, which I did, for the most part shamefacedly enough.

It was a delight to watch the different expressions flit across her lovely countenance, to see them mingle and blend and give way to others – wonder, amazement, awe, horror, terror – I can't begin to name them all. A score of times she interrupted me, but it was always a welcome interruption.

"Stodger's a trump," I concluded. "Think of him jumping up from a sound sleep and throwing himself into the thick of the fray, without one second's hesitation."

"Y-e-s," she agreed, but there was no enthusiasm in her tone. Then she turned warmly upon me.

"I'm thinking, though, that you've been gifted with mighty little sense, Knowles Swift, to have acted so recklessly. The very idea of a sane man creeping through that dark hall and up those dark stairs, and plunging into he knew not what!" She eyed me severely.

"But I did know," I protested meekly. "It was the *etagere*"

There was a solemn rebuke in the slow shaking of her head. "A man swears so," she sighed, "when he does anything awkward, like that."

I remained discreetly silent.

However, she was too much exercised over my "wound" – as she persisted in calling the scratch on my cheek – and the loss of the ruby to encourage any levity. Honestly, at that moment I cared not a whit for the ruby. Besides, there were consolations which I need not record. It *was* real – very, very real; and I was the happiest man in the world.

Genevieve was also curious to learn – and very naturally so – what had transpired between Belle and me.

"How is she now?" I parried. I had concluded that when Miss Belle was again her normal self, she would rather have our little episode forgotten.

"Calm as a graven image," was the reply. Grief and anxiety trembled in Genevieve's voice. "But it is a stony, deathlike sort of calm that gives me the creeps. The poor girl is distracted. She wants to be alone; she sent me to you."

"*She* sent you," said I, with quick interest. This struck me as being rather curious.

"Oh, I know Belle," said Genevieve. "She probably said some very bitter things to you; now she's sorry."

I trusted that the impulsive young lady was experiencing some pangs of remorse; but before I confided anything, I learned how Genevieve came to be locked in Belle's room.

Early in the morning Belle had grown quite tranquil, but insisted upon talking. To humor and soothe her, Genevieve, during their talk, asserted that I could be depended upon to save Royal. She also mentioned that I was expected to call.

After breakfast Genevieve had fallen asleep, through sheer weariness. Belle must have risen cautiously, determined to treat with me herself. Her impulsive decision was manifestly arrived at after I rang the bell, because she had had no time to dress.

Soon after, Genevieve had awakened with a start, to find herself locked in and the bell-button dug out of its socket. She could not summon the servants without creating an uproar. She soon surmised something of what Belle had in mind, but never, until she heard the muffled report of the pistol, had she dreamed that the frenzied girl contemplated anything so desperate and rash.

Well, I softened the matter as much as I could for Miss Belle, making it very clear that I realized from the start that she was not responsible, and that I had been most of the time engaged in calming her and trying to persuade her to return to her room. I even stretched a point about the shooting; I feared that Genevieve would never forgive her for that. I said it had occurred – without intent – while I was struggling with her; which, after all, was perhaps not far from the truth.

"Why should Miss Belle have any reason for despising Alexander Burke?" I asked during our conference, for the girl's patent abhorrence of the fellow stuck in my mind.

Genevieve's expression became all at once very grave. For a moment she sat silent, toying with a plait of her skirt; then she looked up at me, saying soberly:

"It is one of the things that I shouldn't talk about. Still – I don't know," she faltered. "It is Burke alone who has roused her resentment." Then she decided.

"I will tell you this much: She overheard a conversation between him and her father. It filled her with loathing for the fellow – that and – and something else."

"I shall not try to force your confidence, my dear girl," I said. "Tell me only what you think you ought."

"Belle trusts me implicitly," she said simply.

"And I want her to continue to. The something else that makes her loathe him – are you free to speak of that?"

"It's nothing; it's ridiculous." She laughed nervously. "He has tried to make love to her. *Ugh!*" She shuddered at the idea.

"The dickens he has!"

Such a thought had never entered my head; it was impossible to imagine that slippery rascal in the role of an ardent lover. His blood was as cold as a fish's. But now I understood the fellow's animus toward Maillot; his hatred was inspired by jealousy. Belle had never spoken of the matter to Maillot – mortification was potent to hold this confidence in check – but he had instinctively distrusted and disliked Burke in return.

I could not bring myself to confide in my lovely coadjutor my convictions respecting her uncle. I learned that he had left the house that morning at an hour unusually early for him, and I thought at once of the queer memorandum on his calendar. He was still very much worried, declared Genevieve, and when at home kept more and more to himself as time went by. Mrs. Fluette was asleep after the night's ordeal with her daughter.

"If Royal were free to come after her," said Genevieve, not without some bitterness, "he could carry Belle away this very minute; there would be nobody to say him nay. Poor boy!"

"It is more than likely that he shall soon," I offered in dubious comfort. And then we got down to the purpose of my call.

"Do you know where your aunt and uncle were married?" I asked.

"Yes. It was in a little town in Ohio – "

"Merton," said I.

"That's it! But how did you know?"

I smiled at her surprise. "It's Felix Page's birth-place; the rest was inference."

She waited with ill-concealed curiosity for what was to follow. I found it necessary to hold her hands – both of them – while I told her.

"Would you mind making a journey there? – at once – to-day?" Her eyes opened wide; even her sweet lips parted; but she waited.

And now I found it really essential to put my arm around her and draw her to me – she was too agitated to hear otherwise what I had to say. I hastened to explain how impossible it was for me to leave the city just at the time, what with my anxiety to recover the ruby and the necessity of keeping in close touch with Burke.

"I require only one more piece to complete the answer to our riddle," I affirmed, – I really thought so at the time, – "and you can get it for me. Don't bother your aunt; she will keep back all essentials, anyway. Your uncle and aunt and Felix Page all came from the same town, and there you can find plenty of old gossips who can – they'll be only too willing to – give you all the information you want. They'll give you more; but we can winnow the wheat from the chaff after you get back. Do you feel equal to such an undertaking?"

The proposal appeared to overcome her. She considered for a time, then turned to me, her eyes dancing, her cheeks flushed.

"Yes," she said, with bated breath. "I can't do Belle any good; she only wants to be alone. What do you want me to do?"

"Dig up every scrap of family history that you can – the Pages', the Fluettes', and the Coopers'; especially as they affect one another. Being a Cooper yourself, the task should be easy for you; you are compiling a family-tree, you know."

Genevieve gave me a sly look, and retorted: "'When first we practice to deceive' – "

"Oh, no," I assured her. "If you do your work thoroughly, you certainly will have a complete family-tree. So there's no deception about it."

Well, it was finally settled that she would go, and that she would report the result of her journey to me as soon as possible.

She then elicited a confession of my inability to solve the cipher – which confession was yielded up to the accompaniment of an exceedingly sour smile.

"That old house is a hoodoo," I said bitterly. "I have failed in everything I ever undertook inside its walls. The rest of the chase will be pursued on the outside."

"And you didn't even find the little daisy what-you-may-call-'ems – the originals, I mean?" She meant the crazy designs on the cipher.

"I did not." Genevieve laughed.

"Wait till I get back. I mean to have a try at our cryptograph. If the daisies are in the old Page place, I'll find them."

"They're there, all right. I'm sure you're welcome to try – if you'll let me assist in the search."

She wrinkled her nose and sniffed. "Hmf! A lot of assistance I can look for from *you*." Her tone was emphatically disparaging. "No, I'll find them by myself. But I'd be afraid to stay – for long – alone in that empty house."

I cared not in what capacity I served, just so I might be with her.

After making me promise that I would have the scratch on my face attended to at once, she sent me away.

I had not proceeded far toward town when I discovered that somebody was dogging my steps.

21
SHADOWS

It required some little time for me to determine that my shadow was one of the "Japanese"; for it was a most intangible and elusive shadow. Whatever else I might think of these worthies, I could not deny that their ability to hang on a man's trail, and at the same time keep themselves well-nigh invisible, amounted positively to genius. With all my doubling back and lurking in doorways around corners, the fellow never came up to where I could get a good view of him.

Of course it occurred to me that here was a chance to attempt a capture. But was it? The fellow was so slippery and artful that I risked a greater chance of losing him altogether. And then, to capture one of the quintet – or whatever their number might be – would more likely than not merely serve as a warning for the ring-leader of the crowd. Doubtless I could drag nothing at all from the fellow, even though I did succeed in laying hands upon him. If he had been set to watch me he would continue to do so unless I scared him away. I resolved to let him alone for the time being; but the first thing I did after reaching Dr. De Breen's offices was to ring up headquarters and request the Captain to send a man to get on my shadow's trail.

The doctor gave me a bad half-hour. The instant he was through I hurried to a window to learn how events were progressing in the street. Before I had time to ascertain whether my shadow was still on duty, or whether the Central Office man had showed up, my whole attention was absorbed by the appearance of two familiar figures on the opposite side. They were Mr.

Fluette and Alexander Burke, walking along together in the most intimate manner imaginable.

I glanced at my watch; it still lacked a minute or two of ten, the hour Mr. Fluette had jotted on his calendar along with the extraordinary memorandum. Inasmuch as he and his strangely chosen companion were moving rapidly, it was a reasonable assumption that he was even then on his way to keep his engagement.

For a moment I stood irresolute. I was very anxious to follow the twain to the rendezvous, while at the same time I did not want to lose my shadow. I glanced eagerly up and down the street, studying the hurrying crowd on the walk, but could not see him anywhere. Then I hurried out to the elevator, and within the next minute was dropped to the ground floor.

I was obliged to walk fast to get within range of Fluette and Burke again – not an easy thing to do among the crowd – but still I could see nothing of my headquarters man, nor of the Jap. And right then I perceived the last mentioned. He had manifestly only at that instant caught up with the speculator and his companion – though why I had failed to see him before I can't imagine – and he was evidently addressing one or the other, or both of them.

It seemed to me that the fellow was trying to make his presence as inconspicuous as possible. He strode stolidly along, close behind them, looking into the shop windows and apparently not noticing the two men at all. Yet I knew that he was talking to them. I could tell by the surprised way with which both Fluette and Burke swung round and stared at him.

I quickened my steps. Yes, the Oriental was talking, and talking volubly. And, if I might judge by the consternation and anger reflected in the faces of his two auditors, his message was anything but welcome. That is to say, Alfred Fluette's strong features showed these emotions, while, as always, it was difficult to read what was going on behind Burke's impassive mask. Still it was pretty plain that the secretary was utterly at his wits'-end.

At last the three stopped at a corner, where they moved up close to the building to avoid the rush of pedestrians. I dared not draw near enough to hope to hear any of their conversation; I could do no more than watch from a distance, trusting to their absorption to keep them oblivious of my proximity.

Both were now excitedly questioning the Jap, who seemed to be wholly unmoved by their agitation. Presently Fluette turned angrily upon Burke. From his manner it was not difficult to imagine that he was soundly berating the secretary, who, whenever he could make himself heard, was just as plainly attempting to present some extenuating argument.

The entire episode was perplexing enough, but what immediately ensued caught me unawares. Without the least warning the trio separated, each hurrying away in a different direction. At this critical juncture a voice said, right at my ear:

"Shall I stick to Burke? – or follow one of the others?"

I jerked my head round to confront Fanshawe, the man detailed to keep Burke under surveillance. I had not observed him before – not surprising, since he had just caught up with me – but I welcomed his presence now.

"Stay with your own man," I shot at him, and turned to look for the Jap. He was gone.

To make the account of this discomfiting episode as brief as possible, I shall say, merely, that out of the three men whom we were watching, two of them walked away from under our very noses without our having the slightest idea in which direction they went. How did they do it? The momentary diversion occasioned by Fanshawe's arrival, the brief distraction of our attention, had been sufficient. He lost track of Burke, and I never had so much as another glimpse of the Jap.

We had the assistance of another headquarters man, too. The one for which I had telephoned showed up immediately after Fanshawe addressed me. The last-named scurried away to find Burke, while Pennington, my other colleague, and I devoted our efforts to catching the Jap.

"One of those Japs has been shadowing me all morning, Pennington," I advised him. "He's as shifty and evasive as a fox. Fall half a block behind me, and if he shows up again give me a signal and close in. I want him."

But he didn't show up.

It was humiliating to be outwitted by the Oriental – it was the second time for me, too; it would be calamitous to lose Burke. The day dragged along, and when each succeeding minute brought no news of him my anxiety increased by leaps and bounds. Before nightfall, every available man in the department was scouring the city for the ex-secretary.

Subsequent events, however, showed that we might have spared ourselves all the trouble and worry; for one more pertinacious even than Fanshawe clung to Alexander Burke's heels all that day and night.

I found time during my purposeless running to and fro to learn that Alfred Fluette had arrived at his brokers' offices in Quincy Street shortly after ten, where he remained until the Board of Trade closed, and that Genevieve had left on an afternoon train for a brief visit with relatives in Merton, Ohio. Fluette had failed in his engagement; Genevieve had kept hers.

Sometime after dark I boarded a Sheridan Park car, and rode out to the Page place; I don't now know why, unless it was because of the disastrous turn affairs had taken, and that I hoped, in this dismal, dispiriting environment, to find a balm for my depressed feelings.

It was only that morning, in the midst of a blinding snow-storm, thoroughly disheartened by the loss of the ruby, that Stodger and I had left the old house; but as I approached it that night, it bore every appearance of having been abandoned for years instead of only a few hours. No smoke curled from the chimneys; no light gleamed at any of the windows. In its white setting of snow, it loomed silent and spectral.

In the afternoon I had turned the keys over to Mr. Page's lawyer, and how I hoped to effect an entrance – if I had any such intention at all – I have long since forgotten. It may have been because it was here that I first met Genevieve, that I came mooning through the cold and snow. She was gone upon a journey; I knew that I could not see her for days; and perhaps I thought to find some companionship in the more intimate associations clustered about the dreary spot. At any rate, here I was. And I saw nothing else for me to do than to turn round and go back to town again.

However, I started to enter the gate. Next instant I stopped short. The snow bore other tracks besides Stodger's and mine – tracks pointing toward the house instead of away from it. They were fresh, made since the snow ceased.

I advanced a little farther into the yard, where the tracks had not been obliterated by pedestrians on the sidewalk, and soon comprehended that they had been made by two men. Were they in the house now? And if so, who were they? What errand could be so pressing that it would bring anybody here on such a night?

My indifference and discouragement fell away from me in a flash. Cautiously I followed the trail up to the front steps, where at first I fancied it disappeared upon the porch. Still I could not see a glint of light, nor did the most attentive harkening favor me with the slightest sound.

It occurred to me while I stood pondering on the porch that, after all, Mr. White – Felix Page's lawyer – might have been responsible for the tracks in the snow. It was possible that he had sent somebody to look after the place; a caretaker, perhaps, who would stay here until a disposition could be made of the property.

But this idea no sooner occurred than it was dismissed. All at once I noticed that one pair of footprints, instead of mounting the porch steps, had turned to one side. They led off to the east, and disappeared round the wing in that direction. The two persons had not come in company; the first, I presently concluded, had carried a key, and the second had been following him. There were no retreating impresses to indicate that either had departed.

I tiptoed to the front door and turned the knob. The door did not yield. Then for the first time I recalled the window which our housebreakers had forced the night before; unless the latch had been repaired during the day, it would be an easy matter to gain access to the dining-room, which was located in the western wing.

Now it was the eastern wing or gable which sheltered the library, the conservatory, and Mr. Page's bedroom, and it was thither the second man's foot-prints led. I followed them round the corner of the house.

From their appearance it was easy to trace all the mysterious intruder's movements. Evidently after the door had closed behind the first arrival, Number Two had stood for some time at the east end of the porch. Then he had moved toward the same end of the house, pausing at every window and trying the sash to ascertain whether it was fastened. Turning at the corner, he had proceeded along the side of the house, still testing the windows and bestowing particular attention upon the glass conservatory. This was true of every window as far as the bedroom, at least; beyond that I did not explore. Just as I drew opposite the first of the bedroom windows I came to an abrupt halt.

There was a light in the room.

Nor was this all. Some person was in the room, too, and by the silhouette on the blind I could see that he was industriously applying himself to some task, the nature of which I could not determine. The longer I watched the shadow on the blind, the more puzzled I grew. I could imagine no occupation that would account for such singular actions.

The shadow was a man's; I could distinguish that much. He appeared to be bending over something, while his hands flew hither and thither, as if they were performing a quick-step upon a piano. But no sound of music came from the lighted room.

It would be impossible to say how long I stood there, the snow nearly to my knees, fascinated by the remarkable antics of that shadow. Then of a sudden the hands ceased flying. The man straightened and became motionless, as if startled by some unexpected sound.

Well, perhaps within the next second he knew what had alarmed him; I'm sure that I did not. The shadow flashed away from the blind. Then my scalp tingled and the blood seemed to freeze in my veins.

From within the room there came a most unearthly cry. It was weird, terrifying, utterly unlike anything I had ever heard – save once. For it was a repetition of the wild, inhuman note that had thrilled me when I first dashed open the bath room door the previous night.

The terrible cry was not immediately repeated, but for a while the utmost confusion prevailed within. I could hear furniture knocked and slammed about, a tumult of stamping, scraping feet, and once – for the briefest moment – another shadow was projected upon the blind.

It was a hideous, squat, dwarfish shadow. Two long gorilla-like arms were upraised in an abandonment of fury. Then came that awful, blood-curdling scream again, and the shadow's owner seemed to plunge headlong forward.

Another crash followed. The light was suddenly blotted out. The silence was once more absolute.

22

ASHES OF OLD ROMANCE

It was Friday afternoon when Genevieve started on her mission; the following Wednesday morning I received a telegram from her announcing that she would be home that same afternoon. The interim was so uneventful that my note-book mentions only two incidents as being worthy of preservation.

Late Friday night the welcome news came to headquarters that Alexander Burke had been found. He appeared at his lodgings shortly before midnight, looking wretchedly ill and exhausted. Saturday morning a physician was called in, and the whilom secretary was not able to appear upon the streets again until Tuesday. Then it was observed that a change had come over the man. His impassivity had been penetrated at last; it could no longer hide a nervousness and apprehension which kept his head perpetually pivoting in backward glances across his shoulder.

I smiled with satisfaction when Fanshawe told me this.

"Stay with him," I said; "it makes no difference whether or not he knows that you are always close behind him. In fact, I want him to know it; I want to break that man, and I will."

The other incident referred to was a meeting I succeeded in securing between Maillot and Miss Belle — memorable for me as being the first occasion upon which I was favored with a glimpse of Mrs. Fluette.

Sunday afternoon mother and daughter drove up to headquarters in the family carriage. Although the girl had been tactful enough to eschew a heavy veil and sombre apparel, it was plain to be seen that the event was almost too great an ordeal for even her proud and dauntless spirit.

Belle descended from the carriage hesitantly, and then stood looking about with an air of such helpless terror that I approached – I had previously resolved to keep myself effaced during the visit – and conducted her into the Captain's private office, where Maillot was waiting. She gave me an embarrassed, beseeching glance, and murmured a barely audible "Thank you." No more was said. She faltered an instant on the threshold, then, sobbing, rushed in. I made haste to close the door and rejoin Mrs. Fluette.

This lady was slight and frail, with hair as white as snow, and about her there hung an intangible something which gave me the impression that she was a woman who had suffered much. Although I strove to speak cheerfully of the prospects of Maillot's early release, her manner was quite discouraging to all my overtures. When she spoke at all it was only in the faintest of monosyllables – usually with her eyes avoiding mine. She looked at me, when at all, shyly, started at every unusual sound, and trembled during the whole time she sat in the Captain's big easy-chair.

At the end of the allotted half-hour – I wasn't very particular over the number of minutes – Mrs. Fluette's increasing nervousness and impatience moved me to rap upon the private-room door. Belle emerged, her cheeks white and her eyes swollen with weeping. The poor girl pressed my hand when I helped her into the carriage – clung to it despairingly, to be exact – and the tears again gushed to her eyes.

"This is killing me!" she moaned. "Oh, it is! it is! I can't stand it much longer."

"Courage, Miss Fluette," I undertoned assuasively. "Everything is working for the best, believe me."

Ah, but was it? I could not say the words with much assurance. They drove away, two sad, harassed women.

Touching again upon Wednesday afternoon, I was pretty sure that the Fluette carriage would meet Genevieve at the station – very likely with Belle, or possibly Mrs. Fluette. In anticipation of this contingency I had sent a note to the house with the request that she find an excuse to meet me at the earliest possible moment, for I was all impatience to hear her report.

But Genevieve had anticipated also. She arrived armed with a commission from the Ohio cousin, the performance of which would brook no delay. So I had a minute alone with her downtown. She had been thoughtful enough to record a detailed statement of her investigations; it lies before me now as I write; and I shall condense from it those portions that are essential to advancing this chronicle.

In the early '50's Clara Cooper was the belle of the village of Merton. Wooers were many, but favors were few and grudgingly bestowed; and in time all the suitors withdrew, leaving the field clear to Alfred Fluette and Felix Page.

The Coopers and the Fluettes represented the wealth and aristocracy of the community, while Felix Page was a poor, struggling young man whose only advantages and prospects for the future lay in his indomitable pluck and a resolution that was ready to ride roughshod over all opposition.

And Clara favored the poor young man. He went forth from Merton resolved to wrest a fortune from the world and lay it at his sweetheart's feet. She promised to wait for him until he returned with the fulfillment of his ambitious aims.

Alas, though, for the fiery Felix: she was not of a very resolute character, being easily influenced by her sterner parents, whose patrician eyes looked askance upon the presumptuous lover's claims. Besides, Felix was absent – supposedly engaged in his laudable enterprise of wresting a fortune from the world – while Alfred, handsome, polished of manner, patient and persistently attentive, was ever at her elbow.

Then, too, there was Miss Clara's family, to the last one of them espousing Alfred's cause. In the end the girl allowed herself to drift with the current. Felix would have accomplished more to his purpose had he remained at home and married Clara, and then gone after the fortune. At any rate, after one or two letters from Felix, which glowed with hope and boundless zeal, she ceased to hear from him. Doubtless he had come to realize that the wresting operation demanded all his powers; but his silence was easily made to appear of more significance than it deserved. It was construed – for Miss Clara, not by her – as indisputable evidence of forgetfulness. Within the year she married Alfred Fluette.

Six years passed. Alfred Fluette had migrated with his bride to the city. Then Felix Page returned triumphant to Merton. His triumph, however, was short-lived. He was well on the road, even then, to his subsequent commercial success; a good deal of the wresting had been accomplished; but the girl he had steadfastly loved, whom he had never for one instant put out of his thoughts, had married his rival.

To get together most of her report Genevieve had been obliged to labor patiently and painstakingly; when it came to the events associated with Felix Page's return to his birth-place, her task was suddenly transformed from one of gleaning to another equally arduous, of selecting from the plethora of material at her disposal.

One gathers the idea, after reading it all, that his rage was that of a cave-man who returns from the day's hunt to find that his home in the hillside cliff has been despoiled. One thing stands out clear and unmistakable; from that hour his life was embittered, his character warped with the shattering of his ideals. He registered a solemn vow of vengeance against Alfred Fluette, then disappeared.

So much for this portion of the report. Nothing in the subsequent relations of the two men was now obscure.

And here, too, we are given a new light upon Alexander Burke, oiling door-hinges that he might the better spy upon his employer, patiently working out the combination of the hidden safe and running to Alfred Fluette with the old love-letters and mementos – for a price, of course, – playing the vindictiveness of the one against the hatred and fear of the other, and scrupling not to gain profit for himself whenever and wherever he might.

But it is proverbial that a woman invariably reserves the most interesting and important item for the postscript. And it was so with Genevieve's report. I quote the concluding paragraphs *in toto*.

On the very first day of my arrival, and from the very first person to whom I confided the nature of my errand, I received the surprising intelligence that I was not the first to pursue similar inquiries in Merton. Said my informant: "Why, there was a man here two or three weeks ago, trying to find out all he could about the Pages and the Coopers and the Fluettes. Has some one of them died and left a lot of money?"

I did not think so much of it the first time, but when my second victim told me the same thing, I sat up and began to take notice. Then I extended my inquiries so as to cover my mysterious predecessor.

I soon found out that he had ingratiated himself with everybody in Merton who could give him a scrap of information, and that his inquiries were all directed to one end; namely, the family histories of the Pages, the Coopers, and the Fluettes.

Then, from all the people I could find who had seen and talked to this man, I obtained a description of his appearance and (where they were remembered) his personal peculiarities. One description photographed him for me:

"A tall, lean, lanky feller – real sandy – hair, eyes, eyelashes, eyebrows – no, he didn't have no eyebrows; but all the rest was the same light yaller color. He was pale and sickly lookin' – poor man! – and you couldn't tell what he was a-lookin' at when he talked to a body. Any kin o' yourn?"

Who was my mysterious predecessor in the field, if he were not Alexander Burke?

Who, indeed!

23
Burke Unbosoms

Eight o'clock Thursday morning: an hour before, Fanshawe had heard with a sigh of relief that I would take his place that morning. I had since been kicking my heels opposite the rooming house where Alexander Burke had his lodgings.

At the hour mentioned Burke appeared. I retreated into a sheltering doorway, and watched him.

He stood for a moment upon the top step, darting quick glances up and down the street, and intently scanning the few pedestrians who were abroad at the time. Then he came rapidly down the steps, and turned toward the city.

The snow muffled my tread, and he didn't hear my approach – didn't know of my presence until I tapped him upon the shoulder.

"Mr. Burke," said I, "I want you."

With a quick intake of breath, which sounded like the hiss of a snake, he slewed round and fixed me with his expressionless eyes. Also – to complete the simile – his head reared back, like a snake's when it is about to strike. I don't believe that I ever before found such a keen pleasure in arresting a man.

"Want me!" he gasped. "What for?"

"Yes, you." I could not entirely hide my satisfaction. "And because you have reached the end of your rope. I don't intend to stand here and argue about it, either."

In a moment the man was calm – all except his gloved hands. A man's hands will, nine times out of ten, betray him in spite of himself. Burke's fingers were twitching, and folding and unfolding without cessation.

"Swift," he whispered vindictively, "you'll regret this — so help me God, you will.   Curse you!   Why do you persecute me? I'll go with you — of course I shall; how can I help myself when I'm at the mercy of a brute of a giant, like you?"

"Then shut up, and come along. I'll just keep a hand under your arm until we get to headquarters. . . . Never mind!" as he made a move to unbutton his overcoat. "It's cold enough to keep covered."   I had struck down the stealthy hand with considerable vigor, and he winced with pain. The pale eyes flashed a malignant look at me, and straightway became inscrutable again.

Not another word was said until we stood before the clerk at the Central Office.   The matter-of-fact way in which he picked up a pen and poised it over the police docket, the callous indifference with which he inquired the prisoner's name and the nature of the charge, made Burke flinch for the first time.

"Wait, Johnson!" I said suddenly to the clerk, as if on second thought. "I don't believe I'll docket this man yet; I want to keep the pinch quiet for a while."

The game was familiar to Johnson; he laid aside the pen as indifferently as he had taken it up, and returned to his interrupted perusal of the morning paper.

"You come with me," I said to Burke.

I conducted him to the little room behind the Captain's private office — scene of many a heart-to-heart conference — and pushed him toward one of the two chairs which constituted the room's sole furnishing.   It was a dim, silent, disheartening place, and I was resolved to have no mercy upon the man whom at last I had succeeded in getting into a position where I could handle him.

"Burke," I began, "I'm not going to mince matters or stand for any quibbling or lying. I have *you* right where I want you, and whatever leniency you may receive will depend entirely upon your frankness. This is your chance — the last one."

No doubt my expression and manner were grim, I meant them to be and there was no doubt that my obvious confidence in my position impressed the ex-secretary; for the fingers grew more agile, and he licked his dry lips again and again.

"What am I charged with?" he demanded, in a shaking voice.

"Nothing, as yet," I returned cheerfully. "You doubtless noticed that I dispensed with that little formality. Do you know what that means? Just this: no one knows you are here; there is a certain small cell below stairs, dark as Egypt, provided expressly for recalcitrant individuals. You could lie there for a year, and nobody be a whit the wiser. I, for one, wouldn't care how long you stayed."

"Swift," the fellow stammered, "this – this is outrageous!"

"Perhaps," agreed I, carelessly, surveying him with a narrowed look. "I'm not here to excuse police methods; they're not very gentle, I'll admit; but when we deal with crooks we're obliged to hand them the only treatment they're amenable to.

"Burke, you can't excite one bit of pity or sympathy in me for you, for I know you to be a cold-blooded, treacherous scoundrel, and whatever you have coming to you is only what you deserve. I'm fixed to put you through as a principal in the murder of Page – sit down!" I thundered at him, for he had started to rise from his seat. He dropped back limply. "You wait till I'm through. Your chance is coming in just about a minute. I promise not to interrupt – as long as you tell a straightforward story.

"As I said," I went on, "I'm prepared to put you through as one of the principals; the bare fact of your arrest should be enough to convince you of my readiness.

"However, while I haven't any desire to spare you, we are in the habit of trading leniency to a rascal who is

willing to turn State's evidence.   It's a plain business
proposition."

I imagined that he perked up a bit at this.

"Ah, then you are not so sure," he seemed to muse;
"you would have me convict myself for your precious
benefit."

"Maybe you can judge better before I have finished,"
returned I, unmoved.   "You need not tell me anything
about yourself, but I do need a few facts to complete my
case against the others who were involved in this crime.
It's up to you."

I retreated a step, folded my arms, and stood
watching him – and waiting. I knew that he couldn't tell
the truth without filling in the gaps in his own case. I
never am deterred by any compunction over the methods
I am sometimes obliged to use to make an individual,
whom I know deserves no consideration, speak. With a
knave like Burke I would as lief resort to thumb-screws,
the boot, the rack, or even to choking the words from him,
as to trust to persuasion alone. To tell the truth, my
preference lies with the means first enumerated: they are
much more prompt and direct. The worst indictment that
one may bring against the old-time torture is that it was
not applied with judgment and discrimination, nor
always confined to legitimate ends. I fear that I shock
you. But I am not by any means a cruel, blood-thirsty
person. I merely speak from long years of experience.
Whenever I hear a misguided soul deploring the so-called
"third degree" – why, I have something in pickle for *him*.

This, however, is not the place to open the pickle-jar.

Perhaps, though, Burke's suffering was as poignant as
if his ordeal were physical. How restlessly the man's
slender, bloodless fingers curled and uncurled! Still, his
self-control was wonderful; his white face remained
indecipherable, the pale eyes stared at me unblinkingly
and without mirroring a single emotion that I could
discern. Then the change came so quickly that it almost
caught me off my guard. One hand shot to his bosom.

When it re-appeared something flashed dully in the dim light. At the same time, with a cat-like spring, he was out of his chair and upon me.

I concentrated all my attention upon the hand that held the murderous knife. I caught it as it lunged at me; then, with a quick twist, I bent it backward and behind him, until he groaned with pain. The long-bladed knife clattered to the floor, and I shoved him roughly away from me. Then I picked up the weapon.

The fellow acted for all the world like a whipped and cowed panther. He brought up violently against the wall, where, in a stooping posture, he commenced running to and fro the width of the room, spitting and snarling venomously. The pale eyes were no longer blank. The pupils had widened, and the look of them was deadly.

I smiled with quiet satisfaction, for I knew that Burke was – as we specify it in police parlance – "coming through."

After a while he quieted, and at last stood panting in the corner farthest away from me. I pointed to the chair.

"Sit down," I said, precisely as if he hadn't tried his best to murder me but a minute before.

He moved slowly – fearfully – toward the chair, and sank into it. His head was dropped forward, his shoulders were bowed, and the fingers were no longer restless. All the man's defenses were at last down.

"Now, then, Burke," I went on calmly, "I suppose we are ready to get down to business?"

He muttered inaudibly, without raising his head.

"What's that?" – sharply,

"You devil!" he whispered.

"Yes, yes, I know. I've heard that from you before. I don't care to hear it again." I advanced and stood threateningly over him.

"Look at me," I sternly commanded.

Slowly he raised his head until his eyes met mine. The pallid mask was pinched, and it wore a look of torment.

"Once for all, Burke, are you going to speak?" I suppose the quietness with which I uttered it was ominous to the wretch. "Or will I be obliged to drag you to that cell of which I spoke?"

With a quick gesture, he outspread his arms.

"Enough, Swift, enough!" he cried, in a hoarse, distressed voice. "I know when I'm beaten; I'll give up. What do you want?"

"Good," without alteration of tone or manner. "Let's go to a pleasanter place." And we went into the Captain's private room, where a stenographer sat concealed by a screen.

Burke dropped into a chair. I thrust my hands into my coat pockets, and as I slowly paced to and fro, addressed him.

"I'll tell my story. When I'm wrong you may correct me. See that you do it, too, because you won't know when I'm testing you or when I am really ignorant of the facts. You see how much I trust you, Mr. Burke.

"To begin at the beginning, your first treacherous act toward your employer was when you determined to steal the Paternoster ruby, and started in to hunt for it. You had your work all cut out for you, too, Burke; Felix Page was no fool; he wouldn't trust the safekeeping of so valuable an object even to his confidential clerk, nor could that clerk search for it with impunity.

"You've been gifted with the same brand of patience, though, Burke, that keeps a cat glued to a rat-hole for hours upon end; you bided your time. And you never let an opportunity slip by you, either.

"Felix Page was in the habit of talking to himself – a trait not uncommon to people who live much to themselves – so you oiled the door-hinges in order that you might steal upon him undetected, from any part of the house, and listen to his self-communings. No wonder, when you talked with me, that you were fearful of the curtained alcove!

"But I'll be brief. By and by you learned of the hidden safe; then – still with infinite patience – you set about trying to discover its combination. You succeeded."

I halted abruptly in front of him.

"Burke, the opening of that safe door was a revelation; it offered new possibilities which must have overwhelmed you. What did you think when your eyes first fell upon those old love mementos from Clara Cooper to Felix Page? Don't look astonished so soon; wait till I'm done. I'll have no difficulty convincing you that my case against you is pretty complete.

"But your find was extremely aggravating, for you were afraid to make use of it. Without doubt, Alfred Fluette would give a pretty penny to get them from Felix Page. But you lacked sand to brave Page's wrath.

"Then what did you do?" I paused to eye him a moment. "Why, you went down to Merton and dug up all the old family skeletons. Now you were surer of your ground; you were ready to levy tribute – blackmail – not from Page, though, because he would have promptly kicked you out – but again your nerve failed you. That's where you have fallen down, Burke, all the way through. You carried a letter or two to Fluette to prove your claims; then, before their loss was discovered, you brought them back again, and replaced them in the safe. Oh, that old man, in his lifetime, inspired a wholesome fear of him in your soul."

Then, circumstantially, I detailed as a statement of the case, my reconstruction of the tragic night, concluding with his hiding the ruby in the bar of soap. At this point I suddenly wheeled upon him, and asked point-blank:

"Tell me what you were doing in Mr. Page's bedroom Friday night, and what it was that surprised you there?"

He stared at me in amazement. He had been, whilst I was talking, slowly regaining his self-possession –

crawling into himself, as it were, and pulling down the blinds; and now, when he spoke, it was with something of his old manner.

"Swift, my biggest blunder was in underestimating your intelligence. I thought I could play hob with you; but I was a fool." His face gave me a certain impression of slyness, which I didn't at all like.

"Careful now," I sharply warned.

He sat silent for a moment, then spoke.

"I'm not taking any more chances. Swift; don't worry. . . . What was I doing Friday night? I was hunting for the ruby."

"Look here," – impatiently. "I thought you had trifled enough."

He raised a protesting hand.

"Let me finish. Friday was the first time since Mr. Page's death that I have managed to shake off the man who has been following me. When I became convinced that I really had succeeded in doing so, I stayed under cover until nightfall; then – well, you yourself have said that I'm an opportunist. I didn't know the cake of soap had been removed from the bath room; when I discovered it was not there I supposed you had found the ruby's hiding-place, and that you had concealed it elsewhere. I was trying to find it, when – when somebody came in."

"One of the Japanese," I supplied.

"They're not Japanese," he corrected, with a provoking air of superior knowledge. "They are Burmese."

"Whatever they are, you have been playing them and Fluette against each other. Burke, I suppose you can't help lying; it comes easier for you than telling the truth. You know that those fellows managed to steal the bar of soap – "

"While you were watching it," he interpolated. " – and," I went on, ignoring the thrust, "they notified you and Fluette of the fact Friday morning."

"Yes," he said slowly, after a pause, "they told us they had secured the bar of soap."

"If that's so," I fixed him with a level look, "why did the intelligence floor you so?"

"You draw your conclusions so admirably that you ought to be able to supply the answer to that question yourself."

"I'm not here for that purpose," – curtly. "Come, speak up."

He sat for a long while silent; then, –

"Well," said he, "it would come as a shock to any man to be bluntly told that he had just been deprived of a fortune. Mr. Fluette, confident that he was within a step of securing the stone, blamed me with being the cause of his disappointment."

The fellow's demeanor angered me beyond endurance.

"Burke," I cried heatedly, "do you think you can make me believe that a man of Alfred Fluette's caliber would purchase the Paternoster ruby from you, knowing that it was not yours to sell? Bah!" I was filled with disgust.

"Ah, Swift, Swift," the rogue said, complacently wagging his head at me, "there are some things of which even you are ignorant.

"Here is one of them – listen: the Paternoster ruby was no more Felix Page's than it is yours or mine. It is the property of the king of Burma; it was stolen from him years ago, and the Burmese nobleman who is at present in this country with his retinue – "

"Tshen-byo-yen," I said quietly, and had the satisfaction of beholding Mr. Burke favor me with a startled glance.

"Yes," he pursued, with considerably less assurance, "that's his name."

"And one of the 'retinue,' as you are pleased to call his gang of thugs, is that hideous, misshapen monster that shrieks like a ghoul. I suppose that he too was hunting for the ruby Friday night – after having stolen it the night before." My sarcasm failed to touch Burke. He shuddered, saying:

"The dwarf? He's a mute – Tshen's slave. Tongue's been torn out. And – truly – believe me; you may easily verify what I say – Tshen is the properly accredited representative of the king of Burma, invested with full power and authority to dispose of the stone. Does the fact that it was stolen from his royal master – that it has for some years been out of the king's possession – in any way lessen or invalidate his right to it? Surely you would not dispute that?" "I don't propose debating the matter with you." And then I pointed out: "If his claim is good, there are the courts."

Burke's shoulders twitched in a tiny shrug.

"Who can fathom the Oriental mind?" said he, oracularly.

I swung on my heel squarely away from him; I had no more patience for such shuffling with words.

"You come with me," I said curtly; "I'll at least get you straight on the police docket – since you seem to prefer it to frankness."

He was out of his chair like a flash.

"No – no – no, Swift!" he implored. "I swear I'm telling the truth. Not that I – not that!" He hesitated a second.

"It wasn't the ruby that was in the bar of soap" – the words literally dragged from his lips. "*I* thought it was. But it was only the paste imitation."

24
CONFESSION

I stared at Burke in speechless amazement.

The tremendous possibilities opened up by this revelation left me bewildered. But the wave of joy which suddenly swept over me was unmistakable.

"Then, how – " I began, and stopped.

If I could not understand, it was only too clear that Burke could not tell me what I wanted to know; for it was also plain that he too was utterly at a loss to account for the circumstance. This, then, had been the intelligence imparted by the Burman on Friday morning, which had so upset Fluette and Burke.

But again, why in the first place should Burke have informed the Burmese of the supposed gem's hiding-place? And how could it have been the replica instead of the real stone? The whole thing was fraught with many perplexities; something here, which I could not seize upon, flaunted itself in obscurity, and if I wanted to learn more from Burke it would not do for him to discover how far I was at sea. Was it possible that he still fostered a hope of getting his fingers upon the real gem?

I was again surveying him with a cold, suspicious eye.

"Burke," I said, "just how did you come to put the gem – or the paste replica – in the soap?"

For a long time he sat contemplating his hand, first the back and then the palm, and then closing the fingers and scrutinizing the nails. Finally, with another shrug and a little gesture in which I read resignation, he said:

"I might as well tell it. As you say, I knew the jewel-box – and I honestly thought it contained the ruby – and the Clara Cooper letters were in the safe, and I never had an opportunity to take them till Tuesday night a week ago. The assurance that Page was going to Duluth that night, combined with the backing Tshen would give me, put me in a position where I could take the ruby and defy Page. I was so sure that Page was going to Duluth that night that I arranged a meeting between Fluette and the Burman at Page's house.

"For you surmised correctly when you declared that Fluette would not buy the ruby on the strength of my representations alone. The purpose of that meeting was to convince Fluette of the good faith of Tshen's claim to the stone, whereupon I was to procure it from the safe — the letters, too — and he was to pay over a certain sum of money for them."

"How much?" I bluntly demanded.

"Two hundred thousand dollars."

So this was the reason why Alfred Fluette must needs help himself to Genevieve's patrimony. That rapacious monster, the Wheat Pit, had exhausted all of his legitimate resources, and so mad was his obsession that he scrupled not to steal.

I entertained only hard feelings for him at that moment. He had not bought the ruby, however, and doubtless Genevieve's fortune was still intact.

"Go on," I commanded curtly. "What happened then?"

"Well, Maillot's arrival demoralized everything. Fluette was to come at ten o'clock, and Tshen at ten-thirty. I didn't know what to do. I had no way of getting them word at that time of night, and I soon realized that Page had given over the trip. I contrived, however, to smuggle all of them up to my room, without anybody being the wiser.

"I explained the state of affairs, and assured them that I would fulfil my part of the agreement as soon as Page and Maillot retired and the house grew quiet.

"Some time after eleven I heard Page and Maillot coming up-stairs. The light was out in my room, and, peering through the crack of my door, I watched Page bid Maillot good-night. The old man was holding a lighted candle in one hand and the small leather box in the other. I *know* it was the ruby he showed Maillot – "

"I suppose you were in the curtained alcove while he and Maillot were talking," I interrupted.

"Not all the time; I didn't dare be. The old man was as sharp as a fox. He didn't trust anybody.

"However, I carried out my part of the programme, all right; but just as I reached the top of the stairs I felt the magnetism of somebody's presence. I looked back and saw Page – he looked positively diabolical – following me. How he enjoyed catching anybody in such a predicament!"

"And then?"

"Well, then – why, I must have lost my head. I started for my room, but the old man commanded me to stop, and I stopped. People generally did when Page told them to. Fluette heard him and came into the hall to learn what was the matter. Page could not see him then because of the angle in the corridor, and the old man paused by the *etagere* to light the candle in the iron candlestick.

"After that the old man walked right up to me and held out his hand for the box and the bundle of letters; but before I had time to give them to him, Fluette rushed in between us. His appearance startled the old man so that he recoiled a pace or two. This gave Fluette the opportunity he needed to take the things from me. He smiled at Page, and said:

"'By God, Felix Page, you shan't thwart me this time; for once I've got the upper-hand of you, and I mean to keep it.' Fluette, you see, had put in the time while waiting in my room listening to Tshen's story and examining his credentials.

"That infuriated Page so that he went clear off his head. He set down the iron candlestick upon the floor, and plunged right into Fluette. Quicker than you can think, they were wrestling furiously for the box and the bundle of letters.

"'I ran into my room and told Tshen what was going on. Three of his party were with him, and they were all so excited that I could scarcely do anything with them. Next I ran back into the hall, where the two men were still struggling and threshing about. They saved their breath for their exertions, each trying with might and main to wrest the precious package from the other.

"All at once the jewel-box was wrenched open. The ruby – or what I thought was the ruby – flew out and fell at my feet. I stooped in a flash and picked it up. As I straightened upright, I saw that Page had succeeded in recovering the jewel-case, although Fluette had the letters. With an oath, Page cast the empty box away from him. 'I'll cut your heart out for that!' he snarled, and started for Fluette. Fluette hastily jabbed the letters into his coat pocket, grabbed up the candlestick and threw it above his head. The light was extinguished, and the candlestick crushed upon Page's head.

"It was an inspiration that made me press the ruby into the soap; I couldn't have found a better hiding-place if I had searched the house over."

I was no longer heeding him. The last doubt had been removed. After all, then, Alfred Fluette was the guilty man.

My heart ached for the three women upon whom the blow would fall the hardest. The tangle was unraveling in accord with my theory. I had warned Genevieve of what she might expect – indeed, she had apprehended the probable outcome herself; it had been hopeless to attempt to prepare Belle. But all this failed to relieve the situation any.

However, the ruby presently rose uppermost in my mind, and with it came a conviction that Burke had not told me everything that he might have respecting the gem. If it had not been in the bar of soap, where was it? Then light flashed upon the enigma.

Burke and the Burmese had been afforded more time than I in which to speculate upon the substitution of the false for the genuine stone, and Burke had not gone inconsiderately to the Page place on Friday night, but, quite the reverse, to prosecute a definite plan of search. How near he came to the goal I didn't appreciate till later.

The discovery by the Burmese that the soap contained merely the paste replica, made them suspect Burke of duplicity. Hence, after Fanshawe and I lost them Friday morning, the Burman had continued to dog the ex-secretary until relieved some time during the day by the misshapen dwarf, who, in turn, had followed him to the Page place after nightfall.

The mute – whose ugly visage Genevieve had seen at the alcove curtains – had attacked him, perhaps in the belief that Burke had found the gem, and that he had been deceiving them respecting it.

It was this struggle in the bedroom which had created such a tumult, frightening Burke within an inch of his life, and driving him pell-mell away and to his bed, where he had remained until the following Tuesday. Both had utterly vanished by the time I effected an entrance to the house.

"I can truthfully say, Burke," I confided, "that I never underestimated your intelligence. You did not go blindly to the Page place Friday night. You reasoned that, if Mr. Page displayed the genuine ruby to Maillot, and if the jewel-case contained only the replica when you robbed the safe an hour or so later, why, the substitution must have occurred somewhere between the library table, where Maillot and Page had been sitting, and the safe. Consequently you were encouraged by the assurance that the scope of your search would be restricted.

"I believe you argued correctly. And to keep you out of further mischief, or from setting your precious Burmese upon me again, why, you may stay here a while and think over it."

Despite his protestations, when I left headquarters the last glimpse I had of him was through the bars of a cell door.

I went directly to the Fluette residence to inform Genevieve that her apprehensions and uncertainties had at last crystallized into dread reality. I shall not dwell upon this wretched conference; it is quite enough to say that the poor girl was torn with grief, yet not wholly convinced.

"Knowles," – she was clinging to my arm, her voice hoarse and distressed, – "it is too terrible – too monstrous for belief. I can not do it – can't believe it – unless I hear the words from Uncle Alfred's own lips. He is here now; he didn't go down-town to-day. The horrible charge has been made – confront him with it. He's up-stairs with Aunt Clara."

"Very well," I quietly returned. "You go and ask him, as calmly as possible, to come down to his study. Don't alarm Miss Belle or her mother; it may not be necessary."

Moving blindly toward the stairs, she paused on the first landing and turned to me a tragic face.

"Courage!" I whispered.

Then she found the strength to carry her on to the end of her revulsive errand. I went direct to the study, and waited.

Fluette came in hastily, his manner wild, his face white and haggard. Genevieve, distressed and heart-broken, followed close behind him. She closed the door. The man began speaking at once, incoherently, in a harsh, strident whisper that signified constricted throat muscles.

"So! It's come at last! You – keep it from – from – my God! keep it from my wife and daughter!"

I answered him roughly, in an attempt to keep him from breaking completely down.

"Pull yourself together, man! What sort of way is this to act?" I surveyed his abject figure an instant, then added with some bitterness: "It is not I that you fear, but your own conscience."

I was thinking of the women.

He slumped into a chair, clasped his out-stretched hands upon the writing-table, and allowed his head to droop between his arms. At that moment I heard Belle calling "Papa!" She was running lightly down the stairs. Again she called, and I knew that she was coming swiftly toward the library.

Genevieve made a move as if to bolt the door, but I checked her with a gesture. Of what use would it be to bar the way of her who came so impulsively? The dreadful truth must be broken to her. It was a task that no third person might assume; let her hear it wrung from her father's unwilling lips.

"Papa!" She was approaching quickly. How youthful and self-reliant her voice sounded! The sweet, girlish contralto jarred painfully upon at least two of our tense, waiting group. And Belle continued to advance all unsuspectingly.

"Papa, where are you? Why don't you answer?"

Genevieve ran over to her uncle, and laid one arm across his bowed shoulders.

"Uncle! Uncle!" She shook him, striving in an agitated way to rouse him to a sense of realization. "Uncle! Sit up! Don't go all to pieces, this way! Belle is at the door!"

And sure enough, as the bent figure painfully straightened a light rap sounded upon the panel, and Belle's fresh young voice again called:

"Are you in there, papa? May I come in?"

Genevieve drew suddenly back to a shadowed corner, wringing her hands with a helpless, despairing gesture. Fluette rose unsteadily to his feet. Then the door opened, and Belle stood framed in the doorway.

The man's look darted feverishly between the two girls – Genevieve well-nigh overcome, while the smile on

Belle's handsome face quickly gave way to an expression of bewilderment, and then to a dawning one of alarm. Next she rushed into the room, and stopped abruptly. Bending a look of anxious inquiry first upon her cousin and then upon me, she finally confronted her father.

"Papa," she faltered, her voice quaking with the fear that suddenly gripped her heart, "what is it? What does this mean?" Then, as she started blindly toward him, she uttered one piercing, agonizing cry: "Papa!"

Unconsciously he brushed aside her beseeching arms. He did not answer her directly; his words were a response to the charge that I had not yet made.

"Man, you are right," he said huskily, "it is my conscience. It is not you that accuse me, but the pure eyes of these two innocent girls – the unspoken reproach of that broken, white-haired woman who sits in silence up-stairs – those fling the charge into my face – sear it into my very soul – every minute of the day and night.

"Take me. I am guilty. It was I who killed Felix Page."

25
"THIMBLE, THIMBLE"

It is needless to dwell upon the scene in Alfred Fluette's study; I shall take up merely such details as constitute an integral part of this memoir, and hurry along.

After Genevieve had led Belle away, Mr. Fluette quickly mastered himself. The bitter moment of the confession once passed, it seemed as if his mind had been relieved of a great burden, and he talked to me with comparative unreserve. But his appearance was in pitiable contrast with what it must have been before he wandered into devious ways. He was crushed, his mien one of hopeless submission to whatever the future might have in store for him.

"First of all," he began, with impressive earnestness, "I want to emphasize the fact that when I snuffed out that man's life I was in imminent peril of my own. When I snatched up the candlestick, if ever a man had murder in his heart Felix Page had at that moment.

"The rest was automatic; I could no more have stayed the deadly blow than I can now hope to escape its consequences. Revolt from almost a lifetime of pitiless, persistent persecution filled me with an irresistible impulse to destroy and rendered my arm invincible."

I went with him, step by step, over the ground that is already familiar. Felix Page had ever been the thorn in his flesh.

"It wasn't as if I had a tangible enemy," he declared; "he wouldn't come out into the open and fight. His aims were always petty, he perpetually annoyed and harassed me by mean and ignoble ways, which I was obliged to bear with an assumption of ignoring them, or else lower myself to his level to meet them. Any bold, decisive stroke would at least have won my respect; but no, the cunning hound knew that my disposition could not forever turn aside his sly thrusts; he knew that, by degrees but inevitably, he was warping my nature, slowly but surely destroying all that was best in me.

"Well," bitterly, "he has succeeded. He has ruined me not only financially, but body and soul as well.

"Time and time again he flaunted in my face some old letters which my wife wrote when she was a mere girl. They were such as any artless, inexperienced girl might write to a man who has for the moment captured her fancy; but how could that be made clear to a public ever greedy for scandal? How would those letters read in the light of my wife's years and the dignity of her present position? Yet the scoundrel has threatened me times without number that he would scatter them broadcast.

"Then – the ruby: that was a crowning stroke. He deliberately stepped in and wrested it from my grasp simply because he in some way found out that I had set my heart upon it for my collection. It was as if he perpetually had his fingers upon the pulse of my desires and intentions; he seemed to divine and anticipate my every move.

"But I was soon reconciled to the stone's loss, and I would have remained so had it not been for that creature, Burke. When he put the idea into my mind that perhaps Page had no legal title to it, I was tempted – and I fell. He presented to me too good an opportunity to retaliate for me to let it pass.

"It was a foolish thing for me to do, going to his house that fatal Tuesday night; but there was no other way. Burke was willing to procure the stone from its hiding-place, but flatly refused to assume the risk of conveying it through the streets. Page was to be away from town that night, so in an evil moment I decided to take the chance.

"You know what happened. I failed to get the gem that night; your unrelaxing vigilance prevented Burke from getting at where he supposed he had hidden it, and at last the Burmese determined to make the attempt Thursday night. Friday morning I was to have again met Tshen-byo-yen to close the deal for the stone, when one of his henchmen notified Burke and me that the attempt had been a failure, that they had succeeded in securing only the replica. We both charged Burke with double-dealing."

I started suddenly at his last words; a possibility had flashed into my mind, so huge and significant that I could comprehend it only by degrees. I spoke with quick eagerness.

"Mr. Fluette, do you think the Burmese would have devoted all these years to recovering the jewel, if they were willing to sell it to the first would-be purchaser that happened along? Doesn't that strike you as a bit peculiar? – as being inconsistent with their unflagging zeal, their tireless efforts to regain what they contend was once stolen from them? Those fellows are very far from home, please bear in mind."

"I never before regarded it in that light," he thoughtfully returned.

He was not interested, and did not press me for an explanation. But his suggestion of Burke's double-dealing had given me an idea which was clearing away one dark corner of the puzzle: the possibility was opening up more rapidly. I looked at him shrewdly.

"Just how did Maillot's story of his experience with Page impress you?" I asked.

He gave me a quick glance.

"It was amazing. I could not believe that Maillot was willfully fabricating; yet, to accept his extraordinary story left me, as the only alternative, a conviction that Felix Page had either undergone a change of heart, or else had lost his mind."

"It didn't occur to you that Page might be trying a game of his own?"

"No."

"Did you ever see the replica?" I asked.

"Yes, many times. It is a remarkably excellent imitation — silicate of alumina; the weight, color, and hardness, the measurements — table, girdle, and *culasse* — all correspond exactly with the original. It lacks only in density, and perhaps a trifle in — but no; it would require an expert test to determine that it was not a true ruby."

"Then," I eagerly pursued, "even an expert might be imposed upon by the replica?"

"Well," he slowly admitted, "perhaps — yes. But not for long; men who deal in precious stones after a time develop a sort of sixth sense that protects them against imposition. It is too subtle to define; but any diamond merchant will tell you that the most perfect imitation will raise a doubt in his mind as to its genuineness; a true stone, never."

When I considered his special knowledge of the subject in general, and of the Paternoster ruby in particular, I was astounded at his obtuseness. Later, I was no less astounded at my own.

"Is it possible, Mr. Fluette," I went on, with an enthusiasm which he did not in the least share, "that it never occurred to you what Burke's game might be? With the connivance of these Burmese, he was deliberately attempting to swindle you; he meant to practise the old familiar game of 'switching' the false for the real stone. The Burmese want the stone, not the money without the stone; but for a generous share in the proceeds, they were willing to lend themselves to Burke's fraud. There's the Oriental for you."

The man stared at me dully. I continued, warming with the subject.

"And Felix Page — he was craftier than even you give him credit for. Mr. Fluette, there's nothing extraordinary in Maillot's story of his Tuesday night adventure — except our stupidity in comprehending its real significance.

"Remember Page's strict injunction to Maillot not to let the jewel-case out of his possession until he and Miss Belle were married; think of the alacrity with which he acceded to Maillot's request; think of his sly chuckles and furtive manner, of his attitude during the whole of that remarkable conference, and tell me what it means if he, too, didn't intend palming off the false stone on you? Maillot and Miss Belle once married, then the young man – in complete innocence, to be sure – would have handed you, not the ruby, but – the replica."

Slowly the dull look died out in Alfred Fluette's eyes, and in spite of his distress, his face flushed darkly with anger.

"The hound!" he muttered through his clenched teeth. "What a dupe I've been. But," he added, with kindling interest, "where *is* the ruby, then?"

"Ah, precisely. That's what I would like to know myself. I think, however, I have the key that will unlock its hiding-place, when I learn how to use it." And I showed him the cipher. He shook his head over it; it was utterly meaningless to him.

There was one phase of our conference concerning which I insisted that the wretched man be minutely circumstantial. Our talk touching upon this point was much too painful for me to reproduce here in its entirety; but after I had almost literally dragged from him every minute detail of the actual tragedy, I felt justified in offering a word of encouragement.

It is sufficient simply to record now the point brought out, to supplement it with certain details acquired from Burke, and to state that it had a vital bearing upon the outcome of the case. The Page affair was by no means closed yet.

When Mr. Fluette struck the blow with the candlestick he was standing at the angle of the balustrade nearest the rooms which Burke and Maillot were occupying. Mr. Page was facing in that direction –

that is, toward the west – and consequently his left side was opposed to the balustrade. Such were the respective positions of the two men at the instant the candlestick was snatched from the floor.

Immediately after the blow was struck both Burke and Fluette were thrown into a panic. The latter at once ran wildly down the front stairs, stumbling over the body on the landing, and out at the front door and away. Burke followed hastily after him, his teeth chattering with fright, and promptly bolted the front door. The act was accomplished so soon after the flight that Fluette, overcome with horror at his deed, distinctly heard the bolt shoot while he was speeding down the walk.

Burke had already informed me that after he made fast the front door he ran back to the rear stairs – he was afraid to pass again the body on the landing – where he observed the rear door wide-open. This he also closed and locked, then hurried up to the second floor, being governed by only one idea – to secure, as quickly as he possibly could, Maillot's companionship.

Between the instant he started to follow Fluette down-stairs and the time he stood rapping at Maillot's door, he had consumed much less than a minute. Some time later he thought of the Burmese, but when he looked into his room it was empty. The open back door accounted for their absence.

When I departed from Alfred Fluette – and I did that very thing; walked deliberately away from him, leaving him hopeful in the midst of his household – my heart was exultant, although I had in contemplation a task that might have dismayed Hercules.

But sometimes, usually when we are least expecting it, or when we are getting our affairs into too much of a muddle. Providence intervenes, and with a decisive stroke straightens matters out for us. After all, it is ridiculous wasting so much time and energy in rough-hewing our ends, when the shaping lies with other hands than ours. On this day of days Providence appeared in the guise of Dr. Wentworth De Breen.

His buggy drew up at the curb beside me.

"Hullo!" was his gruff salutation.

I was pleased at the meeting.

"The very man I was wanting to see," said I. "How many hospitals are there in the city and the immediate vicinity?"

He eyed me in his customary serious, intent manner. I amplified: "I haven't the least idea, you know. Perhaps I could name a dozen, perhaps a score; but there might be five hundred. Anyhow, I have to search them all − or, until I find what I want."

"The deuce you have!" he jerked out. "Anything to do with your ruby case?"

"Everything," said I.

"Well!" He stared at me a moment, then with a sudden movement whipped the fur lap-robe aside. "Get in here," he commanded, in his abrupt manner.

The next instant I was seated beside him, and his spirited mare was dashing along the street at a pace which I regarded as altogether too reckless. Dr. De Breen had a weakness for spirited horses, and he handled them with a careless ease that never failed to excite in me a secret envy; for − I here confess it − I always have been a bit afraid of horses, whether spirited or not; not much, but just enough to make me cautious. I never take any liberties with even a blind and spavined derelict.

"What d'ye want to find?" he bluntly asked, after we had ridden the better part of five minutes in silence.

"A disabled Burmese," was the reply. "I trust to find some part of his upper-works in a more or less damaged condition."

"Burmese!" he echoed in an exclamation. "Good. I win. Larrimer bet me a five he was a Javanese." The doctor sniffed scornfully, "Devilish lot Larrimer knows about ethnology." He then became lucid.

"Larrimer's head at the Drevel Hospital, y' know; deuced clever at the operating-table, but set in his ideas. Lord, dynamite wouldn't move him; stubborn's no name for it.

"Your Burmese is there: triple fracture of the left parietal, left clavicle and bladebone badly crushed; trephined him last night. Beggar'll die."

"It certainly sounds serious enough," commented I. "Is the parietal a part of his upper-works?"

He jabbed with the tip of one gloved finger the side of my head nearest him, which happened to be the right.

"That's your right parietal," he explained; "the left one's on the other side."

"Thank Heaven for sending you across my path this day!" – fervently. "That's my man."

The doctor was a good deal of a scoffer. "Heaven had nothing to do with it," said he, with unnecessary asperity. "I knew you'd be wanting to see him; I was hunting for you. Beggar speaks English fairly well, and he let out a word or two that made me think he knew something you ought to know. . . . Whoa! Jump out!"

We entered the hospital, and soon were at the bedside of the dying man. The operation had relieved the brain from the pressure of the fractured skull, and the man's wanderings were interspersed with rational periods, during which his story was taken down in shorthand, with infinite difficulty, by the hospital's stenographer. I have taken the liberty of preparing a summary from the long rambling account, sufficient to show my justification for anticipating that the case was on the eve of taking an unexpected turn, and to satisfy the curious respecting certain aspects of the ruby's history.

The man, whose name was Chaya, was a priest of the temple at Tounghain, Upper Burma, "where the sublime Da-Fou-Jan sits in eternal meditation among the thousand caverns that lie beyond Mandalay." His companions were also priests, and Tshen-byo-yen was a wealthy noble of the district, whose family was accountable to the king for the safeguarding of the temple's sacred relic – the "Heart of Budda." Thus was the great ruby known, and the rich crimson jewel was averred by tradition to be nothing less holy than the actual blood of "the Perfectly Enlightened One," bestowed upon mankind in an imperishable form.

Naturally, the gem was greatly venerated and not to be profaned by impious hands. But in the time of Tshen's father, it was stolen from the temple by an English adventurer, who succeeded in escaping out of the country with it and making his way to London.

However, a curse went with the ruby. In the temple its influence was beneficent, its crimson glow benignant and abounding with blessings for all true believers; but when desecrated by the plundering vandal's touch it became a great power for evil.

Therefore it came to pass that by the time the reckless Englishman set foot upon his native soil he was only too glad to part with his ill-gotten treasure at almost any price. He was in rags, starving and broken in health.

Thus it was that the rough, uncut gem passed into the possession of Luca Paternostro.

The recovery of the Heart of Budda straightway became a sacred charge upon all the priests. Tshen's father devoted his entire fortune to the cause. With infinite patience, laboring tirelessly, the Burmese never lost sight of their precious relic; but in England they soon found that conditions were vastly different from those of their home country. It was impossible to approach the object which they coveted; and their opinion of legal redress was based upon their familiarity with what passed for justice in Burma. But they never grew disheartened; and at last their opportunity came.

It was Tshen's father who slew Paternostro. It was he who won undying honor by recovering the jewel. It was he who, hard-pressed by the police, was obliged to seek the nearest sanctuary, which happened to be France. The rest we know.

But the gem still carried its baleful spell, for we also know how the expert whom the Paternostros carried with them to Paris, was drowned just as the homeward-bound vessel was entering Dover harbor.

So much for the ruby's eventful history.

Chaya's declaration also confirmed my conclusions respecting Burke's designed imposition upon Alfred Fluette – which, by the way, he seemed to regard as perfectly legitimate. And then it concluded with the most important matter of all.

On the night of Felix Page's murder, while his companions were all in the second story, Chaya had remained on guard below. He had watched Page following Burke up-stairs, after the robbery, but could not warn the thief without alarming the pursuer.

After the struggle began in the hall, Chaya harkened to it a while, then dashed up the rear stairs to take a hand, in case the jewel was to be snatched from his companions at the very moment of victory. He passed through the bath room during the brief period Burke was in his own room informing Tshen of the state of affairs, entered the hall, where, by the dim light of the solitary candle, the two men were locked in combat. The struggle was so furious that his presence was not noticed. He proceeded to the *north-east* angle of the balustrade, where he crouched around the corner and followed through the balusters the uncertain issues of the fight.

He watched the two chief actors so intently, in fact, that he failed to perceive Burke snatch up the supposed ruby from the floor; but he did see Page wrest the leather case from Fluette.

Now was the time for him to act. He was armed with a black-jack – a ball of lead wrapped in leather and with a short, flexible leather handle – and just as Fluette grabbed up the iron candle-stick he plunged forward.

At this instant the light was extinguished, and he received the full weight of a human body as it staggered backward. He supposed it to be Page's. He struck out blindly with his own cruel weapon, at the same time shoving the body away from him. He felt his bludgeon crush upon his victim's head; and then he was himself felled to the floor with a tremendous blow that blotted out everything else for him. The base of the candlestick had found a mark wholly unsuspected by any one.

He knew afterwards that his companions had carried him down the rear stairs and away; that they tried to doctor him until they grew alarmed at the seriousness of his injuries; whereupon they deserted him in his room, after notifying the landlord, who had in turn notified the hospital authorities. Chaya was well supplied with funds, so there had been no difficulty on that score.

And thus was my deduction proved to be correct. Felix Page's *left* side had been toward the balustrade at the instant Fluette snatched up the candle-stick; on the balustrade was a deep indentation where the base of the improvised weapon had impinged, after glancing; and the fatal blow had struck upon the victim's *right* temple. A single descending blow cannot very well pass down one side of a man and end upon the other.

But while Chaya's story gratified me beyond measure, at the same time it was incomplete; it threw no light upon the ruby's resting-place, and for the simple reason that he knew no more about it than any of the rest of the individuals interested in discovering where it had been hidden. I was satisfied that the cipher, once I had interpreted it, would lead me to the gem. Therefore, it remained for me to find it.

Well, the cryptic writing was solved, pretty soon; but the solution came like a crash of thunder, revealing the one twist toward the end that I had least expected.

And, worst of all, I should have known!

26
THE CIPHER SOLVED

Chaya's ante-mortem statement, properly attested by Dr. Larrimer, Dr.

De Breen, the hospital secretary, and myself, together with the otherwise complete case I had, was sufficient of course to open the prison doors for Royal Maillot. It should also have lifted the cloud from Alfred Fluette; but, alas! it did not.

To make my story end as all well-conditioned stories ought to end, I should here be able to wave my wand, or invoke some good genie, or however it is that the writer-folk bestow happiness at a stroke upon the helpless creatures whom they have been ruthlessly dragging through a sea of trial and tribulation, and show you the actors in my own drama transported with joy. But I am recording what actually happened. It was a strange fatality that cast itself into the lives of these people. They were dismayed, overwhelmed, rendered helpless, left uncomprehending. However much I may desire to do so, therefore, I can not twist the truth to give my own story precisely the ending that you or I might desire it to have.

As for myself, I couldn't carry the news fast enough to Maillot and to Mr. Fluette, and to Belle and Genevieve. My enthusiasm met its first damper when the cell door swung open, and the young fellow walked out a free man. It is true that his gratitude was immeasurable; he could find no words to express it, and he wrung my hand until – strong man that I am – I had to tear away from him.

But after his elation had time to cool, he grew morose and gloomy; he was more inclined to cling to what he had gone through, than to accept the extremely satisfactory assurance that he stood clear and as far above suspicion as Caesar's wife.

"No use talking, Swift," he responded to my attempts to rally him out of his humor; "the taint will stick to me. People will say I'm the fellow who was arrested for killing his uncle so that he could inherit his fortune. They'll always point me out and shake their heads and say I was released only because the police couldn't find evidence to convict me. I hope to Heaven the old man made a will giving all his money to charity."

"Faugh!" Such morbid talk was thoroughly exasperating. "Mr. Fluette had a much narrower escape than you did."

"Perhaps," he admitted heavily. "But nobody knows it outside of you and his family. I can't go to Belle with the odor of prison clinging to me. And what's more, I sha'n't."

"If you don't," I said quietly, "you'll break her heart. Your suffering has been as nothing compared with hers." Then I lost my patience completely. "Maillot," I flung at him, "you're a damned fool!" And I swung on my heel and strode away.

"Hi! Swift! Come back here!" he yelled after me. In the next second he had caught hold of my arm and jerked me to a standstill.

"Good Lord, man! I didn't know you had such a nasty temper! Here you come and drag me out of jail, telling me I'm innocent and all that sort of thing, and because I don't strike out hot-footed and throw myself into the presence of the cleanest, sweetest girl in the world, you think I'm an ass.

"Look here. *I* knew I was innocent; but at the same time I didn't try to blink my compromising predicament. I wouldn't blame *any* fair-minded person for being suspicious of me. But everything's happened so sudden – I can't understand, – and – well, hang it, Swift! you haven't made yourself clear, by a long shot. If you think I ought to go to Belle, why, I'll go."

"Then let's go together," said I.

And we did.

After we had boarded a car, I reverted to the matter of the will.

"I don't think it's likely that any will will turn up," I told him. "I have talked with Mr. Ulysses White about it, and he said that Felix Page was one of the sort who have a holy horror of last testaments. If the old gentleman ever made any such disposition of his property, Mr. White had no hand in it."

To dismiss the matter, I will say here that no will ever did turn up, and that Maillot inherited the entire Page fortune. I merely mentioned this topic to pave the way for that of the ruby.

"Not the least part of the estate," I pursued, "will be the Paternoster ruby."

The young fellow interrupted me impulsively.

"By George, Swift! it's yours. Find it and keep it – or sell it and keep the money. I'll not have the ghastly thing – chuck it into the lake first."

"That's no proper way to dispose of it; and later on you might regret such a gift to me. This was what I was going to suggest.

"I believe the claim of the Burmese to be just, for I suppose they're honest according to their lights. They would have a pretty hard time establishing it, though, if you are of a mind to contest the matter."

"Great Scott! Forget that cursed ruby; talk about something else. I want to get the thing out of my mind and never think of it again."

"All right. I sha'n't mention it after to-day. But let me get through. Here's an easy way to settle the matter.

"Let the Burmese have it after reimbursing the estate for what your uncle paid for it; it would be only fair – at least, in a measure.

"I want to hold Tshen and his entourage of mild-eyed cutthroats until I put Burke through; they're my best witnesses. We can't hang the rascal, but we have an excellent ease against him for burglary, attempted swindling, and attempted blackmail. After I find the ruby you can do the bargaining."

He agreed to this. After a bit he favored me with a quizzical regard. "I don't mind explaining that ring episode – now," he said, in response to my look of inquiry. "When you first pointed out the true import of the wax impression on the candlestick, it brought to my mind at once Fluette's capricious notion of wearing a ring on the middle finger of his right hand. I was keeping tab on you the day of the inquest. I knew that he was going to attend, and that the circumstance would be of considerable significance to you. I saw your look dart to his right hand – -saw you watching him – "

"And you thought you'd confuse me, eh?"

"Exactly. When you saw the ring on his finger only, the circumstance was pregnant – portentous. When you had *two* rings on *two* right hands, why, you were puzzled, but the effect was scattering and weak."

I approached Mr. Fluette with an enthusiasm decidedly tempered, and so I was not as disappointed as I might have been. My good news seemed to produce not the slightest effect upon him. He appeared to have aged twenty years; and from that day until his death, which occurred only four months later, he remained melancholy and without interest in anything whatever.

However, I was placed in the most embarrassing position that I ever experienced in my life. Before explanations were half made, Miss Belle flew at me – I'm not attempting a pun, either – with a glad, impetuous cry, threw her arms around my neck, and, drawing herself to her tiptoes – *kissed me*! I had been far more at ease under her levelled revolver.

In the afternoon Genevieve and I repaired to the old Page place. She was so confident that she could find the originals of the designs on the cipher, that I was anxious to give her the chance. Besides, she was afraid to go alone, and I simply had to accompany her. Belle could not without Maillot tagging along, and – well, we didn't want anybody else.

First of all, Genevieve had to be shown the dent made by the candlestick in the railing of the balustrade. She placed the tip of one little finger in the depression, and drew back with a shudder.

"Let's go," she said, in a hushed voice. "I never expect to come up these stairs again. Let's find the daisies, and go."

She understood as well as I did that Felix Page must have substituted the stones somewhere between the library table and the hidden safe in his bedroom. She proposed to start at the table and examine every object, if necessary, between the two points mentioned.

Our progress was slow until we reached the bedroom. Genevieve drew to an abrupt halt on the threshold.

"There was a table there, by the head of the bed," she said; "where is it?"

"Lying on its side in that corner" – I pointed. "It was hurled there last Friday night, when the dwarf surprised Burke here."

She went over to it, while I raised the blinds. Instantly she recoiled with a cry, and then in a flash was fairly wild with excitement.

"Knowles, Knowles!" she screamed. "Here they are!" And sure enough, there they were – the brass tacks with which the artificial leather cover had been fastened on. Their heads were ornamental, with just such crenellated edges as might have prompted the circular figures at each end of the cipher.

I stared at them in stupefied silence. The row of gleaming tacks staggered me. How many times had I lingered by that very table while I racked my brain to remember where I had seen the peculiar figure! Why, once I even had paused and drawn the design in the dust on the leather cover! What a dunce – how blind I had been!

The cipher was not difficult to read now. At once I recalled Burke's shadow on the blind; he had been bending over this table, and the agile movements of his hands were no longer mysterious. He, too, had some knowledge of the cipher, and he had been rapidly running over the tack-heads, hunting for the combination that would reveal a concealed compartment.

After a while we grew rational again. I got out the cipher, and once more Genevieve and I put our heads together over it. Here it is; you may follow us while we dig it out:

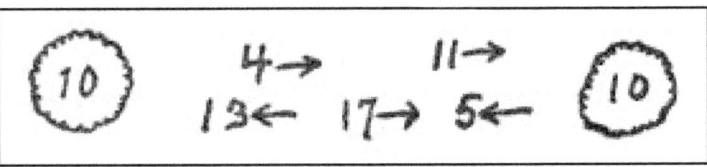

The Cipher

"If you remember," I said presently, "I told you that very likely it would have to be interpreted in connection with something not on the paper. Count the tacks along the front edge."

There were nineteen of them.

"Counting from either end," I went on, "the centre tack will be ten. It's as simple as A-B-C. That's our starting-point from which to find the others. Find the fourth one to the right of the centre tack – number ten."

She placed the tip of one forefinger upon it – a bit gingerly, I smiled to see.

"Why, it gives!" she announced in surprise.

"I'd be terribly cut up if it didn't," said I. "Now, then, the eleventh to the right."

This carried her to the third one around the side; number thirteen was the fifth on the left side, number seventeen the ninth on the right side, while number five was on the front edge, of course, close to the centre. Each of them yielded a trifle beneath her pressure – until she came to number five. Here she drew back and clasped her hands tightly together.

"Oh, I can't!" she cried excitedly. "I'm just so nervous that I can't put my finger upon it. You do it."

"Nonsense!" said I. "If you don't find the ruby, it will never be found. That's the last one."

At last, with shining eyes and parted lips, the little finger went slowly down upon the fateful tack-head. She screwed up her eyes and closed her lips tightly, as if she feared something would explode, then pushed with all her might. The tack gave; but nothing else happened.

We stared at the table, our faces long with disappointment; then we looked at each other in unspoken questioning. Genevieve's expression was so woe-begone that I laughed. The nerve-racking suspense was broken.

"How silly!" she exclaimed. "There!"

With a quick movement, she bore down upon the centre tack – number ten – and lo! a section of the table edge flew outward, disclosing an aperture perhaps six inches long and a quarter of an inch wide. It was very much like a slit in a door for letters.

But there was no ruby yet, nor any aperture large enough to accommodate the one for which we were looking. I leaned over with a puzzled scowl and peered into the slit.

"There's a folded paper in there," I announced. My fingers were too large to force into the opening, and Genevieve promptly produced a hat-pin. Next moment we had the paper out – or papers, for there were three sheets folded together.

Across the back, written in Felix Page's small cramped hand, was this inscription:

Memorandum of Agreement between
Felix Page
and

Cristofano Paternostro, Michele Paternostro
and Filippo Paternostro.

"Well, we're hot on the scent, at any rate," was my comment, as I unfolded the papers. Then I quickly folded them again, without a glance inside.

"Wait!" said I. "This is a solemn occasion, and it should be recognized with some fitting observance."

"Oh, don't tease!" cried Genevieve, dancing up and down with impatience, and trying to pluck the papers from my hand.

"I'm not teasing, my dear," said I; "I'm terribly serious. We are pretty near the end of the trail, little girl; after we have read this imposing document we will have reached the end. I'm halfway sorry, too, notwithstanding the grim tragedy that has hung over us. We must celebrate the last event with an appropriate rite – a fire upon the library hearth."

She flushed with delight, and consented to wait until I had the fire going properly. It was a most successful fire. We dragged the library table up close; I jumped Genevieve to a seat upon it, and then seated myself beside her. She placed a hand upon my shoulder, and our heads were again very close together.

"Now, then!" I shook the papers open.

The more imposing one – the agreement – I placed beneath; its dry legal phraseology was not at all inviting. The other sheets were, however. They too were written all over in Felix Page's hand, but bore the blunt, direct phrases of a man used to expressing himself without any rhetorical embellishment or nonsense.

And this is what we read:

This explanation is written to clear up any misunderstanding or doubt, that may arise after my death, over the stone called the Paternoster Ruby.

In June, 1884, I learned that Alfred Fluette was trying to buy it from the Paternostros. I at once determined that he should not have the stone if money could prevent it. So I too became a bidder.

The first figure set by the dealers was almost prohibitive, but as Fluette seemed willing to meet it, I was ready to go him one better. But the wily Italians hedged. They set us to bidding against each other, and as the price rose my resolution to get the stone grew more set.

While the bids mounted, I was given ample satisfaction for the weight of whatever financial obligations I was incurring by Fluette's increasing worry and chagrin. He was like a pup that doesn't know whether the bone is going into the soup-kettle or the garbage-can. I swore to have that bit of red glass if it took every cent that I could rake and scrape together – and I had a few of them.

Finally Fluette drew out, cursing me. I brought the Italians to a showdown.

Still they hesitated. I became suspicious.

One night Cristofano Paternostro, the head of the firm, called at my hotel. He was nervous and ill at ease. He informed me, with many hems and haws, that the ruby Fluette and I had been snarling over was lying at the bottom of the English Channel, and that they would be unable to deliver the goods. He had a good deal to say about the prestige the ruby gave the firm, and much more to the same effect, until I cut him off short. I told him that the ruby was nearer to making him ridiculous.

It seems that after they recovered the stone in Paris, the expert who accompanied them couldn't resist the temptation to steal it. Besides being a gem expert and an expert thief, this fellow was accounted an expert swimmer. When the boat was near land he tried to get away with the prize by jumping overboard, under cover of night, and swimming ashore. He did succeed in reaching the nearest land – which is to say, straight down. And that was the last of him, the ruby, and pretty nearly of the three Italians.

Since the ruby couldn't be recovered, they agreed to make the best of it. They agreed to keep the matter among themselves, and to continue to reap all the advertising benefits which the supposed possession of such a costly trinket gave them.

It was a joke, that. Here was I, like an old idiot, trying to spend good money for something the other fellow didn't have to sell.

But pretty soon I saw a way to reach my end just the same as though I'd beat Fluette in the deal. It was a whole lot better than that, in fact. I could get out from under without it costing me a cent, and still make Fluette and the world believe that I had bought the ruby.

"Nice thing for the Paternostros," says I, "when all this comes out."

Cristofano turned green. He begged me not to tell. He promised me the pick of his gems if I'd only keep the secret.

I looked at him pretty sour. "Very well," says I at last. "You give me the imitation stone. I'll never disclose the fact that you didn't have the original ruby, if you will announce to the world that it was sold to me for $500,000. As long as you keep your mouth shut, I'll keep mine."

He was tickled to death. Nothing would do but he must have in the rest of the firm (his brother and cousin). When they came I had a written contract prepared for them, setting forth the terms of our agreement and binding them with a penalty heavy enough to keep them from blabbing. (Contract memo. attached hereto.)

How long we remained silent in the midst of a speechless wonder, I haven't the least idea. Words were wholly inadequate even feebly to express the mingled feelings with which we slowly digested the full force and import of this remarkable document.

So the very heart and essence of the tragedy, the crimson woof that knitted together the dark warp of its fabric, had all along been unreal and without substance!

For a gem that cannot be applied to its ordained function can scarcely be said to have an existence. Yet the Paternoster ruby had been potent to project its maleficent influence from the depths of its watery grave, and shape the destinies of the living. Verily, Fate never played a grimmer joke.

My thoughts drifted back to the night of the murder. Why had Felix Page paused beside the table while going between the hidden safe and Maillot, who was waiting in the library? I could imagine only one explanation: as he passed the table he was seized with a sudden impulse to impart the secret to the young man, even going to the extent of setting down the jewel-box so that one hand would be free to manipulate the tack-heads. But a second thought had prevailed. He picked up the box and proceeded on his way.

Genevieve, round-eyed, sat staring into the dying fire. (That was a jolly fire!) Presently her head bent over to my shoulder, and without looking up she quoted a familiar couplet which must have occurred to the reader ere this:

"Full many a gem of purest ray serene
The dark, unfathomed caves of ocean bear."

I mention the circumstance because it prompted an idea which suddenly set me to laughing. Genevieve looked at me in alarm.

"What in the world!" she marveled, for the silence had been very sedate.

"Little girl," I at last enlightened her, "it will pay you to go with me when we leave here – to the Central Station. There's something I want us to enjoy together; it will compensate for a deal of your late trouble and anxiety."

"What is it?"

"I want to hand Alexander Burke these papers, tell him they're what was hidden in the table – then quietly watch him while he reads."

I meant to do it, too. But Genevieve failed to enter into the spirit of the suggestion.

"Mercy!" she shuddered. "I don't want to gloat over the poor wretch." I said no more about it, but – well, the result was all that I had anticipated.

Genevieve reminded me that we should be thankful for having been relieved from a final perplexity.

"I don't understand," said I. "Why, we haven't the ruby to dispose of; that would have puzzled even you."

"I don't know about that. Royal gave it to me. I see where I stand to lose a fortune. Five hundred thousand – *whew*!"

Suddenly she snuggled closer and clasped her hands tightly upon my shoulder. Her hair teased my cheek, and the delicate perfume of it made me light-headed. Twisting her pretty head sideways, she flashed an arch look at me from under her lashes, then glanced quickly away again. Blue eyes and long dark lashes are a potently disturbing combination.

"Well," she sighed, "the Page case may have cost you a fortune, but – it gave you me. And I – for one – am very content and happy, Mr. Swift."

THE END

Now from the Resurrected Press

The Hampstead Mystery

High Court Justice Sir Horace Fewbanks found shot dead in his Hampstead home, a butler with a criminal past, a scorned lover and a hint of scandal. These are the elements of the *Hampstead Mystery* that Detective Inspector Chippenfield of Scotland Yard must unravel with the assistance of the ambitious Detective Rolfe. But will he be able to sort out the tangled threads of this case and arrest the culprit before he is upstaged by the celebrated gentleman detective Crewe. Follow the details of this amazing case at it plays out across Hampstead, London and Scotland until it reaches a stunning conclusion in the courts of the Old Bailey.

The Hampstead Mystery
by John R. Watson & Arthur J. Rees
RPM -101

Visit www.resurrectedpress.com to order now.

Other Resurrected Press Mysteries

From the pen of R. Austin Freeman

Dr. John Thorndyke - Lecturer on Medical Jurisprudence and Forensic Medicine. Before Bones, before CSI, before Quincy, M.E – there was Dr. John Thorndyke solving the most baffling cases of Edwardian London using the latest tools of medical science. Read about his cases in:

The Eye of Osiris
John Bellingham, noted Egyptologist has vanished not once but twice in the same day. Now Dr, Thorndyke must unravel the tangled claims on his estate, solve the riddle of the missing man and find the "Eye of Osiris".

The Mystery of 31 New Inn
When Dr. Jervis is whisked away in a coach with no windows to an unknown location to treat a man in a coma from undivulged causes it is Dr. Thorndyke who must come up with the solution.

The Red Thumb Mark
The first of Dr. Thorndyke's cases finds him trying to prove the innocence of a young man accused of being a diamond thief despite the fact that his finger print was found at the scene of the crime.

John Thorndyke's Cases
More cases of medical mysteries as told by his trusted assistant Jervis, M.D. Eight stories of crime and deduction in Edwardian London.

Visit www.resurrectedpress.com

Other Resurrected Press Mysteries

Mysteries on a Train

Before the Orient Express there was:

The Rome Express by Arthur Griffiths

A man is found dead in his first class sleeping compartment on the express from Rome to Paris. Who was his murderer? The Countess? The English General? His brother the clergy man? The maid who has disappeared? Is the French justice system up to solving the crime? Read about it in The Rome Express.

The Passenger from Calais by Arthur Griffiths

Colonel Basil Annesley finds he is the only passenger on the train from Calais to Lucerne. That is until a mysterious woman shows up at the last minute to book a compartment. Who is after her? What is her secret? Is she a criminal or a victim? Read about it in The Passenger from Calais

Visit us at www.resurrectedpress.com

The Fictional Detective
by Greg Fowlkes

Who killed Ezekial O. Handler?

A beautiful dame, a hard-boiled private eye – and a dead body.

It started like any other case. When a famous writer dies in a mysterious car crash, private detective Frank Slade is called in to find answers, but all he finds is more questions. Who killed Ezekial Handler? Who is Janet Nielsen and why is she so interested in finding out? Who is leaving the neatly typed clues? And as Slade tries to find answers to these questions he starts to wonder if the ultimate answer will threaten his very existence.

Read about it in
The Fictional Detective

Visit www.thefictionaldetective.com

About Resurrected Press

A division of Intrepid Ink, LLC, Resurrected Press is dedicated to bringing high quality, vintage books back into publication. See our entire catalogue and find out more at www.ResurrectedPress.com.

About Intrepid Ink, LLC

Intrepid Ink, LLC provides full publishing services to authors of fiction and non-fiction books, eBooks and websites. From editing to formatting, from publishing to marketing, Intrepid Ink gets your creative works into the hands of the people who want to read them. Find out more at www.IntrepidInk.com.